THE ATHENA PROTOCOL
CARRION VIRUS BOOK2

MW DUNCAN

SEVERED PRESS
HOBART TASMANIA

THE ATHENA PROTOCOL

This book is dedicated to the memory of Henrietta (Nettie) Davidson.

As usual, there is a huge amount of people to thank who have helped in many ways to get this book completed. Without you all, writing this would have been a gargantuan task. Thank you for helping shoulder some of the weight. Stephanie, Pauline, Heather, Jane, Bex, Hannah, Jon, all my friends and family and of course Honey and Alice. I heard that writing can be a lonely pursuit. This hasn't been my experience of writing, not when I have you all around me. Thank you all and I am very much looking forward to the next chapter. Until next time.

MW Duncan
April 2016

So many great nobles, things, administrations, so many high chieftains, so many brave nations, so many proud princes, and power so splendid; in a moment, a twinkling, all utterly ended.

- Jacobus de Benedictus

THE ATHENA PROTOCOL

One Week Before Outbreak

Brutus slipped into a doorway seeking respite from the constant rain. His breath misted and dissipated into the night. Revellers swept past three or four to an umbrella, giggling girls linked arm in arm, loud men singing and swaying. Brutus cast them only a customary glance as he waited. He pulled a cigar from his pocket, held it between his teeth, and patted himself down for a light.

"Help you with that?" A sandy-haired young man, American, suddenly blocked his view of the passers-by, his eyes moving this way and that.

Brutus hissed at being caught off guard, and pulled the unlit cigar from his mouth. "You who I'm waiting for?"

"Ryan Bannister." The American held out a hand. His fingers shook. The man was nervous. He wore a beige raincoat and dark-blue jeans, both soaked by the downpour. So damned conspicuous.

"You're late."

"Flight was delayed. Have you seen the weather?" Ryan withdrew the unwelcome offer of a handshake and smoothed back his hair. "You're Richard?"

"Brutus. Just Brutus."

One of Ryan's eyebrows went up. "How'd you get a name like that?"

His eyes studied Brutus's bulk. The fool wasn't expecting a reply, and he wasn't going to get one.

"This is for you." Brutus placed a small rucksack into Ryan's hands.

The American was not necessary to this assignment. Brutus could have completed the mission on his own, with less fuss, less bother. To this mind, the fewer people who knew what was going on the better. Still, he was paid well not to think too much. All he needed was make sure the package was delivered, and that he and Ryan Bannister arrived at the destination without incident. After that, Brutus was to get him out of the city and onto a flight back to America.

"Follow me." Brutus set a brisk pace through the soaked streets of Aberdeen. Ryan occasionally broke into a run lest he fall behind.

"You know what we're doing here?" asked Ryan, wiping his face free of rain.

"Yes."

"What do you think of it all?"

"You should adopt some savvy and shut the hell up or I'll have to break your goddamned jaw."

They turned off Union Street and onto Belmont Street, a short road flanked by bars and cafes. It was crowded. Brutus methodically placed his hands on shoulders persuading revellers to move aside. They reached a club, booming, music pumping from inside. It once was a church, the dull granite so common and oppressively dark in the wet city. Two bouncers stood at the door, both clad in black to match the night. They cast intrusive glances over patrons entering, no smiles, no nods of the head, no welcoming words. A few IDs were checked but most were simply waved through. Brutus knew he could wreck them both without breaking a sweat. But that would not progress his mission.

Brutus grabbed Ryan by his lapels and pulled him close.

"Here's how it's going to work, stay close to me. Don't say anything to anyone. You see trouble, you let me know. You don't do what I say, I'll break a finger to make my point. Got it?"

"Sure," said Ryan, nodding and furiously blinking rain from his eyes.

"Let's get this over with."

From a set of narrow eyes, the bouncer on the left studied Brutus with particular interest. "No trouble tonight, lads. Alright?"

Brutus flashed a smile. "No trouble from us, pal."

The second bouncer held a stiff, stubby hand to Ryan's chest. "What's in the bag?"

"Nothing that concerns you," said Brutus.

The bouncer looked to Brutus then to Ryan, and to Brutus again. "If you want to come in, that bag stays in the cloakroom."

Brutus considered a cash bribe. But that might encourage further curiosity. "We'll leave it in the cloakroom."

They stepped through the doors and lined up in a short queue.

"We can't let them take the bag."

"Shut up," said Brutus.

The queue emptied quickly and soon they met with a spotty-faced teen. Brutus unzipped his heavy coat.

"This and the coat," he said, pulling the bag from Ryan's grip.

"Five pounds, please," the teen squeaked.

Brutus plucked a handful of coins from his pocket and received a token in return.

"Have a good night."

Brutus gave no reply. Ryan nodded some form of thanks. At least he didn't speak.

The club was a grand building lit by a collection of neon lights and spot lights. The DJ used the former pulpit. Music thundered. The dancefloor was a cache of lively frames, the men in shirts gaudy enough to rival a graffiti alley, and the girls tanned and wearing skirts too short to be called skirts.

Ryan leaned close. "What the hell do we do now? We need that rucksack. You need to get it back. What are we going to do?"

"Have a drink." Brutus steered Ryan toward a small booth with a sofa and a table. "Piss off," Brutus said to a seated male in a pink shirt and white trainers.

A snarl threatened to blossom yet slipped away as he looked up to Brutus. The clubber collected his drink and did as he was ordered.

"Sit."

Ryan did as he was ordered, too.

A blonde girl, tank top displaying a lot of cleavage, tight denim shorts and boots that tried to crawl above her knees arrived at the table with a tray and a collection of shots. She smiled, her teeth impossibly white.

"Would you like a drink?"

"A beer, and a whiskey with ice. My friend here will have a Diet Coke. Leave a couple of those shots." Brutus pulled out a twenty pound note. "Keep the change."

The girl flashed those white teeth again and left. Brutus watched her leave, admiring the way her shorts revealed just a hint of her ass. The way the club operated was so obvious to someone like Brutus. He was as much a student of people as he was of war. He understood what motivated people, how they worked, and how to manipulate. The waitress would spread news of the tip. More of them would descend upon his table hopeful for a piece of his generosity. A quick smile, easy glimpses of the skin often resulted in favours. How many men in the club were falling under her spell, buying drink after drink just for a smile, a few words or a little more flesh? She was pretty. Shame she'd probably be dead in a week or two if the mission went according to plan.

"I don't like Diet Coke."

"I'm here to look after you, not make sure you're comfortable. You're not touching a drop of booze until you've done your part in all this."

"We need to get the bag back."

"I'm working on that."

The waitress returned with the drinks, setting them down on the table. "Here you go, handsome," she said with that killer smile.

Brutus took a long pull on his beer. The club was a hotbox of pressed bodies. He hated the music. Manufactured crap with no soul. The cold beer went down well. How to get back the rucksack? He peeled the label from the bottle, scratching at it until it came free in a shredded mess. He'd already noted the locations of the internal security cameras. They'd avoided all but one, the one in the hallway when they first entered. Bouncers? Two on the outside door, one by the bar, another two patrolling the interior. Timing was everything. The bouncers could all be avoided. The pimply attendant was the issue.

Brutus slammed down his beer. "The cloakroom has a side door. I'll create a distraction, you get in and get the bag, bring it back here."

"Hang on," Ryan protested. "All I'm here for is to—"

"You'll do what I say." Brutus waved over the waitress.

"What can I do for you, sweetie?"

"What's your name?"

"Chloe."

"Nice to meet you, Chloe. Do you know the guy working on the door, taking the coats?"

She shrugged. "Liam, I think."

"That's right, Liam. Well listen, we'd like to buy him a drink or two, but we don't want him to know that it's from us."

"He's working right now, so he's not allowed to drink."

"He knocks off soon?"

"Yes. So, I guess I could get one to him then."

Brutus pulled out two ten pound notes. "Get him a beer and you keep the change."

Chloe's eyes lit up. "Okay." She scooped up the money and went back to the bar.

"When Chloe delivers pimple face his drink, you get the rucksack."

"Why don't we just get the rucksack and leave, go find another bar?"

"That wasn't the plan. Now, you go get the rucksack."

Ryan muttered words that became eaten by the music and headed toward the cloakroom. Chloe pitched a wink at Brutus as she swept past the booth. Brutus lost sight of Ryan. Too many bodies.

It may have been easier to find another club, one that didn't have such a strict door policy but his orders were very specific and he meant to follow them to the letter. He wanted no hurdles to being paid in full, and preferred to keep a tight reputation as dependable, especially with these new employers. He finished the last of his beer.

The crowd on the dancefloor parted slightly and Ryan appeared clutching the backpack to his chest, checking over his shoulder, his face set in grim determination. He fell into the chair next to Brutus, his breath coming fast, and he licked his lips.

Brutus snatched the backpack and pushed it under the table, sure to keep it within Ryan's reach. "Let's get this done."

Ryan chugged on his drink like it was beer and a dose of courage, unclipped the bag, opened the zip, and with the table for cover pulled on a pair of surgical gloves. He fumbled through the bag and lifted out the source of all the worry. It looked like a normal thermos flask, but Brutus knew better. It held something terrible.

"You sure that's safe?" asked Brutus, in a momentary lapse of confidence.

"It's safe. I designed it. It's not dangerous until I insert the timer."

Brutus scanned the club making sure they weren't being observed. No gazes were cast at their booth. Ryan rolled up his sleeve and unfastened his watch. He laid it on the table and pulled the pins from the strap, removed the leather lengths and returned them to the rucksack. He placed the remainder of the watch into the groove on top of the flask. With both thumbs, he pushed it into place.

"I'm setting the timer," explained Ryan.

"How long have we got?"

"The device will open at thirty minutes past midnight."

Brutus looked at his own watch. "That gives us thirty-five to get out of here."

Ryan pushed the device under the seat where Brutus sat.

The device looked suitably innocent, and when found in the morning by cleaners, it would be tossed into a bin. Brutus moved his foot. The floor was sticky. Or perhaps it would remain undiscovered.

"What about the watch? Can anyone trace it?"

Ryan sipped on his drink. His hand possessed an obvious shake. He was right to be afraid. "Not a chance. So what happens now?"

"I get you out of the city."

"Now?"

"Yes, now," said Brutus.

Brutus exchanged the token for his coat and headed out the exit. Ryan stood shivering in the rain. Brutus looked back at the old church. He didn't know exactly what would come next but he knew enough. He had to get Ryan Bannister out of the city and fast. The next time Brutus would step foot in Aberdeen, it would be like nothing before.

Chapter One
The Storm Rages On
Present Day

Eric Mann trampled the virgin snow underfoot. Carter moved to his right and a half-dozen other members of his Black Aquila team followed close by. The snow fell steadily and the wind whipped snowflakes into an intense flurry.

Eric's hand shielded his eyes. Visibility was poor, as was progress. They headed toward a small farm on the outskirts of Aberdeen, responding to reports that an outbreak of the virus had taken hold. With Aberdeen still under quarantine and battles still being fought for control in the city, infection outside the city lines was dealt with swiftly and quietly. Eric's eight-man team could call on military support, but all facets were stretched thin, needed in a thousand places. The waiting period would render the call for assistance redundant.

He gripped his tranquiliser rifle just a little harder as lights ahead blinked through the storm. Black Aquila learned a terrible lesson in Aberdeen, purchased with lives of their operatives, Eric's men. Stun rods and taser weapons were not up to the task of subduing the infected. They could shrug off the 50,000 volts more often than not. Now, Eric and his team carried dart guns loaded with enough chemical toxins to subdue a charging rhino. Nobody in his team carried live weapons. Those were the prerogative of the armed forces.

A dull, amber light pierced the flurry of snow. Eric held his hand up to halt his team's advance. He could just make out the outline of the two-storey farmhouse and outbuildings through the white. His team fanned out on both flanks.

Carter's breath rasped in the cold. "We should have taken the vehicles further. Walking in these conditions is dangerous, Eric. The men are exhausted."

"Better exhausted than dead."

They'd left their transport half a mile back down the rough farm track. At times, the snow sucked at their knees. It was tough. But Eric couldn't risk the vehicles being bogged down voiding any chance of retreat, and even more importantly he couldn't risk the infected hearing their approach. The element of surprise was an integral weapon in their strategies, and sudden sounds aroused the infected from their habitual daze.

Eric gestured toward the farmhouse. "We're going in."

Everyone picked up the pace, legs lifting high and plunging back into the snow. Lactic acid burned in Eric's legs. He pressed on. They all pressed on.

A low, stone wall circled the property. The flimsy perimeter hardly seemed capable of standing against the ferociousness of the weather. The storm was unlike anything Eric had ever experienced. He'd been in snow drifts before, but the snowfall was endless.

His men secured a perimeter, rifles raised, scanning for movement. Nothing natural would be out in a storm so bad. Any movement would indicate the presence of an infected.

If battling a more tactical enemy, Eric's team would have stormed and cleared the building. The infected moving into confined spaces played to their strengths. Eric developed a new technique that worked more often than not.

The perimeter was secured. Eric gave the nod. As one, the team started shouting, yelling, creating a din that was sure to be heard over the storm. Eric sank down to his knees, bracing his rifle on the stone wall. He pulled off his gloves, preferring to take aim skin on trigger.

He'd been on six of these missions since the outbreak at the hospital. Ben Williamson, the CEO of Black Aquila, had promised Eric a period of leave. But his departure was always delayed. Another mission, another shortage of manpower. And he was still trudging through the snow, finger on the trigger, bringing down walking nightmares.

The door to the farmhouse opened, a halting action, a little at first then fully.

Their shouts halted.

A male in his fifties, snarling, clothes heavily bloodstained, stood in the doorway, peering out into the storm. It sniffed at the air like a dog. Eric and his men all wore winter camouflage, but it wouldn't protect them for long. The senses of the infected were above average.

"Wait until it steps out into the garden. I don't want anyone bringing him down and making a choke point."

The order was passed down the line. The infected locked eyes onto Eric's position. It rushed from the doorway, letting out a chilling screech. In a looping stride, it cut through the snow like a plough through frozen earth.

"Take the shot," said Eric.

Carter rose from behind the low wall, took aim and fired. Eric heard the hiss of the dart leaving the barrel. Though he didn't see the missile hit, the infected shrugged, its progress halted. It snatched at its chest before continuing the charge. Two more of Eric's men fired. The infected sank to its knees. Those arms clawed at the air, searching for leverage to move forward, then collapsed face-first into the snow and lay still. One dart would have killed a normal person. Eric and his men discovered long ago that the sure killing of an infected was the only way to bring it down. A rigid way of thinking but a choice made easy when one had witnessed his own men ripped apart by the creatures.

More infected burst from the farmhouse. Three, four, five of them. Three women, an adolescent male, and an older man. They didn't hesitate, charging directly at Eric's position.

"Fire at will."

Pops and hisses came as the men unleashed a torrent of toxic darts, and then came the sounds of reloading. Eric held off engaging, instead watching for any weakness in his strategy.

The infected made some distance before their strength gave way. They fell only a few feet from the wall. The men on Eric's left readied to jump the wall, to secure the fallen.

Carter was about to go over when movement to the right drew both their attention. Another cluster of infected rushed from the outbuildings, seven or eight. They moved at speed, clearing the wall with unnatural agility. Rozek, the closest to the outbuildings, disappeared under an avalanche of bodies.

"Shift fire!" cried Eric.

He fired into the press of bodies. The screams of Rozek cut through the storm. Carter was by his side, also firing. Eric reloaded his single shot weapon. More of the team joined in firing. Rozek fell silent. Two of the infected rose to their feet, their bodies visibly punctured by darts. Carter raced forward, pulling his stun baton from his belt. He smashed the first infected in the face, sending it scrambling back. It tripped on the press of bodies. Eric rushed forward, and placed a foot onto the infected's chest, pushing it down into the snow. He thrust the barrel of the rifle against the thing's forehead and pulled the trigger. The compressed gas spat the dart with such force that it pierced the forehead and created a small crater in the skull. It thrashed in the snow before falling still.

Eric turned to see Carter and two others from the team beating the last infected with stun rods and rifle butts.

In that moment, the infected were not the unfortunate majority of a community succumbed to the awful virus. They were the killers of one of them, killers of a brother-in-arms. And they were treated harshly, anger pushing behind every thrust, every whack.

"That's enough. Hey! I said that's enough."

Carter spat into the snow, his eyes wide, his lungs working hard.

"Carter, get the farmhouse cleared and then the outbuildings. And be careful. There could be more in there."

Carter reloaded and took the team inside.

Eric studied the slain. A young woman. He wondered what she had been before the virus overcame her system. Did she have a career? What were her hopes? Her dreams? What was her name? Did she have two great children, and a husband away on duty? A line of fir shrubs along the garden path at home she love to tend? He was thinking of his wife, of course. Dangerous, for those questions made the creature almost deserving of compassion.

It didn't matter now. The creature and her herd had killed Rozek and had paid the price. There was nobody to answer to, the city was enveloped in chaos. When Eric reported back, he would simply hand over the bodies of the dead infected, and those they successfully subdued. It was as easy as that. And that bothered him.

Chunks of Rozek's neck and chest had been bitten free.

Eric looked away. The sight would bother him at night as they always did. And so would his actions. Could he have done more? Why were so many people dying with his involvement? Was he failing to do what he was employed to do? His conscious could be a mean bastard at times.

"Cottage is clear, Eric. Infected brought down are secured."

Eric turned to Carter. "Bag up the dead. I want a quick sweep for intel in the house and on their bodies. We need ID, anything to put a name to … them."

Eric and Carter shared a moment of silent communication. Carter's eyes went to Rozek. He turned back to the farmhouse to search for ID.

Men dragged up transportation sleds. Eric wiped the snow from his face.

Will I get to go home now?

He looked at Rozek.

He needed to go home to see his wife and kids again.

***

Gemma cried. Hot stinging tears raced down her cheeks. She had not cried like that since she was little, when she lost her eighty-year-old grandfather to a painful battle with brain cancer. The single piece of paper she held in her hands shook as did her body. She wiped her eyes with the back of her hand and looked at the list again. Hundreds of names in two columns and there, highlighted, the name she prayed would not turn up on any list.

Stacey, her friend and dearest companion throughout the chaos of the city's lockdown, was dead. Dead! Gemma could hardly believe it to be true. She so wanted to see Stacey walk into her hotel room, that warm smile on her pretty face, make-up done to perfection. Dead!

They had separated when Gemma resolved to return to the city, camera in hand, chasing a news story. Stacey refused to go. Gemma could not blame her. Leave a warm house with doors that locked? She could barely understand her own decision. Horror lay out there. But horror lay everywhere.

How did Stacey die? In pain like Gemma's grandfather? Terrified? Calling out for Gemma? More tears came to her eyes.

Gemma would give a king's ransom to speak to a friendly face, someone she knew before the world stopped making sense, someone with compassion, someone who hadn't witnessed what they were all witnessing. Out there, in the hallways and the foyer of the hotel wandered stone-faced soldiers, exhausted and spent, and time-conscious scientists trying over and again for an unobtainable solution, and angry faces with creased shirts and loose ties throwing orders with little confidence. Phone lines and the internet were still down. She could not even call her parents to let them know she was alive. The panic and fear they must be suffering. The not knowing.

She threw herself onto the hotel bed. It wasn't yet late, but she decided to turn in. Tears did that to people, brought on the need for sleep. Outside the snow fell, worse than she had ever seen in Aberdeen. She kicked off her boots and wriggled out of her jeans before cocooning herself under the covers. She pulled off her jumper and unclipped her bra, then pulled the covers tight to her chin.

Ben Williamson signed her up with Black Aquila, and put her up in the hotel, protected, dry, warm and fed. Comfort received at the cost of not releasing images to the public, images her camera captured in Aberdeen, and a promise to conduct a little work, dig deeper into the crisis, gather information, investigate. Snoop really. As a reporter all that should have been second nature, but she had worked at a small-time local paper, not a national release.

She reached over and clicked off the lights, plunging the room into darkness. The wind cut into the building, howling, seeking entry to her room. Snow rapped at the window. Engines outside came and went. It was rarely quiet.

Gemma's eyes closed and she almost drifted to sleep. A knock came at the door. She sat bolt upright, disorientated for the moment and breathing frantically. For one terrible second, she thought herself back in the city, back in the clutches of the infected and being chased by that animal in a uniform.

The knock came again.

"Just a second," she called out. She grabbed an ill-fitting t-shirt that hung to her knees. All her clothes were at her flat, and she was left to wear donations. Correct sizing was a luxury she was yet to receive. She answered the door.

The light from the hallway, though not terribly bright still hurt her eyes. She looked away with a squint and a frown.

"Sorry to disturb you, Gemma."

Williamson? Ben Williamson had refused her request for meetings, citing he was too busy. Understandable, but that didn't help Gemma progress her task. Williamson's bulky frame filled the doorway. He checked his gold Rolex.

"It's not late. It's okay." Gemma stifled a yawn. "Come in."

Gemma tugged at her T-shirt, clicked on the lights, then snatched her dressing gown from the bathroom door.

"Please," she said, gesturing to the only chair in the room tucked beneath a desk, and she took a seat on the edge of the bed.

"I know you've been trying to see me for the last few days. I regret it's taken this long to find time in my schedule. Things have been moving rapidly."

"I understand. Sort of."

"How's your research going? I trust you've not run into too many obstacles."

Gemma shrugged. "It's going okay, I guess. I'm still not sure what it is I'm looking for."

"You'll know it when you see it. Just keep compiling reports, first-hand and third. Anything. Think of it as building a case for the prosecution to use at trial. You've covered trials before?"

Gemma nodded. Nothing worthy of front page news. Prosecutions for relatively minor offences, driving charges, minor theft and assault, and a ridiculous neighbourhood dispute that continued for five years before all avenues of appeal were exhausted.

"Good. And see this?" He picked up her Black Aquila ID badge from the desk. "This grants you access to a great many places. Don't be afraid to use it. Anywhere. You might not think what you're doing has rhyme or reason but it does. If not now, it will."

Why was he there? And why now? Something was up.

"It didn't get me access to you."

Williamson smiled, his lips set tight above a stubble-covered chin. "I'll try to rectify that. Unfortunately, it looks like you'll be stuck here for Christmas."

"I guessed as much."

"It bothers you?"

"I wish I could call my mum, just to let her know I'm alive." She could feel the tears coming again, but she blinked them away. Not now, not in front of him.

"I can't make any promises but we have access to satellite phones. I can perhaps arrange for you to—"

"Really? Oh, Mr. Williamson, that would be a dream come true."

"No promises." He stood. "I've got much to do before I call it a night."

Gemma also stood. "How are things in the city?"

"Bad. Really bad. The government has reversed their decision to have only British troops operating in the city. US troops are starting to arrive."

"That's good though?"

"Yes, but the numbers are still not enough. The army is still battling at the hospital, trying to regain control. It's shaping up to be a total loss there. And elsewhere, well let's just say, where the army is not, the infected are. People are dying. A lot. It's a mess."

"There's no good news?"

He paused at the door. "So far, there's only been a few cases outside Aberdeen. We're containing it, but the cost … the cost may be too high to pay. Good night, Gemma. We'll talk soon."

Gemma wished the world would go back to how it was.

***

Dr. Eugene Holden stood in the dull, morning sun, sipping his coffee and watching the snow fall. When this chaos began, he liked his coffee weak. Now, he preferred it strong. The air was biting and his breath misted before him. Even lifting his cup to his mouth was a chore. He was tired to his core and his bones ached. Where was he? Other than somewhere in Scotland, he had no idea.

Holden lifted his glasses from his nose and up to his head. He rubbed his eyes. His mind churned constantly, analysing the *whys and wherefores* of everything. He had been framed for a breach of containment at the DSD building in Aberdeen, an electronic fingerprint damning him to be the one who authorised the opening of the containment tank in the basement. All part of some elaborate forgery. There were possible answers, but none would he speculate out loud. The reality could be too much to contemplate.

Ben Williamson ceased any possibility of prosecution when Holden agreed to join Black Aquila. He was the world's expert on the outbreak of the Carrion Virus. Better to have him working than locked up, was something Williamson obviously believed. Better for Holden to be working than locked up, is something Holden believed.

Holden stood in front of what was his workplace. From the outside, it offered the appearance of a large warehouse at the heart of a sizeable industrial complex. He never saw anyone else other than Black Aquila operatives and the few medical staff seconded to him. His residence was a small cottage on the edge of the woods. The trip to work each morning was a short ride in a blacked-out Land Rover.

Williamson promised that in time he would have the data needed to clear his name. At least someone believed him.

Dr. Holden poured the last dribble of his coffee into the snow at his feet.

Or maybe Williamson doesn't believe me.

"You're getting too cynical, Eugene," he said to the storm raging around him.

From behind, someone cleared his throat. Holden turned.

Hyde, the man appointed to Holden as his official liaison with Ben Williamson, tapped at a watch. A squat man with a wide chest, blinked the snow from his eyes. Holden thought of him as his jailer more than anything.

"We've much work to be getting on with."

Holden pulled his glasses from his forehead. The snow was falling in the forecourt of the complex. It was nice to be outside for a little while.

"Very well. Lead on."

Chapter Two
Deleted Horizons

Eric stomped his feet into the slush and clicked off the satellite telephone. Regular communications down, out in the cold was the only way of making contact. And it was colder than cold. Task completed, he returned to the relative warmth of the hotel, the one Black Aquila used as headquarters, and handed the telephone to the next waiting operative.

Eric shook the snow from his shoulders and headed up to his room. The lobby of the hotel was never quiet. People hurried about every hour of the day. Eric laboured up the stairs, his arms and legs fatigued from trudging through the snow. The death of Rozek hit him hard. Didn't they all? The outbreak had killed so many. And many more were bound to die. He needed sleep, but did not look forward to the nightmares that played movie reels of all the lost men.

At the top of the stairs, at the landing, two women were on haunches cleaning the carpet. Eric looked to his boots and stepped past with a nod of apology. Neither paid him much attention. He guessed it was a never-ending task and wondered about the arrangement for hotel staff. Were their services given in exchange for not being moved into a displacement centre? Eric unlocked his door with a swipe of his keycard.

"Eric?"

Ben Williamson.

"Eric. Good to see you returned safely."

Williamson stretched out a hand. His eyes went to Eric's own, cracked and filthy, tainted with dried blood. He withdrew the gesture. "Your hands. Blood."

"Do you think I'd be wandering around here if it was blood from an infected?" Eric said sharply. He was too tired to deal with stupidity. Eric would never risk spreading the infection.

"No. I suppose not. But I'll wait for you to get cleaned up."

Williamson followed Eric into the room, and sat on a small sofa in the corner. Eric unzipped his tac vest and removed his coat. He went to the bathroom, switched on the light and ran hot water into the sink. He washed the filth from his hands and face, the warm water going some way to reviving his depleted spirit. He dried himself with a towel before returning to the room.

"I can tell by your face it was bad out there tonight."

"It's bad every night." Eric sat on the bed, undid his laces and kicked his boots free. "We lost a man tonight. Rozek. The infected were on us before we could react. Another man down."

Williamson closed his eyes and mouthed Rozek's name. "How many is that now?"

Eric knew the exact number, knew every name and remembered every face. "Too many."

Williamson opened his eyes. "Indeed, Eric."

"I'm going home tomorrow." Eric lifted his legs onto the bed and squashed two pillows beneath his head. "I spoke to Jacqui not long ago. I'm looking forward to seeing her and my kids."

Williamson toyed with the wedding ring on his finger. "I understand, but there's—"

"There's always so much to do, always more hotspots flaring up."

"They need us, they need you, they need Black Aquila. And they need the army."

"If they send the army in it'll be a bloodbath. *They* shoot, and ask questions later. But," he punched at the pillows, and readjusted his position, "perhaps that's what we should be doing."

"They're people out there, Eric. Ill people, not monsters."

"Not monsters? Have you seen them?" Eric pointed to the window. "Those are not people. There's no coming back from that."

"I've seen them," said Williamson in a near whisper. "I've seen what they're capable of."

"And you really think they can recover?"

"I have to believe, otherwise all we're doing here is for nothing."

An awkward silence filled the room.

Williamson stood.

"Go home, Eric. Tomorrow. Spend Christmas with your family. But I need you back here the day after Boxing Day. Carter will take over your role until you're back. How is your wife?"

"Jacqui's worried. It's tough on her."

"I understand. Enjoy Christmas as best you can. Let's hope the new year brings better conditions for us all." Williamson reached for the door.

"Any news on Brutus?" Eric asked.

Brutus was a rogue Black Aquila operative, missing in action. A huge bloke with a huge ego, and a huge debt coming to him. Eric still felt the swelling in his jaw from their last confrontation.

"Nothing about Brutus, no."

"You understand that when we find him, I will kill him?"

"Enjoy the time with your family. Forget about this place for a few days." Williamson closed the door behind him.

Eric could hardly contemplate something as normal as Christmas. It seemed a lifetime since he had enjoyed anything normal. He closed his eyes, hoping for a restful sleep free of nightmares. He would be disappointed.

***

Jacqui stood in the kitchen, hand gripping the edge of the sink. Outside, the two kids ran around in the garden trying to catch the snow as it fell. The white painted the branches of the fir bushes. Small piles of snow were growing higher in the corner of the garden, the beginnings of a snowman more than likely. Thick scarves obscured the kids' mouths but she knew they were both smiling, laughing at the thrill of finally having enough snow to play in.

She turned from the window, back to the empty kitchen. A clock ticked faithfully on the wall. Eric was back doing what he did. She missed him. He promised he'd be home soon. So many promises. Broken promises. But she understood.

It was not too long ago Jacqui cringed at the thought of Eric's return. But he had changed, and much for the better, for her and the kids. The private burden that had caused so much upheaval in their marriage remained, but he'd found a way to keep its tentacles from their home life.

She wanted him home, not just for her sake but for the kids. He would not let anything bad happen to them. She wanted to be engulfed in his arms, to be reassured and feel safe.

"Come back soon, Eric," she whispered.

The clock ticked and ticked, marking time.

***

Dr. Holden entered the secure unit, the place he conducted all his research. A huge serpentine ventilation system hummed overhead, the cacophonous sound echoing through the vault-like room. A research workstation dominated the centre of the room, with flashing computer terminals, cameras monitoring every square inch, and steel surgical implements lined up and arranged by types in boxes. It was state-of-the-art. Unlike his previous workplace, instead of one huge containment tank to hold the infected, there were ten separate holding cells. And each contained one infected. They stood in confinement, hands pressed against the glass, their bodies shuddering in constant motion.

Armed guards stood watch around the clock, observing every move made by the infected and the research staff. Such a measure would have been beneficial in his previous work place, when he was framed for the security breach, a witness to prove his innocence.

Few medical staff worked with Holden. Doctors appeared and disappeared. Specialists and nurses did the same. For all he knew, this was one of many research stations located on the complex. He had no real way of finding out. Everything was kept hushed.

Holden took his usual seat, and flicked through the pages of waiting reports detailing data gathered on the endurance levels of the infected.

"Ah, Doctor Holden."

Hyde, the manager of the facility, walked his way followed by two females. Holden swivelled in his chair to face the new arrivals. Hyde flashed a rare smile, one that did little to comfort Holden.

"I'd like you to meet Doctor Helen Benoit," he said. "An expert in viral infections."

Dr. Helen Benoit was the older of the two women. A pair of thick-set glasses balanced on her nose, her greying hair pulled back into a bun.

"And this is Jane," said Hyde. "I'm sorry, dear, I seem to have forgotten your surname."

"Appleby," she provided.

"Of course. Jane, Jane Appleby," Hyde introduced again. "Jane is a theatre nurse with extensive experience in tissue viability and trauma. They are now on your team, and I'm sure both ladies will prove invaluable to your research."

Hyde stepped away and spoke to one of the armed guards. Dr. Benoit shook Holden's hand in a weak fashion. "It's a pleasure to meet you in person. I've attended several of your lectures in London and read much of your research."

"Well, thank you, Helen."

"I'll set up over there, shall I?" She pointed to the workstation.

"Certainly. And you, Jane?"

The new theatre nurse watched the containment tanks with a peculiar focus. Fear? Surely this scene was not new to her?

"Your quite safe, my dear. Won't you sit down?"

"Are there only ten of them?"

"For the moment, yes."

Jane was a pretty thing with dark hair combed back behind her ears, shining blue eyes and pale skin too pure to be blemished by make-up.

"What kind of work are we doing here?"

"You've not been told?"

She shook her head.

"We'll get to that," said Holden. "I'd like to know a little more about you, if I could? You've experience with the infected."

"Is it that obvious?"

Holden touched her shoulder. "Yes."

"I was in Aberdeen. I worked in the hospital. I was on a bank shift when the outbreak hit. The hospital was overrun. We would have been, too, but a policeman, Nick, he held us together, barricaded the ward and we held out. We were rescued by Black Aquila. Nick, he didn't make it. Not many of us did." She spoke the policeman's name with a touch a love.

"I'm sorry for your loss, Jane."

"I was offered this job. If I refused I'd have to stay in a displacement centre. So here I am."

"You're safe here, Jane. I promise you that." Holden leaned closer. "Do you know where we are?"

"You don't know?"

"No. Like you, I have little choice."

"We're still in the north-east but I don't know exactly where. When I asked, they told me never to ask again. And I won't. Everything has been a whirlwind. The NHS won't allow me into the city to care for the injured. At least here I can do some good. Can't I?"

Do some good? The doctor started out doing good. Now, he was not so sure. There was too much cloak and dagger, snippets of information here, snippets of information there, rarely marrying.

"Of course you can do some good," said Holden in his most convincing voice.

"So what are we doing here?"

Holden shuffled through his notes before pulling a single sheet free from the stack.

"We are conducting trials on the endurance of the infected. We need to understand their tolerance to certain environmental factors. Varying degrees of temperature, for instance. We must also seek to understand what they're capable of. We know they're resilient to inflicted wounds that would kill a normal person. If we are to combat this outbreak, we need to know how best to bring down infected should there be no other option."

"No other option?" said Jane, too loud.

Dr. Benoit looked up from her laptop, peering over the rim of glasses. Holden waved his hand weakly and she returned to setting up her workstation.

"Jane, you must understand we struggle to identify the presence of the virus in a timely fashion."

"They have a vaccine for the early stages. I saw it on the news."

Holden gave Jane a weary smile. "I need to be honest with you, Jane. If you're working here I want us to have honesty. Yes?"

"Yes."

"There is no vaccine for any of the stages of the virus."

"What?"

"The reason for this? Well, can you imagine how many people wouldn't come to hospital if they knew that it was an inevitability they would succumb to the virus? That what we offer is a placebo? It's nothing more than a way to keep track of all those infected. They would go to ground, we'd have outbreaks all over the country and lose control. So far, the media ban is working. For how long, I can't say. This is an impossible situation with no real solutions."

Jane bit her lip, her eyes downcast. "I don't know if I can do this."

"We don't have any choice. We have to do this. Come. You'll be okay. I promise but we need to work."

***

Far from the research unit and its noise, Holden led Jane through the facility's quiet corridors. Motion-activated lights flickered to life. Holden's footfalls echoed. Jane walked lighter, her trainers occasionally squeaking on the floor. Not for the first time, Holden wondered what the facility was designed for before its current purpose. Above ground it looked like a nondescript industrial complex. But the subterranean vaults contained a darker secret. Was it purpose built for the outbreak?

This possibility disturbed Holden a great deal. It indicated somebody knew the carrion outbreak was coming, and also knew its potential.

Holden wiped at his forehead with a handkerchief from his pocket. His hand shook. He paused, resting a hand on the wall.

"Are you alright, Doctor?"

"A funny turn, my dear," he lied. "Nothing to worry about. With everything that's going on, and well, I've not been sleeping much. I'll be fine. Just give me a moment." Holden gulped down some air. "Shall we continue?"

They arrived at a large, double security door. Holden punched in the security code and the doors slid open. The first time Holden entered the cavernous room, it felt much like the DSD containment centre in Aberdeen. As time passed, he picked subtitle differences. While the DSD containment facility was a construction of necessity, fragmented and fluid, with temporary walls, and makeshift rooms, here every part had a definite purpose. The room was segregated into sections, each one containing an individual area for holding an infected. More personal for study.

An armed guard gave them a sombre once over before allowing access. Jane's eyes were wide and her mouth ajar. Holden silently took stock of his own reaction. Nothing. He had been at this task too long, too desensitised. The door slid shut behind them and automatically locked.

Within the open-plan lab several pods stood evenly spaced around the interior. Each pod contained a research station, a small containment facility for a single infected and a line of computers and cameras. Documenting the work was key to progress. Nothing could be missed. Clean and sterile like an operating theatre.

Holden did not enjoy the work but he understood its importance.

Due to his skill set and position in the research team, Holden was given an additional workspace, a small office to work from, away from the rest of the lab. Jane followed him like a lost puppy, staying close.

"Sit down, Jane. Let me explain what we're doing here. Out there, each pod contains an infected. The work being conducted will yield important information about their durability. We know the virus grants the infected superior strength, a superior sense of smell and hearing, and similar endurance. They need little sleep, can run for hours when stimulated and can tolerate injuries that would cripple a normal man. We've seen some indication that the virus bestows limited regenerative properties; however, we're in the early stages of understanding this. The virus and all its hallmarks are still very much a mystery. Do you have any questions so far?"

Jane's eyes flicked from Holden to the floor and back again. "How long does infection take to occur?"

"Initially, we believed that infection travelled all three stages in seven days. More recently, specifically those who have contracted the virus through a bite or similar succumb to the infection in a matter of hours, sometimes less. It could be a natural immunity that sees the disparity, but we simply don't know."

"And treatments?"

Holden pushed his glasses up to his forehead. "There are none at this time."

Jane sat back. "On the news, they said there were treatments for those in the first two stages."

Holden shook his head, with genuine regret.

"A story told to prevent a situation where those with symptoms would refuse to report to the authorities. A white lie to protect lives. If there was any other way, be assured we would have taken it." His words of assurance sounded hollow to himself. He stood. "Come, it's time. I need to inspect the work."

Jane followed without comment. Holden lead her to each pod in turn. Each one contained an infected, strapped down, powerless, no longer a threat, now just a source of data. Some of the infected were being deconstructed, limbs surgically removed. Others had their core temperatures increased or decreased. Many were intentionally wounded to study the regeneration the virus gifted. A few were to be starved, some blinded and a few remained untouched for now. It was a grisly sight, one reminiscent of Victorian battlefield surgeries.

Jane hid her shock and outrage poorly, remained quiet, stunned to silence. Holden could understand. It bothered him a small amount that he was devoid of those reactions now. They were lost some way back on the path he now walked.

Chapter Three
Pressure

Ryan Bannister stirred in his bed. The sharp screech of a cell phone cut through the calm of the apartment with a rancorous certainty. He had not heard that ringtone before. He sat bolt upright. The tone came again. He leapt from the bed and ran to his desk, pulling open the top drawer with such force it came free, crashing to the floor and spilling all its contents. Ryan scrambled until he found the cell.

"Hello. Who is this?" He knew it could only be one person.

"This is Mr. Nippon."

Ryan mustered a grunt of acknowledgement.

"You're coming to us. Your flight leaves tomorrow. The details have been emailed to you securely." Mr. Nippon's voice, normally eloquent and serene, was electronically distorted.

"Why?" The word slipped out in an automatic plea.

There was a pause, the soft crackle of the voice disrupter and the rain hitting the window the only sounds.

"We have some loose ends to tie up, Mr. Bannister. I trust you've been watching the news?"

The line went dead. Ryan threw the phone onto the bed. Outside, Seattle endured another rainstorm. The dreary grey matched his mood. Since returning from Scotland, Ryan isolated himself from people, spent days in bed, dreaming, regretting, wishing. Since Aberdeen with Brutus, Ryan questioned himself like never before.

He picked up the television remote control, his finger hovering over the power button. Sweat trickled from his unwashed armpits. He pushed the button. The television burst into life. It was on mute. He flicked through several channels. All covered the same story. Words flashed across the screen streaming updated reports.

Gunfire heard within the city.
Military aircraft flying into the heart of the city.
Naval ships patrolling offshore.
No contact from within the city.
Power outages.

Reports of mass loss of life to the infection.

Ryan dropped the remote to the floor. The back sprung open and the batteries spilled out. He sank down to the floor next to them. He shivered. He wasn't cold. He watched the television without sound. He did not need to hear the words.

"What have they done?" he sobbed into his hands. "What have I done?"

***

Brutus watched the blades of the fan spin above the bed. It was still dark outside. The Thai woman lying next to him did not stir. He reached out and casually caressed her nakedness under the light sheet. He had paid for her company and it was money well spent. Not that such a monetary decision was a concern. Brutus had plenty more cash. His services in Aberdeen had been well paid for. The dollars allowed him to disappear, to escape the snow and blizzards of Scotland, and become anonymous in Phuket, Thailand.

For the first few days he discovered the city, drank in many open-aired bars, brushed off pushy pedlars, and found countless women ready to spend the night with him for a relatively small fee. Afternoons were spent on Hua Beach, beautiful and secluded, golden sand touching crystal water. It all provided a measure of peace, an indulgence of sorts. And it remained only momentarily, for Brutus was a man of war. The chaos of conflict was food to Brutus, and so often in life it called to him in a way that was impossible to ignore.

The sea breeze danced in through the patio doors. The distant waves could be heard, the heartbeat of the ocean rhythmic and eternal. Perhaps a few more days and he would move on to a different part of the country, or perhaps jump on a plane and head for somewhere new, somewhere south, somewhere north, east or west. His eyes began to close. The girl next to him moved from his reach, turning with a stretch.

The satellite phone rang as he knew it would. He reached under his pillow, felt the reassuring presence of the Glock, and next to it, the phone.

"Do you know the goddamned time?"

Andor Toth, a double agent at the DSD gave a slight chuckle. "I'm enjoying my lunch, Brutus. You failed to provide a longitude and latitude, so consideration of an opportune time is mere guess work."

Brutus heaved himself off the bed and walked to the patio doors. "What do you want?"

"Are you alone?"

He looked back to the prostitute. She slept. In any event she did not speak much English, only enough to effectively ply her trade.

"I'm alone."

"It's time for you to go to work, Brutus."

"I'm on holiday."

The playful tone in Toth's voice disappeared. "Things are moving faster than we anticipated. You're needed."

Brutus cultivated a silence. He looked over at the holdall, stuffed full of cash, mostly American currency. How difficult would it be to disappear permanently? Easy to fall off the map and live comfortable for several years, but permanently? It was not that simple. It never was. He knew just enough to be considered a liability. If they could unleash the Carrion Virus on Aberdeen then knocking off Brutus would be a breeze.

"When and where?"

"Cairo, in two days. We've sent the assemble order to your team. I'll meet you on the third day for a briefing." The line went dead.

Brutus switched off the phone and placed it on the table. He pulled the Glock from beneath the pillow, placed the edge of the barrel against his forehead, the cool metal interrupting the persistent heat.

The girl stirred again. She pulled her long dark hair from her face, fixed her eyes on the gun, and broke into a babble of broken English.

"Get out," said Brutus.

She continued with her noise and crawled to the far edge of the bed.

Brutus lifted the gun, the sight set on her forehead. With his free hand he pointed to the patio doors. "Get the hell out. Now!"

She grabbed her clothes from the floor and dashed out the door.

Brutus grabbed a cigar from the table and sat it between his lips. Two days to get to Cairo without alerting the authorities to his passing. It was tight, but doable. Tomorrow he would go back to Hua Beach one last time. He did not know when he might get another chance. The work that was to come would be bloody, of that he was sure. It was the only type of work he was good at.

***

The midmorning traffic crawled along at a frustrating pace, at times almost to the point of a gridlock. Brutus wrapped a knuckle against the half-opened window of the taxi. The driver sang along to a tune on the radio. Brutus could have left earlier in the morning, instead, he spent a few hours on Hua Beach drinking fresh, fruit juice and enjoying the sun. The beach was a perfect place to be, but he had to get back to work.

Toth expected him to leave first thing in the morning. He disliked being summoned like an obedient dog. Tardiness was an apt protest. That's why he left later. Well, that and because he did not fully trust Toth or the people he worked for. The difference between getting on a plane to the next objective and having his throat slit while he slept was as thin as an assassin's blade.

He kept his arm resting on his holdall while scanning out the window. "How much longer?"

"Not long, mister," said the driver.

Brutus gave the window a final wrap. He could see the airport ahead. "I'll get out here."

Brutus threw a bunch of crumpled notes at the driver, and stepped out into the midday sun, slinging his bag over his shoulders. He slipped on his aviators and closed the taxi door behind him. It may not have been more time efficient to walk the remainder of the distance, but the driver's singing was getting on Brutus's nerves. He pulled his mobile from the pocket of his shorts and punched the only number stored.

"Freddie. It's me. You ready?"

"Ah, yes, Mr. Brutus, sir."

"Meet me at the drop off point in five minutes."

"Very good."

Nodding Freddie, as he was known, due to his habit when speaking, was a fixer of sorts. Brutus was put in touch with Nodding Freddie by an old acquaintance, Ash Gibbons. For the right price Freddie could negate all security measures, sneaking you through passport control and customs. Nodding Freddie was a backdoor in and out of Thailand.

Brutus powered on, picking up his pace. Since Aberdeen, he was confident his face would be on a watch list. He touched at his eye, beneath his glasses. The scar still hurt, made worse by the hours spent in the sun. If anything, that bitch made him more recognisable. A scar on his face. It was not a death sentence but it made international travel more difficult.

Nodding Freddie in a garish Hawaiian shirt, yellow with green palm trees, waved Brutus over.

"Inconspicuous shirt."

Freddie nodded. "Sorry, Brutus, sir. Should I change?"

"The flight is in an hour. I need to be on it."

"Of course. I will need the … ah …" He rubbed his thumb and index finger together.

Brutus gripped Freddie on the back of his neck and pulled the slender man into an embrace. While close, Brutus slipped enough cash to keep Freddie in alcohol and hookers for the next few months.

Freddie nodded as their bodies separated. "Very good. Follow me."

Brutus paused at a waste bin, pulled out his Glock which was wrapped in a plastic bag, and threw it onto the pile of trash. He would never make it through security with the firearm, despite the money he was paying. He felt naked without it, but even unarmed Brutus was a dangerous man. Besides, he trusted Freddie just enough to know that he was not stupid enough to cross him. Brutus had a reputation and in some instances it was better protection than bullets.

***

Eric stepped out of the car and into the cold night. A light covering of snow whitened the ground underfoot. It was nothing like the adverse weather in Aberdeen, but enough to excite children on a day off school. The house was quiet, the windows dark except for the dull light in the living room.

Eric raised a hand to knock, frowned, and pulled a key from his pocket. The grandfather clock in the hallway ticked its perpetual tempo. He locked the door behind him, dropped his pack, removed his coat and placed it on the banister. Christmas cards hung on a string extending over the far wall. A small wooden advent calendar sat on the table, the numbered drawers waiting to be opened. A familiar scent struck him, a perfume that Jacqui wore for special occasions. He bought it for her on their one-year anniversary. It reminded him of better times.

The living room door creaked open. Jacqui gave an optimistic smile. She rushed over and he took her in his arms.

"Thank God you're back."

Before Eric could speak his wife placed a firm kiss on his lips.

"Not here, the kids are asleep. I don't want to wake them." She led him by the hand into the living room and closed the door.

The last time he had been home, things were strained. The kids did not warm to Eric, and Jacqui seesawed through phases of hating him and rescuing him. When they parted, Eric felt there was hope for something better than they had before. So far, that hope was being proven true.

Eric eased himself into the armchair, Jacqui sat across from him. He longed to sit next to his wife, have her in his arms but a nagging caution urged him to sit where he was.

"I was so worried, Eric. I didn't know if you were safe. It doesn't make sense what they're reporting on the news, and the few times you called, well, you could never say anything."

"You know the rules when I'm working."

"I know. I know. I'm not blaming you."

Eric felt his face harden. Not in anger, but in thought.

"What happened there, Eric? Can you tell me now?"

He let a long moment of silence pass. What to tell her? The whole truth would frighten her. Not enough of the truth would underprepare her.

"It's complicated, Jacqui."

"Try me. Please."

"You know it's a virus?"

She nodded.

"It's more widespread than reported. People are getting sick all over the city. There's nothing the government can do. There's no cure."

"And the sick people?"

"Locked away until they can be treated."

"So they can be treated then?"

"Not yet. Nothing's been discovered."

Jacqui tucked her legs up and hugged them to her chest. "Did you lose people?" Her ask was soft.

He didn't answer.

"Eric?"

"Too many. Too many."

Jacqui unfolded her legs, crossed the space between them and sat on the floor. Her hand kneaded his thigh. "We're safe, aren't we?"

Eric forced a smile. "Of course. I'll not let anything happen to you and the kids. I promise." He brought Jacqui's hand to his mouth and kissed her palm. "Can we go to bed?"

Jacqui smiled. "You want your Christmas present early, huh?"

***

Their lovemaking had been awkward at first, two people once so close, trying to rediscover that intimate familiarity. After, they lay together, Eric pulling Jacqui close. He could feel her heart beating against his chest. He was safe, even just for a night. Outside the wind flurried, snow tapping at the window. He stroked Jacqui's hair, breathing in all that he had missed for so long.

"Eric?"

"I thought you were asleep."

"Are you going back?"

"I have to."

"When?"

"Boxing Day."

Jacqui let out a sigh, her fingers pushed into Eric's chest with almost enough force to hurt. "You'll come back to us, won't you?"

"Nothing in the world will stop me."

"Don't break your promise, Eric Mann. I need you. The kids need you."

"Do you?" Eric recognised an element of desperation in his voice.

"Obviously more than you know."

"I thought you would try to stop me."

"I would love to. But I've come to understand that sometimes events take you along for a ride, and you either hold on or fall off. I know you too well, Eric, so any protesting wouldn't have done any good. You'll go back until you're satisfied you've done all you can. Martin was the same."

Martin's name still struck a raw nerve. They'd buried him only a few months ago. A good man who died under Eric's command, and died looking out for Eric. That fate was bound for one of them.

Eric gently removed Jacqui from his chest so he could look at her fully in the dull light. Her eyes sparkled. She was beautiful. He had to remind himself of how close he came to losing her with his stubbornness and his lack of control and his lack of trust. It brought a chilling fear but also a poignant reminder to never let things spiral out of control like that again.

"What is it, Eric?"

"When I'm away, you need to keep your eyes and ears open. You hear anything about people with rashes or unusual behaviour in the area you take the kids and leave. Go out into the country. Check into a bed and breakfast somewhere quiet."

"Why? It won't come here, will it?"

"No. I don't think so. But I need to know that you'll do what's needed if it does."

"What's happening in the world?"

Eric had no answer. He did not understand events anymore. Everything soared from nightmares to reality and he was thrust in the middle of it.

"Merry Christmas, Eric."

Eric hugged her close. "Merry Christmas, my love."

What kind of Christmas would the people of Aberdeen have?

***

Brutus had not visited Cairo before. As was promised, he made it through airport security without so much as a question being asked, or an eye sent his way. He kept a small wad of cash in his pocket in case a zealous official challenged him. None did, and he swept through the throngs of humanity crowding the transport hub and hailed a taxi. A grotty, somewhat rusted car pulled up. Inside, the stench of stale sweat and cigarettes choked Brutus.

Downtown Cairo, and onto a part of the city the rest of the world never saw, he found the stygian of the renowned capital of Egypt. It was not unlike any other sullied portion of a city. Cut a little deeper through the visible layers, and Brutus could read the streets as well as a lifelong resident. Street vendors selling all manner of ware, some mundane others illicit. The roads filled with cars and lorries. A swarm going about its usual business, many clad in caftans. He may not have spoken the language but Brutus understood all too well.

The taxi stopped in a narrow street away from the crowds, the light of the sun fading. Brutus threw a clump of crumpled notes to the driver and the taxi pulled away.

The air was heavy and a musk polluted the street. The windows on a dilapidated and discoloured, two-storey building were shuttered with boards. If anyone observed Brutus he wasn't aware. The building could have been abandoned and perhaps that was the intention, a camouflage designed for plain sight. The door was the only clue there was more to it. Sturdy, made of steel, well-kept and relatively new with a sliding panel at eye level. His new accommodation was an urban fortress.

Brutus banged on the door, and stepped to the side before the shutter opened. Cautious? Perhaps. But it served him well. A loud click, and the slider moved from position.

"Who is it?" called a voice.

"Santa Claus. And his elf."

"Brutus?"

He stepped into view. "Open the door, Niall."

A few more clicks and the door opened.

"No presents?" asked Niall Campbell with a smirk. He looked tired. Several days of stubble added a number of monochromatic tones to his face.

Brutus raised his middle finger. Niall laughed at the gesture and slipped his Glock into the waistband of his combat trousers.

"Is everyone here?"

"Mostly. A few are out in the field as instructed."

Niall lead Brutus to the rear room. A collection of men sat around a square table, cleaning weapons, loading magazines, typing on a laptop or just leaning back in a chair, their baseball caps pulled down over their eyes. Multiple bodies confined without proper ventilation. The room stank. Brutus recognised all in the room, all former military men, elite soldiers now working in the private sector. These men represented a portion of the collective trust Brutus retained in the world. Magnus Munson, Stuart Taylor, Freddo Macleod, Daniel Ziaber and Graeme Sinclair.

"Season's greetings, gentlemen."

Greetings were returned.

Niall pulled up a chair for Brutus and they sat next to a weapons rack that held AK-47s and a PSG1 sniper rifle.

"Where's Ry Watson?" Brutus asked Niall.

"He's at the airfield, making sure our transport is serviceable."

"Craig Muir? Roy Smart? Ash Gibbons?"

"At the location. We last had contact from them two days ago."

"Good. We'll move out tomorrow, be there the day after."

Niall leaned in close, and said in a low voice, "What are we getting into, Brutus?"

These men were hired on his recommendation, on his assurance that he could control them and apply them to the task ahead. The money that secured their services for the next two weeks was better than any could hope to make elsewhere in a year.

"I wouldn't be involved if it wasn't worthwhile," was all Brutus offered.

"The money is worthwhile. It's the risk I worry about."

"My contact will be here in the next few hours. Then we'll all know."

"I won't stick my neck into a noose. I'm here to make money."
Niall leaned back, and edged his chin toward Brutus's face.
"Collected another scar?"

Brutus touched the wound. A little deeper and he probably
would have lost the eye. That bitch and her knife. He should have
broken her neck when he had the chance. He shrugged. "We're all
scarred. I just wear mine for the world to see. Get some rest. We're
moving out tomorrow."

***

Gemma stepped off the bus into a snowstorm. Christmas Eve
and she was riding along with a force of CAF soldiers and DSD
agents. It had taken some persuasion before any would entertain
the idea of allowing her to witness them in action. She dropped
Williamson's name enough and finally the DSD agents relented.
She chatted with Danni, a female agent while they rode the
commandeered bus. The sheer amount of displaced peoples in
Aberdeen looking for shelter far exceeded the anticipated numbers
so the CAF now looked to open more areas of the city to house
these people until the containment was lifted. Several of the larger
hotels in the centre of the city had been cleared out by the military;
all traces of infection were removed and they now were readying
to receive the displaced. It was a mammoth task but a necessary
one. So Danni told her.

Gemma clutched her camera. Her aim was simple, document
everything and latch onto anyone who could provide leads or
snippets of information. She pulled her coat tighter, trying to
huddle against the cold. The shivers that ran up her spine and
through her neck were not due to the weather, but due to the act of
stepping back into the city, the place where she lost Stacey, the
place where she was forced to strike a man with a knife to save her
own life. She had seen so much horror, and knew there was more
to come.

*Don't think about it. Concentrate on moving forward. Stacey's
gone and you have a job to do.*

The CAF soldiers alighted from the bus, rifles and packs in
hand. The bus station was covered in a thick layer of snow. Armed

men stood at the doorways, weapons held at the ready, their faces hidden by thick balaclavas. Gemma followed the group toward the hotel door. It was one of the largest in Aberdeen, several storeys high and housing hundreds of displaced people. Now filled to capacity, no doubt strangers would be forced to share rooms.

They trudged along the corridor, sweat and dampness mingling in the air. The carpet beneath their boots showed hints of once being bright and immaculate, yet was now dull and ruined. Gemma loosened her scarf. Ahead, a sergeant shouted orders. She followed the procession up the stairs, filming as they climbed. Her foot burned. Glass had lacerated her foot two weeks ago, and regular cleaning of the wound and changing the dressing had not brought about any signs of healing. But she had less to complain about than most.

Nothing happening around her sprang out to her as majorly important. She was taking standard run-of-the mill footage, the movement of displaced people and the redeployment of military personnel, a mass of panic-filled faces, people herded from one place to another, the everyday misery that haunted Aberdeen.

Gemma rounded a corner, finding the soldiers stowing their packs in the bar area before moving out. Danni waved her over and indicated the free chair next to her.

"Sit down. Thought I'd keep you in the loop," she said with a smile, one that Gemma guessed would disappear in a few days.

"What's happening?"

"We're starting to bring in the displaced. The soldiers you saw will be stationed on every floor. None of the room doors will be permitted to close."

"And if someone does close a door?"

"Everyone coming here signs a contract of behaviour. Anyone breaking it will be removed and detained indefinitely."

"No kidding?"

Danni shrugged. "Dangerous times, Gemma. The actions of one person can endanger many more. We need to be strict. The CAF aren't screwing around. That's live ammunition in those rifles."

"Where do they go?"

"Who?"

"Those who don't follow the rules?"

Danni checked over her shoulder, a slight movement that many would have missed. "I don't know. Nowhere good I suppose." She smiled again. "But still, we hope that won't happen. The first coach load will be here soon. We'll be processing them. Feel free to stick around."

"Actually, I was hoping to tour around the hotel a little, see some of the conditions."

Danni tapped a pen to her teeth. "That's at the discretion of the CAF. That badge," she pointed her pen at Gemma's Black Aquila ID badge, "won't get you very far. The CAF is the law here."

"Guess I'll stick with you, then. Can we get a coffee?"

"Sure. Over there."

She pointed to a table lined with large canteens for the preparation of hot drinks.

Gemma made herself a cuppa. Only plastic cups were provided. Her cold hands welcomed the warmth, then as her fingers seemed to thaw, the cup was difficult to clasp.

"Government issue," said Danni. "Would kill for a good porcelain cup and saucer."

Something niggled at Gemma, and it wasn't the heat of her drink. For all the structure and organisation there seemed to be a vagueness to what she was told. Control was a fine thing, the CAF and DSD maintained it only through circumstance. How thorough were the new arrivals screened for infection? It would only take one lapse, one rare case that didn't display symptoms in the assumed time to turn the sanctuary of the hotel into a nest of infection.

The thought roused a great fear, one strong enough to have her think on running back to her small hotel room and the safety of that warm bed. It was not a real option. Only a fool would risk making their way through the city alone. She remembered being fearful to walk home alone in the dark not too long ago; now it wasn't people lurking in the shadows that she feared, it was something far worse.

***

The small cottage was warmed by the wood burner Holden kept fuelled. The cottage lacked any kind of decoration to mark the time of year, nor was there anything that could be considered a personal touch.

Holden had been drinking for some time before Jane arrived. An unusual circumstance. Since the crisis began he had not stopped to think about himself, or do anything other than work. He slept little, ate between appointments and spent hours in the company of monsters. And none encouraged the indulgence of a drink. This day was different. He looked forward to some chatter. And he troubled to hide the effects of his early start. But Jane was quite morose from the moment she arrived. She said little, and contributed nothing to the conversations Holden generated. It was utterly understandable, yet still annoyed him. If he could pretend the world was not going insane why couldn't she?

Two plates of food and a bottle of wine were placed on the table by an armed guard.

"Shall we begin?" Holden poured two fresh glasses, the liquid sloshing as he upended the bottle too quickly. No damage was done. "Jane, shall we begin?" he tried again.

Jane looked up, blinking as if she just returned from the recesses of her mind.

"The food smells good and is hot. Please."

Jane pushed a chunk of turkey around her plate, chasing a river of thin gravy. "What's going on, Eugene?"

Holden placed a slice of his turkey into his mouth and chewed. "What do you mean?" he said with difficulty. "I thought it would be nice to have a meal together."

"Not this," she said waving at the table. "I mean back there. Back in the laboratory."

Holden threw down his fork, far harder than he meant. Or perhaps not hard enough. He swallowed his mouthful.

"I thought you'd understand, Jane. I thought you had seen the infected at their worst, lost people you cared about. I'm trying to stop this. That is what's going on."

"What was done in there, what you did, what you asked me to do, it was torture."

"Don't be so naive. They are no longer human."

"You don't know that."

"I do. I've fought this infection from day one. I've seen the limitations of medicine and the potential for cataclysm. If we don't stop this at the root then it will flourish. I cannot allow that to happen."

"So you'll torture innocents?"

He snatched up his glass of wine. "I lost everything to this. I've given everything but my life. And here I am, a professor, spoken to like a fresh-faced student, and by a nurse? My research is respected throughout the world." He raised a finger to her. "I won't be lectured by you on issues that you barely comprehend."

"Don't pass what you've done as something for good." Jane stood from the table, her chair slipping back and falling with a loud crack. She moved toward the door without turning to face Holden. "I'm leaving tomorrow. I won't be part of this. I thought you were different. You're just like all the others in that slaughter house. I won't go back."

Ire slipped from Holden like blood from an open wound. Jane was not the source of his anger and frustration, merely an opportunistic excuse. "Jane, wait, please. Sit down. I have something to tell you."

She turned, scepticism written all over her face.

"No more excuses. No more skirting around the questions you have." He waved a hand over to her seat. "Sit. Please."

Jane stood for a moment at the door, unmoving, before turning and righting her seat. "Go on," she said sitting.

Holden grasped his wine in both hands. "No more lies or half-truths. The outbreak in Aberdeen, we were containing it in the basement of the DSD building. Someone or some people deliberately opened the containment facility and liberated several hundred infected. Somehow they falsified the electronic signature to my name. I'm being blamed. Framed and blamed."

"What?"

"It's true."

"You've been drinking, Eugene. Are you imagining things?"

"Peterson, the regional director of the DSD at the time had a part in it, others too, I'm sure. The sudden release caused the loss of a great number of military and Black Aquila personnel. You see, I lost hundreds of people on that night. Probably thousands." The sensation of a tear on his cheek surprised him. He was not an emotional person. He gulped from his glass. "I had no part in the deception or sabotage. I've only ever wanted to help people, to save them. Williamson believed in me enough to place me here so I could continue to be of some benefit. I receive his protection from prosecution in return for my continued work. I know what we're doing here is immoral, evil even. So it's useless lecturing me. I convinced myself that the end result would be worth it, even repeated it like a mantra. But, I see the horror in your eyes, and that reminds me that all my lies simply fortify my denial. What we're doing is wrong. There is no research being conducted to heal these people. The only solution left is to kill them, slay them like beasts."

"So why not leave? Why not call Williamson and tell him what's going on here? Get out now?"

A hiccup erupted. And then another. "Oh, do pardon me, Jane." Holden held his breath for a few seconds. "You've felt it here, perhaps you've never admitted such, but we're prisoners."

Jane's eyes went wide. "No."

"You've met Hyde, that odious little man. He's our jailer. I've not worked out the ins and outs yet. I'm not sure in what capacity he is employed. Does he report to Williamson? I'm not sure. I'd like to think he doesn't. So, you see, my dear lady, we're stuck here. The Black Aquila guards say little and remain professional. I've no doubt that if one of us stopped cooperating they would involve themselves with their considerable cloud. As much as I'd like to leave, to go back to something simpler, we can't."

He drained the last of his wine and coughed heavily. It didn't go down too well.

Jane's look of surprise was replaced with one of defiance. "I won't be a prisoner."

"These are dangerous and unusual times." Another hiccup. "We survive only as long as our usefulness remains intact. You jeopardise that and you might not live to see it."

Holden's vision swam. He placed a hand to his forehead. "I believe I may have drunk a little too much."

"I think you may be right." Jane crossed over to him. "Let's get you to bed, Eugene."

She wrapped an arm around him and pulled him from the seat.

The small, plain single bed almost filled the tiny bedroom. Holden sat down on the bed with a bump. Jane knelt down and removed his shoes. She swung his legs into the bed.

"I'm a professor. My research is respected throughout the world. I should be doing this myself."

"You're a drunk professor, and I'm a nurse. I've gotten a lot of people ready for bed, you know?"

He felt the covers being pulled up to his chin.

"Sleep well, Eugene. Tomorrow, we're going to plan how to get out of here."

***

Gemma remained silent. A procession of refugees skulked into the hotel lobby. Men, women and children, all frightened, clutching their meagre possessions. They kept their eyes down. Children huddled close to parents. Some alone, wept. Who knew what horrors they'd endured before reaching the safety of the displacement centres and the watchful eyes of the CAF? Gemma knew all too well.

It was a slow procedure. All identifications needed to be checked and double checked before rooms were allocated. The soldiers of the CAF kept a close eye on the newcomers. Danni sat behind a folding table sufficing as reception, logging the new arrivals.

From the doorway, someone shouted. "Down on the ground. Everyone down!"

Soldiers raised their SA80 rifles. Mother's lifted their children. One of the officers shouted for calm, but he struggled to be heard over the growing panic. Women screamed. Danni, in her rush to comply with the orders knocked her table flipping it over, scattering her files. Gemma filmed it all through shaking hands and heavy breaths.

Soldiers pushed their way through the crowd without a hint of softness. The throng parted with a single male remaining at the centre. Rifles were pointed at the man.

"Down!"

"Down!"

"Down now!"

Dark-haired, no older than twenty-one, the young man did so without hesitation, and when commanded placed his hands on the back of his head. Soldiers in protective clothing restrained his hands behind his back, and placed a spit-guard hood over his head. The soldiers lifted him to his feet and ushered him through the crowd. He shouted and screamed his protests.

"I know where the outbreak started! I need to speak with someone!"

The officer-in-charge shouted for everyone to get back in line. Danni, pale-faced, lifted the table that toppled during the rush, while her fellow DSD agents picked up the strewn paperwork. Gemma caught her attention and smiled but Danni's eyes were unfocused.

The restrained man was marched down a corridor. Gemma made to follow. A soldier moved to block her.

"I'd like to speak with the person you just took away."

"That's not possible."

Gemma pulled her Black Aquila badge from her coat. He cast it a customary glance, his attention mostly fixed behind Gemma, his task to reorganise the group.

"He's being screened for infection."

Gemma pushed the badge up high, close to his eyes. "I'd like to see that man."

"I told you, lady. That's not going to happen. Step back."

"Look," said Gemma with false confidence, "don't make me get your officer involved."

"I told you, get back." He pushed Gemma at the shoulder, not hard but with enough force to make her stumble back a step.

She could not blame him. Caution was a necessity. One thing was for sure, Gemma needed to talk to the man taken away. It's what Williamson employed her for, to poke around and uncover what others may have missed. And his claim could not be ignored.

Danni appeared at Gemma's side. "Gemma, the last transport heading back to the airport is leaving in the next few minutes."

"What about you?"

"We'll be here all night."

It would be cold, noisy and uncomfortable, but she had to speak to the man they took away. "You know, maybe I'll stay. I can grab a few hours on a sofa over there and head back tomorrow."

***

The kids tore into a present together, one of their joint gifts from Father Christmas. Eric sat in his armchair, a mug of coffee in one hand. Jacqui sat on his lap, smiling at the excitement only Christmas morning could bring. The children still had not acclimatised to Eric's presence in the household, memories of the turbulent period the family went through still fresh in their minds no doubt. Still, Christmas had a way of washing away past pains.

The mobile in his pocket vibrated and Jacqui jumped at the sudden interruption. Eric moved to pull the phone free. There was only one person who would be calling on this day, and it would not be with tidings of Christmas joy.

"I better take this, love."

Jacqui slipped from his lap. "Daddy will just be a minute, kids. Help me pick up the wrapping paper."

"I'll be quick," he promised. Once out of the living room, in the hallway, he answered his phone. "Williamson?"

"Yes, Eric. It's me."

He sounded drunk, or tired. Probably both.

"Things are bad, Eric. I need you back here. Tomorrow evening at the latest. Christ, it's a mess. The CAF have been using lethal force. It's only a matter of time before this gets out. We're losing men, too many. Some are refusing to go out into the field. You know what? I don't blame them. I'm close to halting all our operations. We're not rat catchers, Eric. I need you back here."

It was a pleading repetition.

"What about Carter?"

"He's twisted his ankle on a mission. He's hobbling about, not fit to lead. A car will pick you up tomorrow morning. I'll see you in the evening."

The line went dead. Eric stood in the hallway for a time, the children were still cleaning up the fallout of their gifts.

"You have to go back?" Jacqui seemed to appear from nowhere.

Eric nodded. He didn't want to say the word. His chested ached.

"When?"

"Tomorrow morning."

She touched his cheek. "We still have today. Let's make it special."

"The kids?"

"They'll understand. Their Christmas joy will keep them elated."

Eric took hold of Jacqui's hand, harder than he meant to. "You remember what I said last night?"

She nodded, her eyes full of quiet strength and yet some doubt. "I remember." She kissed Eric. "Always come back to us."

"I will."

Chapter Four
Days Of Uncertainty

While Ryan Bannister sat on the plane flying over the darkened world, a thought struck him. How little understanding people possessed of each other. On the outside, he likely seemed a normal holidaymaker, perhaps heading to see loved ones for the holiday season. In reality, he was a gifted and integral part of the facilitation of something stupendous.

It was a fleeting retrospection, no doubt his mind scrambling in its cataclysmic attempts to rationalise his role in all things. In the lonely hours he told himself that all he did was deliver the package, one of his design of course, but someone else would have been paid to take his place. No matter what he told himself, deep down Ryan Bannister knew he sold his soul for a huge sum of cash and entered into a conspiracy he wished to know nothing about.

The landing was turbulent. He took his first steps on Japanese soil in the rain. The journey was particularly arduous, with time-consuming screening for infection at every transfer point. And it was all about to start again.

Another blood test was required at the arrivals section at Boarder Control. Japanese Defence Force soldiers wore protective gloves and surgical masks, their rifles rested on slings but all kept their hands resting close to the triggers.

Ryan was toward the back of the queue, underwent the blood test and passport checks and was then ushered through to baggage collection. Soldiers patrolled every corner of the airport. It was the Christmas period. Ryan expected to see more commuters. At times there seemed to be more armed personnel than travellers.

Announcements in Japanese were made over the public address system. People elbowed each other vying for a prime spot at the carousel. A baby screamed in its mother's arms. A child clinging to its father's leg looked up at him with an inane curiosity. A couple kissed. A large man's finger was busy digging into his ear. A woman behind him sneezed and sneezed and sneezed again. A young man, too tall for his coat sipped on a can of Diet Coke. He wished he was elsewhere.

Ryan shook his head at the absurd direction his life had gone of late. Poor decisions lead to screwed-up situations. He knew that.

He slipped his arm through the second strap of his backpack. It was the only luggage that he cared to bring. How long would he be in Japan? The opportunity to hammer out the finer points of the trip never presented itself. Or, more so, Ryan was shit-scared and plodded along leaving his brain in his arse where it couldn't get him into more trouble.

A Japanese man in an expensive dark suit headed his way, his bald head still damp from the rain. Ryan looked away, hoping the man was focused on anyone but him. His intense look and subtle confidence bothered Ryan.

"Mr. Bannister?"

That question and a fixated look from a heavily lined face suggested his bother may have been warranted.

"Mr. Nippon sends he regards. I am to take you to him." The man spoke with a heavy accent.

"Now?" It was late. Ryan expected to be taken to a hotel, settle in and see Mr. Nippon in the morning.

"Follow me, please."

The man turned on his heel and marched toward the exit. Despite being almost a foot shorter than Ryan, he found himself breaking into a trot to keep up. Why was he always meeting people in a hurry?

Outside the airport felt busier. Arrivals or departures, Ryan could not tell. He swam through a sea of umbrellas, uttering apologies as he knocked people in his haste to keep up with his nameless guide.

The slapping sound of their wet shoes echoed on the first tier of the multi-storey carpark. The unlocking mechanism of a red Mazda clicked, and Ryan slid into the rear seat.

"Where are we going? Will it take long?"

"The Owls' Nest."

Ryan fastened his seatbelt. The guide's eyes studied Ryan through the rear-view mirror. Again Ryan wished he was somewhere else, perhaps back in his bed, living out his crappy life, just as he was up until a few months ago.

Greed can blind a man, and Ryan only now began to regain some of his sight.

***

Gemma scribbled some notes on her thick notepad, a record of observations, leads to follow, names and contacts, reminders to herself. Details of all her memory cards, the date, time and event. For a few hours she watched the displaced arrive, be logged, and assigned rooms.

She yawned and rubbed her eyes. The sofa she sat on was a typical hotel piece of furniture, built to endure and look classy but not necessarily for comfort. Her foot burned. She'd run out of fresh dressings for her wound. If she asked one of the soldiers, she was sure one of them would have a medical pack but she was doing her best to stay out of their way. Most were now on different floors, guarding their respective areas.

Danni sat across from Gemma, her chin slumped down to her chest and snoring softly. Her hair was coming loose from the bobble she used to tie it back. She looked a mess. Nobody spoke in the lobby. The radios crackled and operators occasionally relayed a message back, but otherwise all endured the silence. Gemma's breathing seemed too loud. She found herself stalling her breath, counting the seconds she could last comfortably on one breath. Eighteen seconds was the best she could do.

Gemma finished her note and closed the pad, and put it to one side. She stretched out her legs, kicking them up on the table.

A young radio operator looked her way. "Long night?"

She gave a weary smile. "I don't seem to have any other kind nowadays."

Gemma turned her coat into a makeshift duvet. She wriggled herself down into a lying position. A stiff back was likely in the morning. The gentle hum of the lights, the snoring of Danni, and the rhythmic footsteps not far off were her lullaby. Eighteen seconds was still the best she could do.

Voices. Sudden. Gemma's eyes snapped open, and for one terrible moment she believed the infected were at her throat. She managed to suppress the scream before it left her throat. The man detained earlier was being marched across the room, an officer gripping the back of his neck and speaking words Gemma could not make out. Their quick steps took them up the stairs.

Gemma sat upright. Her belongings cascaded to the floor. She swore, hurriedly picked everything up and stuffed it all back into her bag. She slung her coat under her arm and took off toward the stairs.

"Where do you think you're going?" The officer eyed her with eyebrows raised.

"I didn't think I'd be staying here all night, sir." Why did she call him sir? "I was thinking of trying to get a bed for the night. I know you're not at capacity here yet."

"You're the Black Aquila lady, right?"

"Yeah. Gemma Findlay."

"I know Williamson, many years ago now since I last saw him."

Gemma flashed a smile, but the officer seemed to allow his thoughts to wander to another time. Was that fear she detected? Perhaps not fear, anxiety more likely.

"Do you think I can get a bed?"

"Fifth floor. There's a handful of displaced persons bedding down there tonight. Don't be disturbing anyone. They've been through enough."

"I'll be the perfect guest. I'll even make the bed in the morning." The humour, probably inappropriate, remained unanswered by the officer.

Gemma entered the stairwell, looking up. Five flights of stairs. *This better be worth it.*

It looked miles away, and she didn't think of herself as an athlete. She would have taken the lifts but they were all deactivated, a security measure she was told.

Her foot still burned, and she hobbled with hands grasping at rails, levering herself upward and around, and upward further, Gemma's breath grew laboured. *Maybe I need to join a gym. Thirty-two years of age and I can't handle five flights.*

A CAF soldier on the fifth floor sat a little too relaxed on a chair. His eyes were heavy, his head slumping. He gave Gemma one quick look, turned and saw his colleague checking rooms, and then returned to the task of fighting sleep.

The first two rooms were occupied, the beds used by adults, the makeshift cots on the floor taken by children. Two suitcases lay open next to the children, clothes spilled and scattered about the room. The third room she came to was empty, the bed made perfectly, and rolled up mats stacked in the corner for the extra guests that would no doubt be squeezed in at some point.

Gemma sat heavily on the bed, throwing her bag and coat down behind her. Finding the man they detained was her main concern but the fire in her foot compelled her to attend to that first. Her foot throbbed. Taking her weight off it helped a little but not enough. She pulled off her boot and sock, stifling a moan. The bandages were stained crimson and as she unwrapped the dressings. It felt like the inside of her foot sought to break through the skin. The smell was not pleasant.

"Ma'am?" A handsome soldier, olive-skinned with stubble darkening his chin, stood in the doorway. "May I come in?"

Gemma nodded, the pain having robbed her of the ability to speak. He knelt at her side, pulled on some protective medical gloves and took her foot in his hands.

"This looks nasty. You've ruptured a stitch. There's a smell to it, too."

Gemma felt her cheeks reddening.

The handsome soldier looked up and smiled. "Sorry, I didn't mean that to sound how it did."

"It's alright, I know what you mean." Gemma's chest heaved as he pushed around the wound, and with the last push she sucked in a breath between her teeth. "You do know what you're doing, don't you?"

"I need to go get something to clean this up." He stood. "I'll be back in a moment."

Under normal circumstances she may have been intrigued by his good looks, intimidated even. But then and there, with the smell lining her nostrils, she didn't feel too attractive, and was more intent on having the pain disappear. The soldier returned, a small medical pack in hand. He set his rifle down against the wall and returned to kneeling in front of her. Yes, he was good looking. Those blue eyes were bright against his skin.

"I'll make this as painless as possible. So what's your story? How'd you get this cut?"

"What's your name?" countered Gemma.

"Dylan Lee. Yours?"

"Gemma Findlay."

Dylan cracked open a plastic vial of saline and emptied the contents onto some medical swabbing. He dabbed at the wound. The pain and the cold fluid sent shivers up her foot.

"Broken glass," she said through clenched teeth.

"And what were you doing walking on broken glass?"

"I assure you it wasn't intentional." Gemma spied a slight smile break upon those handsome lips. "An infected broke into my flat. The only means of escape was—"

"Across the broken glass," he finished for her. "Well, you should have been off your feet for a week or so."

"If you know anywhere I can relax in this crazy city I'd sure love to know."

Dylan looked up at her. "Yeah, you have a point there. I've never seen anything like this before." He wrapped her foot in a clean bandage far tighter than was comfortable.

"There," he said, standing. "Stay off the foot as much as possible." He scooped up the medical kit and retrieved his rifle. "Will you be okay?"

"Yes, thanks."

"I'd better get back to my duties. You take care of yourself, Gemma."

"Dylan?"

He turned at the door.

"Why did you help me with that dressing?"

"What do you mean?"

"You didn't have to."

Dylan shook his head. "I've been here every day. I can't do much, but what I can do, I will. Get some rest."

***

So this is The Owls' Nest?

Driver, as Ryan had named his guide, pulled up at an ultra-modern, sleek, black skyscraper. The building's windows had been darkened, or it could have just been the oppression of the night creating such an effect.

Ryan followed Driver to the door, looking left and right and behind to make sure they weren't followed. That possibility didn't seem to worry Driver. He strode onwards as if walking into a bar to catch up with some buddies after a game of football.

The large, opulent lobby spoke of power and wealth. Their shoes clicked on the marble floor. Two security guards sat behind a desk, their dark-blue uniforms immaculate and gleaming.

Driver did not break step, instead carrying on past the reception toward a set of lifts. The two guards sat up rigid at their passing. One of them bowed, a slight movement toward Driver which he did not acknowledge.

Inside the lift, a familiar tune played, performed in a traditional Japanese style with flutes and a twangy stringed instrument that made everything sound sad. The elevator ascended fast, far quicker than what Ryan was used to. He felt light. Downtown Tokyo fell away as they climbed higher, the lights fading to small bulbs in the sea of dark.

The lift beeped, a female voice announced something in Japanese. Ryan was not sure what to expect. Perhaps some kind of high-end restaurant, the kind of place that society's elite would feast at, with waiters that rarely spoke, expensive wines and rare foods on the menus. Perhaps fish tanks as tall as he was. He was thinking movie stuff.

Nope.

An open-plan room, the centre boasting three leather sofas orbiting an ornate glass table that may have been crystal. A compact, yet bountifully stocked bar slipped into an alcove in the wall. The windows would no doubt provide a spectacular view over the city come day. On the other side of the room, a wood-panelled double door waited.

"Sit. Wait here."

Driver disappeared through the doors. Ryan stood alone with the sofas and the table, his head swimming with possible outcomes and theories as to what was going on. The more he thought about things, the more elaborate and desperate his situation became. He imagined the doors would swing open and a group of men would set upon him. Or the vents in the room would release some kind of noxious fumes. Maybe there was a deadly animal somewhere in the room, stalking him? A panther? A cobra? Only silence met him.

He moved to throw his bag onto the closet sofa, but checked himself, and placed it neatly on the floor, then moved up to the bar. Did he dare? This seriously, bad day deserved a shot of something, and it was equally possible that he was in fact a guest at this place after all. He plucked out a tumbler and poured himself what may or may not have been whiskey. He sipped. An expensive, smooth scotch. He took his drink back to the sofa, sat awkwardly as if his presence would somehow dirty the fine leather, and upset his captors, if it actually was a pair of captors that lay on the other side of those door. Ryan studied the craftsmanship of the table, the cuts in the glass, the reflection of the lights overhead in some of the sharper angles. At home his feet would have climbed onto that table and rested. Not here.

Ryan nervously flicked his fingers one at a time. He gulped from his glass, and winced as it went down. Surely if they wanted him dead, he would already be bloated, floating face down somewhere in Seattle's harbours. He only guessed facedown because that's how bodies are discovered in crime shows.

Ryan knew only what was required for the mission he undertook. No more than that. No names. No faces. No phones. No questions. What if they wanted him to repeat such a task, invade some poor, unsuspecting city and unleash another wave of the Carrion Virus. He placed two hands on his glass. What if they now wanted to become a host to a new strain of the virus?

No opening mechanisms or locks appeared on the windows. No escape. Anyway, he was pretty high up, he'd splat like a pancake. If he bolted for the lift, it would *bing* and that Japanese lady's voice would call out a warning.

The double doors opened at the far end of the room. Driver appeared.

"Mr. Crispin will see you now."

***

Gemma knocked on the open door. The sleepy guard, charged with watching the captive, paid little attention when she flashed her ID badge. At best she was stretching any authority she might have. At worst she was breaking the law. Gemma was not sure which way Dylan would see things. She felt a little guilty, but only a touch. This is what she was employed for after all.

The young man stood at the window, peering out into the dark of the night. Snow fluttered against the window. The man wiped his hand against the glass, clearing the build-up of condensation from his breath.

"Yes?" he asked, turning toward her.

"Can I come in?"

"That depends on who you are and what you want."

The man seemed calm, perhaps resigned to the fact he was marooned on an island of desperation.

"Well," said Gemma, stepping into the room, "I'm Gemma, and I want to hear your story. I heard what you said to the soldiers in the lobby. Nobody wanted to listen."

"Nobody's ever wanted to listen," said the man, sitting down on a small wooden chair next to the table. "That's the problem."

"I'm here to listen, and to help. What's your name?"

"George Reign."

"Rain? As in?"

"Kings and queens, not horse equipment or water from the sky."

"You don't mind if I record our conversation and make some notes?"

"Why? What are you? A reporter?"

Gemma smiled. "I'm just trying to piece together this crazy event." Gemma clicked on her recorder and opened the notepad.

George looked tired, defeated, dark circles hung below his eyes. In other circumstances he may have looked trendy in a teenage way. Sandy hair, with a long fringe, tanned, unnaturally white teeth. He shrugged.

Gemma sat down on the edge of the bed. It felt as if she lived most of her life from a hotel these days. "So, downstairs you were shouting about the outbreak. Do you want to tell me about it?"

He leaned back in the seat, and wiped a hand over his face. "It's been so long. Let me think about things. I've not slept in a bed for ages. I'm so tired."

"I know it's difficult, but try, try to remember," said Gemma, applying a soothing tone. This young man was keen to tell what he knew, but perhaps needed some gentle coaxing, a measure of patience, something he hadn't been shown since his arrival here.

"Okay. I worked as a barman in the club on Belmont Street. The Church. You know it? It was a normal night, nothing out of the ordinary. I was on lates."

"When was that?"

"Three weeks ago? Maybe longer. I was sweeping the floor, clearing out all the plastic cups that had been dropped. I swept under one of the seats and found something weird."

"Weird? Try to be specific."

"Like a thermal canister, one that old people use to keep their soup warm on picnics or something. But it was different, not like one I'd ever seen before. It was stainless steel, cold to the touch and the lid had some sort of clock face on it. The lid was open. I tried to fiddle with it, close it down but it wouldn't close. I left it for my manager to see the next day when he opened up."

Gemma scribbled away on her pad, using the shorthand she'd learnt as part of her trade. "And what happened with it?"

"Nothing. I forgot about it. I didn't even really think about it much until after all this happened. But there's more. About a week later, all my friends who were either at the club for a night out or working there came down with the flu, you know, the confusion and the bleeding sores. And all of them were taken to hospital. I've … I've not seen them since."

Gemma knew not seeing a friend for a period meant they were either dead or worse. Either way, they were beyond hope.

"So why weren't you taken ill?"

"I wasn't there for long. I guess I missed the moment that everyone was exposed to it. Gemma," he said, looking directly into her eyes for the first time, "I've seen movies and I've read stuff online. This outbreak isn't natural. It was deliberate and all the signs point to that canister being the thing that released it, in The Church."

Gemma leaned back on the bed, and stretched out her back, cracking her spine the way it always did after she had been seated for too long. What George was saying was the first piece of interesting information she'd received, despite how farfetched it seemed. She heard rumours about the outbreak not being a natural occurrence, or maybe even a bio-weapon. What sort of human would unleash such horror and devastation?

"You think I'm crazy, like the soldiers? They didn't want to hear what I had to say either. They told me that if I caused a panic like that again, I'd go to jail, and for ten years."

Gemma scribbled down the last few notes. "I'm sure they're scared, too, George. I wouldn't take it too personally."

He returned to the window. "What do you think about what I've just told you?"

Gemma scratched the back of her ear with the pen. "I think you're very brave for speaking up, George. It might be nothing. It could be something. Either way, I'm glad you told me. It's got to be investigated."

"Is that something you can do?"

"Perhaps. I'm not sure yet."

George's voice took on a monotone quality. "I've given you something, and now you've got to do something for me."

"What's that?"

"You've got to get me out of the city. I don't want to stay here anymore."

"George, I can't—"

"I don't want to hear that. I'm useful. I know things. I want to get out of the city. I want to get out of this building. I'm not stupid. I know you work for the government. Why else would you be interested in what I have to say? So you can pull strings."

While Gemma did not work for the government, George's assumption was right, she was more than just a curious mind. But how much pull did she have?

"George. You're safe here. Out there in the streets, it's dangerous, even with an armed escort. Stay here, wait for the crisis to blow over and I promise to get you before someone high up."

"You think this is safe? Let me tell you something about safe, Gemma. I've been to another displacement centre and it's not safe. They missed one of them. The infected. Oh yeah, everyone was asleep, then screaming. Shouting. Shooting. It was a massacre. Those soldiers here to protect us? They were killing everyone. Didn't matter." He moved closer to Gemma and she saw the pain in his eyes. "I saw old people on their knees with their hands up, holding grandkids around their waist, shot dead. Nowhere in the city is safe. Nowhere."

Tears came. Gemma reached out, touched his shoulder. He recoiled as if Gemma sought to do him harm.

"Don't touch me! I won't let anyone touch me here."

"Okay, I'm sorry," said Gemma, her hands raised in apology. "I'm going to do my best for you, George. I'll look for you in the morning."

"Nowhere is safe," he repeated.

***

Ryan marched through the double doors expecting the worst in a situation he did not understand. Instead of cohorts of henchmen waiting to dispose of his body in the most untraceable of ways, he found a solitary man scribbling furiously at an opulent desk, tubular table lamps at two corners. *Mr. Crispin?*

Crispin was unsmiling, and set aside his pen, sat back in his chair and tented his fingers. "Welcome, Ryan. Please, take a seat."

Ryan smiled as if meeting a good friend — it couldn't hurt — and took the offered seat. The man before him was older, maybe late sixties, small fashionable glasses perched on a slightly hooked nose. He wore a beard, more grey than black now. When he spoke, he did so with an accent of education. English, with the fading hint of an expatriate.

"I trust your journey here was uneventful despite the new restrictions at the border?"

Ryan nodded. "Yes, sir, Mr ..."

"I'm Hector Crispin. You've come to know me as Mr. Nippon. A silly, little title designed to protect my identity when dealing with unknown factors. You should know, Ryan, that very few people meet me face to face. Our meeting tonight isn't by chance. Everything results from a perfectly calculated decision. Had we not seen something in you that was worth our investment you would not be here."

Ryan cleared his thought and shifted in his chair. "Of course, Mr. Crispin. I mean, Mr. Nippon."

There was no clarification as to what title this man expected.

"What I require of you will become evident over the next few days and weeks. We'll be spending time together. You proved yourself useful once to us, Ryan, and assets that prove useful are compensated for their efforts. There is no limit to what we can achieve together. Now, for the next few days, I'd like you to acclimatise yourself with your surroundings. Some of our associates will no doubt make themselves known to you. I would ask that you do not leave this building for the time being. Tokyo is a vast city, easy to become disorientated in when you don't know where you're going. Is all understood?"

"Yes … um, what do I call you? Mr. Nippon?"

"Mr. Nippon has served its purpose between us, Ryan. You may call me Hector. If there's nothing else? I'm sure you're fatigued."

"Who are we, and who is us?" The words hung in the air. For one terrible moment, Ryan believed he stepped too far.

"We are The Owls of Athena, Ryan. And you are made welcome."

***

A hand clamped down on Gemma's mouth, violently rousing her from sleep. She fought the unseen assailant, fingernails digging into skin, her legs kicking out.

"Gemma. Gemma. It's me. Dylan. You need to calm down." He shook her. "Be quiet."

The sound of the soldier's voice reassured her enough to stop the fight as the bonds of sleep fell away. Dylan knelt on the edge of her bed. She pulled the covers tight to her chin. He pulled his hand away from her mouth. In the dark of her room it was difficult to focus, the light poor.

"What is it?" she hissed.

"Trouble. I need you to stay calm. Get dressed."

He went to the door, rifle in hand, watching the corridor. Gemma grabbed at her discarded clothes and using her bedcovers to maintain some dignity, pulled them on. Not that Dylan took any interest. He stayed at the door, his back to her. She slipped from the bed and pulled on her boots. She had no idea how long she had been asleep.

"What's happening?"

Dylan moved from the doorway to the corridor window. He motioned for Gemma to join him. She peered out into the night. The streets were empty, yellow streetlights guarding against the night.

"I don't see anything."

"Over there, to the right, beside the shop."

Gemma leaned closer to the window until her forehead touched the cold glass. Nothing. Darkness. Snow. She was about to question him again when movement caught her attention.

"Jesus. No."

Lurking in the shadowy recess of the building, a horde of infected, their jitters and jolts and circling betraying their affliction.

"We've got to warn everyone." Gemma pushed back from the window.

"They already know. We're trying to secure the building. There's only one way in."

"Why are they waiting?"

"We've seen this before. A group forms. It's like they wait for their full strength before charging."

"Like strategy?"

"Could be. It gives us vital minutes to prepare. I better get downstairs."

"Why did you wake me?"

He turned. "This is why you're here, to document stuff like this, right?"

"What do I do now?"

"Start documenting. But stay in your room and wait for one of us to tell you further."

He left, his footfalls echoing in the stairwell. Gemma went back to the room and grabbed her camera. She filmed the infected as best she could from behind the glass. The picture blurred and was distorted by the snow. Opening the window would grant her a better picture, if she could negotiate the safety locks, but something about the sealed window reassured her.

George's words revisited her. *Nowhere is safe.*

***

Gemma waited for as long as she could. She could take it no longer. The infected still clustered in the shadow of the shop. She crept to the stairwell. The stairs were empty and she descended as quickly as she could. The main lobby, in contrast to her floor, was a hive of activity. Gemma snapped open her camera and filmed the men at work.

Soldiers moved sacks of sandbags to the entrance, building a wall already to the height of Gemma. Along the base, they created a firing step, where two men could conceivably stand side by side to look over at whatever enemy lay on the other side. One soldier stepped up and rested his rifle on the parapet. He held a pair of binoculars to his eyes, scanning down the corridor and out into the dark.

Dylan stood off to the right, checking weapons and magazines. It was clear they expected the worst. The officer that spoke to Gemma earlier in the night barked orders to his men. Their situation was reported repeatedly by the dishevelled radio operator, but no acknowledgement came back.

Gemma counted the soldiers. Sixteen, including the officer. Not the most comforting of numbers when guarding against a charge of many hundreds.

"You there," shouted the officer. "Get back up to your room and stay there."

Gemma lowered her camera. The officer stared. She understood his impatience, and dared not defy the order a moment longer.

She headed back upstairs to her floor, and looked out the window. Some of the infected stood in plain sight, their focus on the hotel. They knew. They knew people were inside. She was pulled away from the window.

Dylan. "We don't want them charging in here after seeing a pretty, little blonde do we?"

Under other circumstances Gemma may have considered that flirtation, but she was too scared to think that way. "They know we're here."

"And the last thing we need is a panic in here. We've done all we can for the moment."

"Is it enough?"

Dylan smiled, a false expression. It marred his handsome face for all of the falsehood's ugliness. "Of course. You're safe here. You should get some sleep, we'll protect you. That's what we're here for."

"Please help me!" A woman exited her room, she wore a dressing gown that fell open, her pencil-thin body a mess of weeping sores. She raised her hands, palms painted with blood.

"My family," she said coming closer, "they're sick, worse than me. Please."

Dylan raised his SA80 to his shoulder, and Gemma sidled in behind him.

"Stop," he commanded, aiming down the iron sights. "Won't tell you again."

Gemma snapped her camera open and aimed, too. She somehow felt safe behind the lens. It wasn't a weapon, but it created an improbable sense of security.

The woman took another step. Dylan snapped the safety off his weapon. Gemma popped the camera just above his shoulder.

"Gemma," Dylan growled.

"I've got to capture this."

"No. Get back to the stairwell."

The woman's eyes never settled on either of them. They grew manic.

"He said he was there to help. Injected us. We were fine until then. My child ... my husband." Her whole body jittered. "There to help."

"Who? Who said they were there to help?"

Gemma stepped past Dylan. "We can help."

"Gemma!"

The infected woman's eyes fixed on Gemma, bloodshot and losing all appearance of humanity. She moaned. "The medic."

A figure dashed from the room behind her, screaming guttural rage at Gemma and Dylan.

"Her husband?" Gemma gasped.

"Gemma, get out of here now!"

The woman turned. A male, the lines of sores on his body moist, smashed the woman with a balled fist. Her neck cracked, and she fell to the ground, wheezing and clutching at her throat.

Dylan fired off two rounds, the air cutting uncomfortably close to Gemma's ear. She dropped to her knees, her camera bouncing at her chest, and she scrambled away. The rounds struck the infected in the chest. He stumbled, hands raking at his wounds, then charged again.

Three more shots, four, five, tearing into the neck and head. It went down with a gurgle, the body twitching. Dylan raced over to the fallen and placed a foot onto its chest. He lowered the barrel of his weapon and fired a single shot, point blank into the skull. All movement ceased. Dylan turned and executed the infected woman in the same fashion.

She was infected. Of that there was no doubt. But to see someone still able to communicate in some form, and yet killed, chilled Gemma to the core.

"Was there nothing we could do? She was still talking?"

"Her neck was broken. If that didn't kill her, the infection would've taken control of her. It's better that she died quickly before she could hurt anyone else." Dylan checked his weapon. "Stay here."

He entered the bedroom the two infected came from and closed the door behind him.

Gemma whispered to herself, "The woman said her husband *and* baby succumbed. No."

A brief scuffle came from beyond the doorway followed by a single shot. Gemma jumped. A terrified face appeared from a room at the far end of the corridor. Gemma shook her head, waved her hands and gestured to get back into the room. The door slammed shut.

Gemma grabbed her camera and pointed. The woman. The male. Her stomach lurched. She dropped the camera, ran into her own room, pulled the duvet and sheet free of the mattress and dragged them back to the corridor. She threw them over the two dead.

Dylan returned from the room and pulled the door closed. He shook his head, and she understood. *Don't ask.*

"Should we move them?" She pointed at the covers. "Them."

"We don't have the gear to safely move them. They're covered, that's the best we can do."

He moved to the window and swore. "They're moving."

Gemma joined him. Outside, the infected streamed toward the entrance to the hotel. Tracer fire ripped through their ranks but they pressed on regardless. The gunfire sounded distant from the fifth floor.

"I've got to get down there, they need me. Stay in your room." He pointed behind Gemma.

"I'm not staying here on my own."

Dylan looked ready to argue but instead took off for the stairs at a trot.

Gemma followed. Her foot burned. "What do you think about what the woman said?"

Dylan grunted.

"Do you have a medic operating here?"

"Yes, but he only treats us, not the displaced."

"Everyone who arrived here was tested for infection, then suddenly a medic treated them and they get sick?"

"She was delirious, you can't put stock on what she said."

The sounds of gunfire and screaming grew louder.

"There's a rogue medic in this building *treating* people."

"One problem at a time. Stay back here."

They reached the bottom of the stairwell. Dylan marched through the doors. Gemma followed cautiously behind, hugging the wall.

The barricade and sandbags wavered, heaving inward. Two soldiers leaned their weight into the barricade.

"They're on the other side?" But no one replied to Gemma's question. They couldn't hear her, but more so, an answer wasn't needed.

Another two soldiers jumped up onto the firing step, raised their rifles overhead and fired blindly into the screaming mass beyond.

Gemma fired off shots of her own, capturing the scene of chaos that unfolded.

Residents of the displacement centre filtered down the stairs behind Gemma. Some cried, others screamed, most watched wide eyed, shaking with terror.

One weapon was grabbed at from the parapet. The soldier wrestled to keep hold. In a desperate bid, he reached higher up the barrel. That was his undoing. He was pulled high and flew over the wall. Gone. More soldiers took his place, again firing blindly. Gemma covered her ears. It did little good.

"We need to get out of here," shouted one of the displaced. He headed to the large exit that opened into the shopping centre of which the hotel was part of. A heavy security door sealed the barrier between the centre and hotel. "We can open the shutters and get out, close it behind us."

More than a few listened to him, and followed.

"No," Gemma yelled.

The soldiers kept firing. The group grasped the underside of the shutters and heaved against the weight.

"Out there isn't safe!" Nobody could hear her. She pushed through to the ringleader and pulled on his arm. "You can't do this."

He shrugged her off. "To hell I can't. I won't stay here to die." He cried out encouragement to the group.

A woman in a dirty, white blouse and black skirt waved something in her hand. "I worked here. I have the key."

"Can you open the door?" called the ringleader.

"Yes. I think so."

"Then quickly. Before they notice."

"Don't!" Gemma held her arms up. "This is suicide."

But the woman busied with the key, all eyes on the shutters, hoping, praying.

Gemma headed to the reception desk and slid under the barrier.

Infected were spilling over the sandbag barrier becoming mixed with the soldiers who held the barricade in place. When one fell into the lobby, they were quickly surrounded and pumped full of rounds. One soldier, an older man, sat on the floor, his uniform stained in blood. He clutched at the wound and held a pistol in his free hand, firing into the infected when one appeared.

Gemma raised her camera but could not bring herself to take a picture.

Dylan was close to the entrance, reloading his rife, spent magazines and shells at his feet. Gemma called his name but he did not hear.

Gemma weaved her way through the concentration of soldiers, reaching Dylan. The gunfire hurt her ears. Infected fell over the barricade, more than could be killed. They were on the verge of securing a foothold, despite their losses.

Gemma hit Dylan's arm.

"What?"

"They're opening the side doors." Gemma screamed to be heard, and pointed back to where the group wrestled with the shutters.

Dylan looked between the infected and Gemma. "Show me."

She did.

It was a different scene.

The barrier was gone.

The displaced had made it through, and into the shopping centre. But they were easy prey. The infected pulled down the slower women, and the others were being chased or cornered, and simply waiting for the pain. Screams mixed with roars. The caught wailed like sirens, their skin being shred and sliced and ripped.

Dylan sprang into action. He ran to the console and activated the mechanism to lower the barrier. Some of the lucky ones attempted to return. They found no escape. They banged on the door. Their frenzied attempts to return only drew the attention of the infected. Through the slits in the security barrier, Gemma could make out a swarm bearing down on them.

"Can't we help them?" asked Gemma.

"We open that and we're all goners. I won't lose this facility to save a handful."

Back in the hallway, the soldiers were falling back, infected snapping as they fought a retreat. One soldier, his rifle empty swung it like a club, smashing the teeth from the mouth of the closest beast. He was pulled down by a second attacker.

Dylan seized Gemma and propelled her toward the stairwell. The soldiers followed, barring the door after the last member was through.

The captain, bleeding from a scalp wound, breathed heavily and leaned on the banister for support.

"We're losing control. We need to regroup, get the surviving displaced on the top floor and hold out for relief. Did we get a message off to *C and C* before we pulled back?"

The radio operator was dead. An infected slapped at the door, its face pressed against the small square of glass. It battered its head repeatedly, each strike a dull thud until the glass cracked. Gemma took two pictures, snapshots.

"Up the stairs," ordered the captain. "I want eyes on this door. The moment it looks like it might give, I need to know."

Gemma returned to her room, and awaited the flood of displaced. Could the soldiers secure the fifth floor? Was she safe? Was she going to die? Was she going to become one of *those*?

Streams of humanity hurried past her door looking for their own rooms.

Soldiers spoke just short of a shout. "Move quickly. Find space. Move. There's more people to come."

A fear-stricken woman knocked on her door, a child hugging her legs. "May we come in? They're running out of space."

Gemma patted the bed. "You can have my bed. You look exhausted."

The woman nodded her thanks.

Gemma gathered up her few things, and stuffed them into her bag. "You're safe here."

"Are we?" The woman wasn't expecting a reply. She laid her child on the bed.

Gemma moved to the door. Dylan was in deep conversation with the captain.

"It's too risky, Dylan."

"I'm volunteering. I can make it."

"Make what?" asked Gemma.

Neither man acknowledged her question.

"Captain, I know I can do it."

The captain plucked at the bandage on his head. "It's a distance. We're not sure if the radio message got through."

"We don't have any other choice. Most of our equipment's in the lobby I'll get to Marischal College. I'll bring back help."

"Marischal College?" said Gemma. "I'll show you the way." The words left Gemma's mouth before she had time to consider them.

The two men looked at her. "You know how to get there?" they both said.

Gemma knew that Aberdeen City Council headquarters was about a ten minute walk from where they were on a good day. In another time she would use this route to take some exercise. On an evening like this, with the near impassable weather and armies of infected abroad in the city, it could take much longer.

"Better than a GPS."

"That's a brave offer, Miss Finlay, but I can't allow you to take that risk."

"And how long can you guarantee the safety of the people here, Captain? A few hours? How long before anyone comes looking for us? If we go now, we could have help back here in an hour, two at most."

The captain rubbed his chin, he had the look of a man who carried the world on his shoulders.

"She has a point," said Dylan, his eyes locked on Gemma. "Back in an hour and we can clear out this nest of infection."

The captain looked past Gemma at the number of people in his charge. Hundreds, and he had nine men.

"Go," he finally said. "Get what you need and be ready."

"You have a George Reign here. He should come with us."

"Gemma?" quizzed Dylan.

"And why is that?" said the captain.

"That's Black Aquila business."

"You realise I could order you to tell me?"

"You could," agreed Gemma.

"We're wasting time here," said Dylan.

"Captain, it'll be one less for you to worry about."

If the displacement centre fell before they could raise the alarm, at least Gemma would have secured a lead to the outbreak. There was still the case of the rogue medic. He could not go far. Either he was dead, in the failed escape bid, or he was hiding in plain sight. Gemma would deal with him when she returned. If she returned.

***

Brutus stood ready, pistol in one hand, his other hand on the door handle. Andor Toth was on the other side, but times were dangerous and he would not take any chances that someone else joined Toth, someone wanting him dead.

He opened the door. Toth held a laptop under his arm, and was flanked by two armed guards who did a poor job of blending in. They wore white shirts, dark glasses and only partially hid their weapons.

Toth pulled off his shades, revealing tired eyes. He nodded at the pistol in Brutus's hand. "Getting nervous, old friend?"

The endearment irked Brutus. They had never been close, it was strictly business. Brutus unscrewed the silencer, and slipped the safety on. "You're late."

"Don't lecture me, Brutus." Toth stepped into the building. "I've been in three countries in the last three days. I can afford a little tardiness."

"What about them?" Brutus pointed toward the two guards left out on the street.

"They're fine where they are. Close the door. I don't want this to take longer than necessary."

Brutus slammed the door, sending an echo of finality around the small room. Toth marched through to the back room and the assembled men. He scanned each one in turn as if marking them individually, then opened the laptop.

"I'm Andor Toth. I'm the one financing this adventure. You won't have any questions by the time I'm done. You'll be paid handsomely. There's no turning back from this point."

Brutus watched for reactions. None. Not yet. Some would have reservations once the true nature of the mission was revealed. Brutus recognised he was pretty much alone in the world with the way he thought. A unique element. Brutus did not see good and evil, or right and wrong. For him, his guiding principles were do or don't. A simplistic black and white view that served him well. His men would need some convincing.

Toth set the laptop on the table. A map of Egypt. He clicked a button and the map focused on the Sinai region. A red dot flashed.

"You'll be driven to an airfield, then flown to this position. We've observed an outbreak of the Carrion Virus in the local population, a village of no more than two-hundred. You will rendezvous with members of your team already in a forward observation post and detail the behaviour of the infected. Once all available data has been collected, you'll be required to neutralise the threat. All bodies must be burned. You'll be extracted and returned here to Cairo and our contract will terminate. You may be wondering why the Egyptian government doesn't act. I can tell you they fully support our services. They need to maintain deniability and using a group of mercenaries is the natural choice, something that can't be traced back to them."

Toth's eyes, flicked to Brutus. So, Toth was not prepared to share the entire truth? Perhaps it was for the best. Knowing Toth's men first delivered the infection to the village may have proven to be a contentious issue for some, and Brutus needed every one of those men.

"I know some of you may have some reservations about what's to come, but be assured these infected are beyond all medical hope. It's a necessity that they're brought down to avoid an outbreak that would result in the deaths of many hundreds more, many thousands. In Aberdeen an attempt to contain has become a disaster. If you have questions about the infected, my old friend Brutus has become quite the expert and will answer your questions." He snapped down the laptop lid.

And there it was again, the *my old friend* endearment. Brutus could have snapped Toth's neck.

"Three days of work and you'll have rendered a useful service and gained a sizeable wallet to do with as you will. And, there will be more work on successful completion of this task. So, gentlemen," Toth clapped his hands twice, "I'll leave you to get on your way."

Niall cornered Brutus. "We need to talk."

"Not now. Get your things, we're leaving."

***

The rope around Gemma's waist felt like a boa constrictor. The wild wind threw her side to side as the soldiers lowered her down the few storeys to the ground.

Dylan waited below, almost eclipsed by the whiteout. He had scampered down the rope, his military training serving him well. Gemma did not even consider mimicking his descent. It was beyond her physical capabilities. The granite of the wall scraped her hands as she was lowered. She kicked out with her feet, pushing her free of the wall in bounces.

Dylan grabbed her feet. "I've got you," he whispered, untangling her from the rope.

He gave it three sturdy tugs and the rope climbed back up onto the roof above. Everything was blanketed in white. Snow fell in blustering waves. Gemma wiped the flakes from her numb, wet face. She reached down, making sure her camera was safe, strapped tight against her.

An impossible period of time slipped past before a shadow broke the omnipresent white. George Reign was lowered to the ground in a much less controlled fashion, crumpling into the show on impact. Dylan hauled George up by the lapels of his coat.

"You stay quiet, follow me and I'll keep you safe. You don't do what I say and we leave you out here with those things. Got it?"

George nodded, seemingly resigned to his fate. He had not been a willing participant. It had taken the physical imposition of Dylan and promises of escaping the city to get him to agree. As much as his paralytic attitude riled Gemma, she understood why he felt such a way. Fear. He had been through some horrific times, losing friends, seeing death and barely surviving. They all had. He was important and they needed him alive if Gemma was to pick up a clue about the infection and its origins.

69

Dylan brought his rifle to the ready. "Let's go. Stay close and if you see something you have to tell me. I reckon it's a half-hour jog to our destination. Factor in the weather and any infected that we might see, we'll be there in an hour."

Being a trained soldier with long legs, Dylan set a pace. The snow was knee-deep for Gemma's shorter legs. It was like wading into the shallows of the sea. She forged ahead without complaint, keeping an eye on George.

They moved through the streets unnoticed, past abandoned cars swallowed by the storm, past houses with doors broken inward. There was some respite from the weather where the angles of the buildings sheltered the streets enough to see the cobbles of the old city peeking through like an archaeological marvel.

"We're making good time," puffed Gemma.

Dylan suddenly pushed her sideways until all three were crouching in the hollow of a wall.

He pointed with his chin and whispered, "Fresh tracks in the snow."

Gemma followed the confused footprints. A single person, moving this way and that before leading off around the corner.

"Snow hasn't covered them. It could still be close by. Stay here."

Dylan crept forward, his rifle in hand until he reached the limit of the wall. He chanced a look beyond and snapped back a moment later. He held up a single finger. One infected. He slipped his rifle round on its sling and pulled out his combat knife then rapped the weapon against the masonry of the wall. The infected sprinted into view, kicking up clumps of snow as it ran. Dylan sprang like a coiled snaked, bringing the blade up into the jugular. The infected thrashed, flailing its arms but Dylan clung on, bringing it down into the snow, driving the blade deeper and deeper with short thrusts. Gemma closed her eyes, not to banish the killing, but to banish the memories fighting to be recalled, memories of her first encounter with an infected. Fear. Blood. Her friend being charged. Violence. And then escape.

Dylan was before her, his torso and neck splattered with blood. He picked up handfuls of snow, using it to clean as much of the blood from himself as he could. "We need to move on."

"But the blood?" Gemma argued. She knew the risk. And so did Dylan.

"And what do you suggest?" he snapped. "I take a shower?"

She argued no further.

Dylan kicked snow over the face and neck of the downed infected. They passed with no comment, George never letting his eyes drop to the corpse.

They pushed on, past the deserted city. Remnants of normality were laid out, half-buried by the snow. Shopping trolleys, cars with their doors left open. Bags left where those escaping dropped them. The snow hid a terrible tale. Shops, long ago shut for business and left to the mercies of looters stood empty, their once rich window displays stolen, and replaced by shattered glass and snow.

Ahead, over Market Street, and up the adjoining side street, a group of five or so figures moved about, creating as little noise as possible. Not infected? One of the group kept watch, standing next to a Land Rover, the engine a low rumble. The rest, armed with a variety of garden implements, spades and a long-handled axe entered the small Irish bar and carried out boxes of alcohol. Again Dylan pushed Gemma and George down to their knees.

"Looters." He spat into the snow. "Idiots. The noise of the engine will bring infected down on them."

"We can go around, up Market Street, onto Union Street and to Marischal College that way."

Dylan shook his head. "It's too risky. We're better in the side streets."

"We can wait here until they're finished," suggested George.

Dylan shot George a wrathful glare. "Every moment we're exposed like this is another chance for infected to discover us. We need to scare them off."

As if fated was tempted, a milling group of shambling infected entered the street. They were two-hundred metres from Gemma, and not much less from the looters. Gemma touched at her camera, but thought twice. The clicking sound would give away their location.

The new swarm of infected, several scores in strength, make their halting progress down the street. The looters had not yet noticed the approaching danger. The baseball bat one had been carrying was now propped up against the side of the vehicle.

Gemma turned to her two companions. "We have to go back. Those looters see us and they'll make enough noise to bring the infected down on top of us."

"We can't go back. We need to keep moving forward."

George tugged on Gemma's shoulder. "For God sakes, let's go back. What are we doing out here? It's crazy."

Dylan grabbed hold of George's chin and made sure those terror-filled eyes focused nowhere but his face. "You're here and we move forward. You make enough noise and I'll silence you. Understand?"

Whether the words were designed to scare George into compliance or whether they held darker grains of truth, Gemma was not sure, but she was frightened enough to intervene.

"That's enough, Dylan."

His blazing eyes turned on her. "And you'll do better if you take the same advice."

Dylan let go of George's face. Tears ran south along the frightened man's cheeks. Gemma could have cried, too. In the hotel at their first encounter, the handsome Dylan had been so gentle, so calm, so warm and caring, despite his uniform, despite the weapons strapped to his body, despite the horrors of the city. It now seemed things were taking their toll. Inevitable she supposed, but she had hoped it wouldn't happen to this soldier.

The snow lessened for a moment, the veil of white becoming more permeable. Dylan reached into his vest, and pulled a flare free.

"What are you doing?"

"Surviving."

"Dylan, no."

He struck it alight, launched the illumination over the street, his aim good. It landed amongst the looters, and alerted the infected. A charge erupted and those beasts fell upon looters with familiar efficiency. Gemma filmed it all.

"Move," ordered Dylan.

The three ran through the snow drifts, up the street in the direction the infected came. Screams and cries haunted their flight, but no pursuit came. Gemma did not look back, instead willed herself forward. She pushed her burning legs harder, drawing level with Dylan. George was a short way behind, his heavy footfalls crunching through the snow.

Dylan had little sense of Aberdeen, where Gemma knew the city well. They entered Union Street, the arterial passage that ran through the heart of Aberdeen. It was a dark, ghost-land filled with snow.

"This way," she called out and set off again.

Vehicles had trampled the snow to slush. It made for easier going. The three of them ran up the middle of the road, past cars hidden in the white depth. They rounded a corner and finally Marishcal College came into sight. The gothic, granite-fronted building seemed a fortress. They wasted no time in dashing toward the protection it would offer.

"What were you thinking, Dylan?"

"Move, unless you want to stay out here and die."

"But *you* let those people die."

He did not halt his run. "I have my orders."

"I thought you were in the business of saving people."

"They were out robbing a bar. They broke curfew."

"They didn't have to die."

"It was us or them."

"What's going on with you?"

He kept running.

"Hey! I'm talking to you." Gemma grabbed his arm and hauled him to a stop. He turned on her, opened his mouth to speak. Before a word came out Dylan flew backwards, thrown off his feet by an invisible force. He landed five feet away, his chest ripped open, exposing broken ribs and pulped innards.

"Sniper! Get down."

Hands encircled her waist and pulled her back. Where she stood a moment before, a huge spurt of snow erupted. George pulled her further away, to a low wall in the shadows of a building adjacent to Marischal College.

Gemma could not master herself and screams came, her eyes fixed on the wreckage of Dylan. She pushed her face into the snow, letting the ice numb her hot tears of anger. They had been so close, so close. Now they were about to be killed by a trigger-happy soldier.

George slunk down to his belly and snaked around the short wall. He stretched out and pulled the rifle free from Dylan's body then wriggled back.

"What are you doing?"

"We need to let them know that we're not infected. Look." He indicated with a nod of his head toward the plaza before the entrance of the building. Breaking the blanket of snow, here and there, limbs protruded like broken gravestones fighting against the decay of time.

"They're shooting first and asking questions later."

George pulled open his jacket and slipped out of it. He pulled off the white vest he wore under his jumper, wrapping it on the end of the rifle. George held the weapon by the stock and waved it past the cover of the wall and into the open where the sniper was no doubt watching, waiting for a clean shot.

This is crazy, thought Gemma. Part of her wanted to run back the way she came. The rest demanded inaction and so she lay in the snow, watching the person she had become companion to through circumstance.

"Gemma, look."

A five-man squad of soldiers, kitted out in winter camouflage moved toward them, weapons ready. George threw the weapon down and stood, with his hands raised overhead. She did the same, only speaking to confirm her name. Gemma offered no resistance as her hands were tied behind her back and a spit-guard placed over her head. She allowed herself to be taken. They had made it.

***

Work never ceased at the research facility. Staff and guards went about their business. As long as Jane moved with a perceived purpose nobody challenged her, not even the armed guards who watched everything with a predatory interest.

After leaving Holden the night before in his drunken despair, she spent the night formulating some barebones plan to get a message to the outside world. But who to call? Holden no doubt had connections but how many of them knew of the practices here. For many employees, the powers that be would have played with their desire to do good. Some would have been threatened. Some probably complicit in the establishment and maintenance of the facility.

It should have been a sanctuary, a place to share her medical expertise as trade for safety. Hyde, who she assumed was Holden's unofficial minder, had access to a phone. He walked around clutching the thing to his body like it regulated his heartbeat. She needed to prise it from his grip, use it to contact somebody, anybody on the outside that could help.

Hyde's personal office was before her, the blinds of the window drawn, the door probably locked.

"You there. Nancy?"

It took her a moment to realise the voice called to her.

Hyde strode up from behind, the satellite phone ever present. Jane attempted to look elsewhere and not at the prize.

"Jane," she mumbled, pulling her eyes from the phone to his dour face.

"Where is Doctor Holden? He is overdue."

"The doctor wasn't feeling well this morning. I think he's coming down with something." She looked up to the humming vents. "Probably all the recycled air you're pumping in here."

Hyde waved a hand in a dismissive fashion. "He's here to work, we can't afford to not have him working. He's got until the afternoon."

Hyde breezed past. An overpowering richness of aftershave came like an aftershock. He grabbed a key from a cord on his belt and rattled it into the door lock.

"Well, I won't keep you." Jane did not move.

"Piss off," he said in response. The door closed behind him.

Jane burned a hole in the door with her anger. One way or the other, she was going into that office and taking his phone. It had to be soon.

***

Ryan spent the night in The Owls' Nest, his accommodation a room of unique opulence. Every piece of furniture no doubt had been chosen for its beauty. The bed, a four-poster, ornately carved frame, was as comfortable a bed as he'd ever slept in. Paintings on the wall, framed in gilded finery did not look like prints. A vase stood here and there, vases he dared not touch out of fear of breaking them. He suspected none to be reproductions.

He waited in his room, waiting to be summoned, showering in a marble bathroom well-suited for a Roman villa. He still felt majorly underdressed, wearing a creased white shirt and jeans. When he was summoned, it was without ceremony or speech. A knock at the door, and a wave followed when opened.

Hector Crispin, or Mr. Nippon, sat at a table crammed with breakfast foods. Large bay windows commandeered a postcard view over Tokyo.

"Beautiful isn't it, Ryan? For a city with such a massive population it still retains an aesthetically pleasing facade. Sit. Join me. Please, eat."

Ryan heaped a plate with toasted sourdough bread, poached eggs and slices of smoked salmon. Into a glass he poured equal portions of pineapple juice, orange juice, and apple juice. His eyes devoured the pile of pancakes and the jug of syrup, and thought it a little bold to start on that yet.

"Tokyo is one of the few examples of a city where the presence of people does not detract from the beauty. Of course, like any city, scratch a little below the surface and the rank underflow is revealed."

Crispin kept his focus out to the city. His face twisted, as if he chewed on a sour grape. He leaned back, and sipped at a hot drink, probably coffee from the scent. He lapsed into silence, his eyes moving from point to point, pondering some great secret. His lips moved with unsaid words, and then, "The Owls' Nest. Mister Nippon. The Athena Protocol. Grand names, theatrical in a way. I'm sure you're wondering about them. You've heard the first two, of course. The Owls' Nest, here, where we are enjoying a delicious breakfast. Mr. Nippon, well a code name of sorts. The Athena Protocol. One that you haven't heard yet. You probably suspect a great deal, some will likely be astute guessing, the rest I shall reveal. A time of great strife is coming, Ryan. Many will not live to see the resolution. And you, my dear boy, have helped us sow our seeds."

"I didn't know what I was doing would be used in such a way."

Crispin laughed a dry rattle. "Come now, don't play innocent. You designed and built the pressurised storage and delivery system. You personally delivered the virus to a target of our choosing. You did all knowing it would not benefit anyone in the venue. The almighty dollar sign blinded you. Perhaps such a thing would have been inconceivable under different circumstances."

A flush of heat burned its way from Ryan's stomach and into his head, causing his vision to reel. All psychosomatic symptoms he was sure. He attempted to force out a few words in defence.

"Relax, Ryan." Crispin now looked directly at him, a stare Ryan could not hold. "I'm not judging you. There will be no recriminations, no trace back to you. You provided us a service. Of all those in our employ, you are quite the most unique."

"In what way?"

"Well," said Crispin, turning back to the city. "You are the only one we've allowed to live after their task was completed."

How did he allow himself to be there, in The Owls' Nest? Hector Crispin was right, he was blinded by the money. All he saw was a way to make his life easier for a relatively small task. Ryan almost managed to convince himself that he was doing something harmless, even when he stepped off the plane in Aberdeen.

"What do you know of your father, Ryan?"

"My father?"

"Yes, your father. It's important because I'm asking you, and you are here under my sufferance. You will answer."

Ryan blew out his cheeks. "I never knew my father well. He always worked away from home, hardly saw us at all. I know he passed away some years ago. I don't really remember the date."

"A sad thing when a father is not mourned by his child."

"Mr. Crispin, I don't understand why we're talking about these things."

Crispin slammed his hand on the table, rattling crockery and spilling juice. "We are talking about such things because I've made it happen. Your survival is down to me, and me alone. Had you been anyone else other than your father's son I would not have protected you. Your body would never have been found. You would have simply ceased to be. A stain on the annals of history removed without comment or consequence. You are here, talking about what I deem worthy to talk about because I saved your life. Do you understand?"

Ryan nodded, a robotic movement. A chunk of toasted crust sat on his back teeth. He dared not chew. He dared not say another word.

"Your father's legacy is why you're alive. And this is something that we shall explore in due course. You understand there is no going back from this. You are on the inside. Should you even consider breaking that trust, people within our group will have you destroyed in the most painful and prolonged fashion imaginable." Crispin pulled his sleeve back to reveal a golden watch. "In fact, our last loose end will be taken care of in a few hours. Then we'll be ready to move forward. In time, Ryan, you'll come to understand what we do. Why The Owls of Athena do what they do. This has been a good conversation."

Crispin dabbed at his mouth with a napkin. "We shall have another tomorrow. If you will excuse me." He stood. "You have free run of this floor. Entertain yourself as best you can. Do not try to leave. That is unacceptable at this point in time."

Chapter Five
Desert

The convoy's journey to the airfield was unpleasant, the heat so oppressive. Brutus's team was heading into an abnormal situation. All the training in the world, military or otherwise, could not prepare them for what was to come. The airfield itself was little more than a clearing in the desert, a square of flattened sand with high-banked, dune walls. A few Cold War-era military tents rippled in the breeze. On the central landing pad, an aging Mi-17 Russian helicopter waited, the silver chassis darkened by rust. Ry Watson stepped out of the helicopter, wiped his hands on a rag.

"It's been a long time, Ry." Brutus stuck out his hand and they shook.

"I didn't think I'd see you here. When they mentioned your name, I thought it was a mistake."

"Got to make a living." Brutus pulled a cigar free from his pocket and stuck it into his mouth. "Does that thing fly? Looks like it's seen better days."

"Don't let the rust fool you. I had her up this morning. She'll get us to where we need to go so long as the weather stays like this. When do we leave?"

"As soon as possible. There's three of our team waiting in the field. Things are moving fast," said Brutus.

Watson held up a hand. "I don't need to know the details. I'm here to fly you in and out, that's all. There's some crazy shit going on right now. The less I know the better."

There was wisdom to what Ry Watson said. He was a pilot of above-average skill, proficient in flying a variety of aircraft. He never feared breaking a law or two if it meant making a tidy sum. Drug shipment, gun running, covert ops. Watson had done it all, and he possessed a hefty streak of self-preservation and knew to distance himself from whatever was going on.

"You armed?"

"Out here you've got to be." Watson pulled his sunglasses from his head, and onto his nose, then hiked a thumb toward the cockpit.

An AK-47 rested in the pilot's chair. "I've been told that we'll be unhindered in our flight today."

Brutus nodded, padding down his tac vest for a light. "So long as we keep to our course and schedule, yes."

The rest of the men unpacked the vehicles, making ready to load their gear and weapons into the aircraft.

"Tell me the plan again."

Brutus finally found his lighter, lit his cigar and blew out a thick puff of smoke. "You fly us out there, we disembark. Two days in the field and you return and fly us back here. We go our separate ways. You get paid to fly."

Watson nodded. "Gear up. We leave in thirty."

***

The helicopter swept over the Eastern Desert, low and fast. Brutus and his men sat on both sides of the cargo hold, containers and supplies strapped down between them. He leaned back, stretched out his legs and rested them on the cargo. He shifted his AK-47, making sure the barrel pointed down. The vibration of the great engine rattled his bones. Nobody attempted to talk, the noise too great.

A sullen mood descended on the group. The men suspected this mission was something outside the realms of their experience. Brutus remained tight-lipped. Of anyone he probably had the most experience with the infected. He would never let his men face them underprepared, but he certainly would not put the fear of God into them. If only they were more like me, he thought. Fear was a condition Brutus strove to eliminate from his being. The infected scared him to begin with, up until the point he discovered they could be killed. More dangerous than a normal person, resilient to pain and injury but they still went down with a bullet to the head, or a knife to the throat. If it can be killed, there was nothing to fear.

Ry Watson's voice crackled through his headset. "ETA ten minutes."

Andor Toth's pockets must be deep indeed, Brutus thought. They flew over an area of The Sinai. Egyptian security forces fought an Islamic insurgency there. It would be heavily patrolled and monitored, yet the aircraft passed unmolested, unchallenged.

The helicopter shuddered, slowed and began a controlled descent. The men inside were rocked as if enduring a storm on a ship. Brutus clung to his seat, knuckles white. It felt as though the helicopter would rip itself apart. It hit the ground, bounced, struck terra firma once more before coming to a standstill. The engine powered down.

Ry Watson popped his head through from the cockpit. "We've arrived."

Stepping from the cargo hold felt like marching onto an alien planet. Wind whipped sand and dust about in a frantic cyclone. Brutus pulled his shemagh up over his mouth and nose. His companions did likewise. The nature of Brutus's work often took him to places he would describe as a shithole, and here in Egypt, was one of those.

"Stay with the helicopter, Ry." Brutus patted the side of the aircraft. "Keep her ready to get us out of here ASAP."

Ry nodded and retreated up the ramp. The last of Brutus's team jumped from the chopper, carrying weapons and equipment. They were travelling light, packing only essentials for survival in the desert. Nobody grumbled or complained. The job was the focus.

Brutus checked his watch. Ash Gibbons was late. Ash Gibbons, Roy Smart and Craig Muir all kept station near their target, observing the village, unseen and silent watchers.

The ramp of the helicopter closed with a final bang. For a moment, Brutus envied the simplicity of Ry's part in the job.

A single figure appeared through the wall of sand. Ash Gibbons. He pulled his own shemagh down, shouting to be heard. "Storm's coming."

"Tell us something we don't know," shouted Niall Campbell.

"We need to make it to camp soon. The storm'll keep us pinned down in an hour or two."

"How long to camp?"

"Ten klicks."

They set off, the pace hampered by the strong winds and poor visibility. Snow or sand, Brutus hated them both. He pulled his shemagh back into place, his baseball cap low, and held his AK-47 at the ready.

The trek was hard going, feet sank into the soft sand, and visibility was reduced to almost nothing. At one point, they were forced to scramble up a dune on hands and knees. There was no path to follow. They were completely reliant on the guiding skills of Ash Gibbons who led without reservation.

***

Camp site was well chosen. You could have stood a few metres away, and if unaware, would miss it completely. The wind was thunderous. Brutus knew the target village was close, close enough for two men to observe comings and goings without risk of detection.

The camp was little more than a collection of tents, pitched to provide maximum protection, nestled in the protective shallow of a wadi, and obscured from sight by sandbank parapets.

Ash pointed to one of the tents, and Brutus gave him the thumbs up. Brutus unzipped the canvass, stooped low, and threw his pack to the back of the tent. Daniel Ziaber followed close after, and closed the flap, zipping the storm outside. He spat sand from his mouth.

"What do we do now?"

Brutus removed his boots and outer layers. He stretched out, laying his AK-47 on his chest. The storm battered the canvass with little pause. The storm would get worse before subsiding. Once night came the temperature would drop and the situation would become uncomfortable. Roy Smart and Craig Muir were outside somewhere, keeping watch on the village and making sure the camp was secure. They would be more than uncomfortable, but they would keep everyone safe.

"Get some sleep while you can, Daniel." The wind howled a call of promised rage to come. "I doubt we'll be getting much through the night."

***

Brutus was right. The night took its toll. Tents collapsed, and outside, temperatures froze anything that stood still. When Brutus emerged from his tent, it was as if the camp had been swallowed by the desert. New piles of sand hid parts of the camp.

A hundred metres out of the wadi, Ash Gibbons peered through binoculars, a dusty baseball cap sitting backward on his head. His beard was longer than Brutus's and was ruddy-blond in colour matching his ponytail. Brutus rested his rifle on its sling.

"Good morning," said Brutus.

Ash dropped the binoculars from his eyes.

Ash was always the first to laugh, the first to joke, never took any situation too seriously in a superficial way. But his typical humour seemed to be missing that day.

"Everything okay?"

Red eyes flashed at Brutus. "I need to check on Craig and Roy. You should probably come, too."

"How far?"

Ash pointed forward. "Fifteen minutes or so."

The rest of the team stirred, escaping the confines of the tents, stamping cold feet, clapping cold hands. Brutus did not have to tell them how to conduct themselves. They grabbed shovels and began to attack the build-up of sand.

Brutus followed Ash in silence, up dunes and down steep slopes. The morning was starting to warm with the rising of the sun. For that Brutus was glad. The light brought life back into his cold body.

Rising from an unseen location was the target village. They reached a small dugout on the cusp of a dune. A small canvass-cover sheltered the trench from the elements. A figure, clad in a desert ghillie suit, lay in the trench, an M40 sniper rifle next to him. He watched the village beyond with a telescopic lens.

Craig appeared from behind. Brutus had his rifle in his hands before he realised the sudden appearance was friend not foe.

Roy turned, slipping down into the recess and waved to the two new arrivals. Both men looked exhausted. Nights spent in the desert and in the storm would do that to a person.

Roy waved the two men down to a crouch. Brutus followed Craig and Ash into the dugout, sinking into the sand. Brutus pulled out his canteen, sipped some water, swished it around his mouth and spat it out.

"What's the report?" asked Brutus.

"The outbreak occurred five days ago," said Roy. "From what we can tell the population has almost universally fallen ill. Stage two infection should progress to stage three in the next twenty-four hours. As of this morning, there's little movement about the village. Those that tried to leave or arrive have been taken care of."

Craig drew a finger across his neck, then went back to chewing on a fat biscuit.

"Good. We can wrap up here in a few days then. Get back, get paid and go our separate ways."

Craig and Roy knew more details than the others, as their role in the operation dictated. No doubt when Brutus's group came together things would be discussed. It was the nature of operators in their downtime. It annoyed Brutus more than a little that he did not know the full details of the overall plan. He spent so many years following the orders of others that he stopped questioning the reasons behind them. Back at the safe house in Cairo he had several-hundred-thousand reasons not to ask questions. Lately, he felt the need to know more. He could puzzle the pieces and come to a rough conclusion. Together with that kid, Ryan, they orchestrated the outbreak in Aberdeen on a population that was so underprepared for such an event it could not be halted. Now, they unleashed the virus on a smaller community, in a more isolated setting. All data was to be documented on film. This grand endeavour was nothing more than testing the effectiveness of the virus. Whether or not it was in preparation for another deliberate outbreak or to show its potency to entice a curious buyer, it did not matter to Brutus. The Carrion Virus, as far as Brutus was concerned was an artificial construction, a bio-weapon in its infancy. The powers that be would end the lives of thousands, but now, the uncertainty of the plans ahead troubled him. Brutus was not comfortable with guesses.

***

The whole day and night, and through to the next morning had been spent in preparation. They all knew what was coming. The first infected appeared a few hours from sunrise, staggering out of bounds of the village. Brutus granted permission for it to be taken out. Roy, a marksman of considerable experience brought it down with a silent shot from his rifle. It was the first of many that would have to die.

Ash led the group through the sand maze to the observation post. The village itself was small, less than a hundred buildings, set a short distance from a water source. A relatively new road bisected the place, but with the storm there was little traffic to or from. It was a sight that was chosen well. Even the weather seemed in conspiracy with Toth and the plan makers.

Brutus knelt, drawing a rough diagram of the village from memory in the sand. "We'll keep this simple. Sweep and clear, two teams, from both sides and meet in the middle. Once they hear gunfire, they'll charge. Don't think of this like anything you've gone through before. The infected don't possess fear of any sort. They won't stop if you point a gun at them. They're relentless, more dangerous than they look, and can survive wounds that would cripple anyone else. Don't think too much, just bring them down. Roy and Craig will watch our arses and make sure none of them sneak out and around. We do this right, we walk away job done. Let's get to it."

That was the best he could attempt at a warning. Brutus knew that once the chaos erupted it would do more than his words ever could. Nothing was questioned.

The whole team pulled on protective gloves that went some way up the forearm. Brutus readied his weapon, patted himself down for a second time to make sure he carried enough ammunition. All the weapons and ammunition used were locally sourced. There would be no fingerprint left behind to implicate anyone or any group. When the Egyptian authorities got around to investigate, they would fail to identify a suspect. Or perhaps there was already a scapegoat lined up for the fall. It was not Brutus's problem. He would be long gone, somewhere safe, somewhere he could keep his head down and watch the world tear itself apart.

They split into two teams. Brutus led his group down the direct route. Niall circled the second group around to the far end of the village. They moved fast, weapons raised, scanning for movement. Brutus charged over the flat sand before his feet hit the concrete of the road. He paused, letting the team form up. Without the use of radios, Brutus had no choice but to count silently in his head, giving the second team time to move into position and start their sweep.

"What are we waiting for?" asked Daniel Ziaber. "Let's go."

Brutus held up his hand, counting, waiting, peering into the village. In the doorway of one of the closest houses, something moved. Perhaps the wind whipped up a curtain. Perhaps something more sinister. The count was done.

Brutus dropped his hand. "Let's go."

The team moved forward into the ghost-village. Small, open-fronted stores were open, their wares laid out for inspection and purchase. Fruits in baskets waited to be haggled over but nobody came to buy.

From the doorway, movement. Brutus brought his rifle around, waiting. The first infected burst from the doorway, and like a cork from a champagne bottle, the rest followed. They stood for a moment, blinking in the sunlight, sniffing the air, jittering to a silent tune. Then as one, they charged toward Brutus. They moved with a single purpose, their prey in sight.

Distant rumble of gunfire began. Niall's group must have encountered the infected. There was no time to worry about them. Brutus had his own problems, and they all needed to be neutralised.

"Open fire," he barked.

He squeezed the trigger, firing a lethal burst, ripping into the advancing group. His team moved from behind him to his side, firing while they moved. The infected fell in droves. Some struggled back to their feet, others, their legs shredded by the fire, crawled toward them, raw hands ripping at the road.

Each house spewed out their occupants. Men, women and children, all stained crimson, wild-eyed and single-minded in purpose.

The rifle clicked empty. Brutus dropped the mag, and slotted a new one home in a fluid action. Daniel Ziaber appeared at this shoulder.

"There's kids with them!"

Brutus shot down a charging woman, her headscarf unwrapped and trailing like a cape. "Keep firing!"

Daniel grabbed at Brutus's arm. "I won't shoot kids. I didn't sign up to do this."

Brutus never took his eyes from the charging infected. "Get your hand off me and keep firing, or you'll end up like one of them. I guarantee it."

The forerunners of the infected were only fifty metres away. Brutus fired at anything that moved; he did not see people, only things that needed to die. One crawled from the mound of corpses, its mouth stretched back into a nonhuman snarl. The firing from the group died to sporadic rattles of gunfire.

The crawling infected kept their charge, slow and difficult, but there was no surrender. Anything that still moved, the team fired at.

Brutus didn't waste a bullet on one, and instead kicked its head. Something broke with a crunch. He stepped down on the back of its neck, pinning it to the floor. It roared in defiance, and was almost successful in throwing Brutus off. He swore and stamped down twice, and then a third time, snapping its shoulders and neck.

He turned to face his team. All still held their weapons at the ready. Daniel Ziaber's mouth was twisted into ball of anger. If he did not wear dark sunglasses, Brutus was sure his eyes would have burned into him.

Brutus marched up to Daniel. "If you ever pull something like that again, putting me and my team in danger, I'll put you down. You understand?"

Daniel seemed ready to argue. Brutus grabbed him by the collar and hauled him off. He brought him to the slain infected. He pulled out the body of a child, no more than five, her hair a matted mess, her diminutive body riddled with bullet wounds.

"Look at it," Brutus ordered.

Daniel pulled off his glasses. A snap of a few rounds from Roy and Craig took down another infected that made it into view.

"It doesn't matter how old they are, boy or girl, young or old. Once they get the virus they come for you, and they don't just have the strength of a child. Stop thinking of them as kids or as people. They're infected. The only way to stop them is to put them down. Permanently."

More gunfire from Niall's team.

"I've got kids. Around her age," said Daniel.

Brutus softened his tone, something he did not usually afford anyone. "Our friends are out there. We need to link up."

Brutus waved over his team. He pointed at each house in turn. "Grenades and clear every room. None of these things can be left behind."

The team moved off to the first house, tossed in a grenade, and breached after the explosion. Brutus counted the dead on the ground before him. Forty-three. He guessed for the size of the village the overall population would have been somewhere around three-hundred. Unless Niall's team ran into severe trouble it meant that the infected remained inside the dwellings rather than expose themselves to the withering fire. The situation bothered him more than a little. If they all charged suicidal into the path of the weapons then the mission would be wound up in a matter of hours. They kept to the shadows, forcing his men to move into the houses, robbing his men of what advantage they possessed. Grenades were the safest option. Frag anything inside and mop up what was left. The grenades popped, shattering windows, and were followed by bursts of gunfire.

Brutus marched up to his team, expectant that the next house they breached would be a nest of infection. His experience could prove the difference between clearing and one of his team succumbing. The building they were about to breach was two-storey and whitewashed. The alabaster was cracked, the walls pockmarked where rounds impacted.

Graeme Sinclair kicked the door once, twice, and it gave way. He stepped aside and Freddo McLeod tossed a grenade through the doorway. Everyone hugged a wall, or sidestepped out of the blast zone. The grenade erupted inside, throwing dust and splinters out of the doorway. Daniel Ziaber and Freddo McLeod entered moments later, ready to meet the roaring infected. Gunfire bursts came, and the scuffling of furniture knocked and kicked down. The two men returned from inside.

"Clear. Two in there."

Brutus nodded, the rest of the team falling in. So far so good, but they were not even halfway through. Brutus checked his weapon and moved toward the next building.

A sudden impact from behind knocked Brutus forward. He stumbled, fell to his knees, catching himself with hands into the sand-covered concrete. He threw himself round, onto his back, bring his rifle up to the ready. It didn't make sense. His team lay scattered about, all picking themselves up. All except Graeme. He lay face down, an infected grappling at his back, sinking its teeth into his exposed neck. He cried out. Brutus squeezed the trigger, firing a single, well-placed round impacting the infected's cranium. Brains, blood and bone cascaded down on to Graeme. Brutus hauled himself to his feet, and kicked the infected off his fallen comrade.

Graeme moaned, a low sound like a wounded animal. He struggled onto his back, hand pressed to the gaping wound at his throat. His mouth moved and uttered nothing coherent. His eyes rolled back, revealing only white. They returned, his eyes now a deep-red, pupils dilated and unfocussed. Daniel Ziaber stepped toward Graeme.

Brutus threw out a hand. "Keep back. He's been bitten."

"We need to help him. He's dying."

Freddo McLeod stepped toward Daniel. "He's already dead. Look at him. That's not normal. How long before he turns?"

"Minutes," said Brutus. "When the virus is transferred through a bite it progresses to stage three in moments. Graeme is dead." He pointed toward the next building. "Keep clearing. I'll take care of Graeme."

"We shouldn't leave you here alone," said Freddo.

"Go. I'll do what's necessary."

The team reluctantly moved to the next house. Brutus knelt next to Graeme. The man's breaths came in rapid and shallow gasps.

"Goddamn, Graeme. You should have checked the roof." The infected must have launched itself from the flat roof of the building. "You're going to turn into one of those things, you stupid bastard. It wasn't supposed to happen like this."

Brutus pulled out his combat knife and placed the blade point down above Graeme's heart. Graeme flailed wildly. Brutus struggled to hold his arms down. He thrust down, short and sharp. Graeme's eyes closed. A raw rattle sounded from his throat, then he stilled.

Brutus pulled the knife free and ignored the wet sucking sound. He wiped the blade on Graeme's clothes. Brutus never understood why people in his line of work fell apart when bringing death. It was their job. But this one? The infected were to blame, not Graeme. A rage stirred, one that would be sated by violence. Revenge. He would take a heavy toll on the infected. They needed to be wiped out.

Brutus sheathed his knife and brought his rifle to the ready. His team completed another clearing, all members returning unharmed. He was ready to direct them to another building, a shop this time when Niall and his team raced around the corner from another street. They all shared a look of panic.

"Looks like they're coming," said Brutus, grabbing hold of Freddo and pushing him toward the centre of the street. "Stay away from the buildings, three-sixty cover. Keep your bursts short and accurate. This is your bread and butter. Get them on the ground."

They assembled in the centre of the village, reloading weapons, littering the road with spent magazines.

"We found the nest," puffed Niall. He pulled off his sunglasses. "Damn near the whole lot are in there. A big warehouse on the far side of the village. Hundreds of them."

"It's better this way. We needed to draw them out in the open. Going house to house costs us."

Niall raised an eyebrow.

"Graeme's gone. Infected got him."

Niall swore.

"Here they come," shouted Magnus.

The mass of infected appeared. Some fell as high velocity rounds speared through bones and organs. Brutus glanced to where he knew Roy and Craig sat perched, unseen guardians doing what they could to thin the herd. Those that fell without a head wound shuddered upright, continuing their advance. They screamed and roared. Beside him, a few of this team took a step backwards. Despite their military training and countless combat missions this was an enemy that was completely new.

Brutus stepped forward, more to install confidence than to gain any tactical advance. He opened fire, his first burst striking the forerunners. A few stumbled but none fell. His team opened up, unleashing a hail of fire. The combined firepower brought down some of the mass but the rest surged on, unconcerned by losses.

The first infected reached Brutus, manic eyes and grasping with hands. He threw a fist into the dark face, and it stumbled backward as if bouncing off a brick wall. Someone behind shouted for Brutus to move out of the way. He ignored the call, kicked out, landing the flat of his boot on its knee, breaking the joint. He swung again, knocking it down. The snap of bullets rippled past. He fired three shots into the fallen, two in the chest and one in the head.

"Brutus, get back!"

He pulled back. The entire team moved, firing in retreat.

"Grenades," he called.

A handful of the small explosives were thrown at those still charging. The explosions brought some to an immediate halt, and threw others two-foot off the ground. Brutus kept firing.

The momentum of the infected faltered. Only a few managed to break forward and come within twenty feet of the team. They were quickly gunned down.

Freddo McLeod moved forward, swapping his AK-47 for a combat shotgun. He blasted the last infected at close range, a hole as big as a basketball appearing at its chest, one shoulder falling free from the torso.

The village fell quiet. Brutus turned to his team. All still held their weapons ready. They would have to clear the remaining buildings, perhaps thirty to go. Brutus suspected that most, if not all, the infected were now dead. The gunfire would have drawn them out from their nests. That was his experience but he needed to make sure. That was what he was being paid to do, be thorough.

Freddo weaved through the destruction, careful not to touch any of the corpses.

A single infected, a female, naked and bleeding ran from the cover of a building. Freddo McLeod raised his shotgun, pumping it once, an empty cartridge falling to the ground.

"Stop!" An idea flashed in Brutus's mind, born in a spark of opportunism. He ran to Freddo and demanded his shotgun.

Freddo threw the weapon over without protest, and pulled his AK around instead. "What are you doing? Don't let it get close."

Brutus did not take his eyes from the approaching infected. "Get something to restrain it. Plastic ties and something to cover the mouth. Go."

She screamed as she charged. He held the shotgun high, waiting, studying her pace. The girl couldn't have been more than thirteen, a young body only starting to take shape. Brutus knew it was dangerous to attempt a capture, but something told him it was an astute move.

He threw the stock of the shotgun into the girl's face, and hit her again, then flipped the weapon around pushed the barrel, hard, forcing her down and onto the road. With two swift kicks he had her on her stomach, and placed a heavy boot on her head. Daniel Ziaber appeared at his side, his rifle trained down, a boot holding her hips low. Freddo knelt and wrestled the girl's arms behind her back. A vein in his neck pulsed with the strain. Together, Brutus and Freddo secured her arms, strapping them together with plastic restraints. And then her legs. Magnus Munson handed over a roll of duct tape.

"When I flip her over," said Brutus, "cover your faces. If she spits and you get that crap in your mouth, you're in trouble."

They heaved her onto her back. She spat and growled to the left then right, then snapped like a dog. Freddo and Daniel recoiled, but Brutus was not in danger of the saliva. Watching its eyes move from him, he ripped a length of tape free of the roll, and pushed it down over her mouth, then ripping more tape free he wound it round and round and round again. It was not a style of strapping any doctor would own up to, but his messy crisscross patterns sufficed and sealed the eyes and mouth, yet left the nose free to take in air. Brutus stood and stepped back.

"What the hell was that all about?" Niall's barrel homed into the infected. "Sweep and clear, that's what we're paid to do. Not crap like this."

"Relax, it's done," said Brutus. "We needed some insurance."

"Insurance for what? It wasn't part of the mission. You put us at risk, Brutus."

"It's done. Now we'll finish the sweep, clear the rest of the houses and get the hell out of here."

Niall matched his fiery gaze, holding it for a moment before looking away. The team moved to pick up where they left off with the sweep.

Brutus stood over his prize, like a huntsman and his dead deer. The captured infected represented the more cynical nature of Brutus. At best, it was something he could make a little more money from on the side. At worst, it was a form of insurance against outliving his usefulness. He suffered no illusion. He was expendable. The whole team was.

He'd keep completing his tasks, then when the opportunity arose, slip away. He had the money to keep comfortable for many years and that was his plan.

Whatever was coming next, he'd be a spectator not a participant.

***

No more infected were located. The team readied to pull out. Brutus shouted orders. He need not have been so official. The team went about picking up the crates and carrying the bags without prompting. He suspected many of them were happy just to be leaving the nameless village in the Sinai.

Their dead comrade, Graeme, had been placed into a body bag, and the captured infected was thrown into a makeshift canvass carry. She thrashed about, all for naught. The bag was secured tightly at its opening, and layers of tape wrapped round and round offered the last measure of restraint.

Everything was packed and ready. Forty minutes and they would be back to the helicopter and Ry Watson would be flying them back to Cairo.

The team trekked out into the golden expanse, the cruel sun beating down without mercy. The return journey fared better than the first even with one member down and towing dangerous cargo. Brutus still had not formulated a plan in which to offload the infected. Any number of buyers would clamour for a chance to gain access to a live one. States and corporations. Brutus had contacts but none that could network him to the people he needed. If he was to sell, he couldn't do it alone.

Magnus stepped next to him. He carried a large bag, plus his pack. His rifle swung on its sling at his back. "What are we going to do with Graeme? We can't just rock up to a hospital or the consulate and tell them he died in his sleep."

"Toth will make arrangements. We'll get him back home."

Magnus made a face, seemingly unconvinced.

Brutus quickened his pace.

They trudged on, Ash at the front, leading them onward. Finally, the rolling dunes fell behind them and they found the makeshift airfield, the helicopter now covered with a sand-coloured canvass.

Ry Watson popped his head over a sand bluff, dropping his binoculars. He stood, an MP5 weapon in his hands.

"Guys!" He waved at them, and ran down the bluff to meet them.

Ry stuck out a hand and Brutus shook.

"How'd it go? Get the job done?"

"Job's done. How have things been here?"

Ry looked around. "Nothing to report. It's weird here at night, freezing. You start imagining things, you hear things, voices. It's just an empty, creepy place."

"Graeme didn't make it, Ry."

Ry swore.

"Get the bird prepped for launch. I want to be out of here ASAP."

Ry unsecured the lines holding the canvass down and pulled it free. He dropped the rear ramp and the team loaded their cargo. The infected continued to roll about in its bag. Freddo McLeod gave it a swift kick and spat. Brutus said nothing. If only his team knew the reason why he insisted the infected was brought along. Better they didn't know.

Once the gear was secured, the team took their places, fastening themselves into position. Brutus walked the length of the helicopter, past the growling infected, past the still body of Graeme and into the cockpit. Ry talked into his headset, hand pressed against the earpiece.

"What's the hold up?"

He did not turn. "We can't go yet."

"Why not?"

"I can't get through to Toth. We don't go until we do."

"Screw that. Come on. We need to get out of here."

Ry shook his head. Brutus was about to say something when Ry answered an unheard voice. He pulled off the headset and handed it back to Brutus.

"Toth wants to speak to you."

Brutus slid the headphones over his ear. The signal was full of static, crackling and buzzing.

"Brutus here. Go."

"Ah, Brutus," said Toth, the hint of mockery in his voice. "The party was a success I take it?"

"All went as planned. One of my men was killed. We'll need to bring him home."

There was a moment of silence. "That can be arranged. Put me back onto your pilot. We'll speak again when you're home."

Brutus returned the headphones and sat in the empty co-pilot seat. Ry gave one and two word responses. Nothing could be discussed on an open channel. He hung the headphones up and turned to Brutus.

"When do we fly?" asked Niall.

"As soon as we're loaded," said Ry. "I'm not spending any longer out here than necessary."

***

The rotors of the helicopter powered up, the chassis shuddering. Ry gave a thumbs up and the helicopter lifted from the ground.

Brutus held tight. The flight kept a low altitude, skimming over the terrain, eluding the radar of any who may be watching.

The land sped past. Brutus watched from the shallow window. Something caught his eye. A blimp in the otherwise pristine landscape. He was about to call to the others when a fireball ripped apart the rear of the helicopter. The explosion rocked the aircraft knocking equipment and bodies around. Ry struggled with the controls. Black smoke filled the compartment. Brutus grasped the handrail with both hands.

Ry shouted, "We're losing altitude. Engine's shutting down."

"Hold onto something," ordered Brutus.

"We're going in hard!"

The ground raced up to meet them, the sea of gold ready to welcome the helicopter.

Someone shouted, "Good luck."

The engine screeched a final death rattle. The impact shattered the aircraft and turned Brutus's world into a void of black, filled with pain and confusion.

***

Brutus woke, a thundering ache in his forehead. He reached up, his hand coming away warm and wet. Brutus lay a few metres from the helicopter. It was a miracle he was alive, having been thrown clear on impact. Where was the infected? That canvass bag?

An acrid smoke billowed. Someone cried out in pain. He couldn't tell where. Brutus pulled himself to his feet, a wave of nausea churned and churned. He gave over to it, and threw up into the sand. Daniel Ziaber lay a few steps to his right. Brutus shouted for help. He stumbled over to his mate, and dropped down next to him.

Daniel moaned, unable to open his eyes. His left leg sat at an awkward angle.

Brutus patted him on the shoulder. "Daniel, the infected, the canvass bag?"

Daniel made no reply.

"I'll get help. Hang on."

Brutus freed himself of his rifle, made his way to the helicopter, and forced his way through the ruined cockpit door. Splintered metal bristled in the doorway. Ry Watson was dead, his torso crushed beneath a sheet of the machine, his eyes wide and his hands gripping levers. He made a grotesque hybrid, man and machine. Brutus pushed through to the cargo hold. Several of the team were outside, whether thrown clear on impact or escaped after, Brutus was not sure. Craig Muir lay in the gangway, dead, the back of his head sheared off. No sign of the canvass bag. Did the explosion shred it to smithereens?

"Brutus." Niall moved up to his side, and helped him out of the helicopter.

"Ry and Craig are gone," said Brutus.

"What brought us down?"

"Daniel's hurt bad. See to him," said Brutus.

What brought down the aircraft? The anomaly that caught his attention moments before the blast. Something in the desert. A flash that did not resonate at the time. "What was it?" he said to himself, rubbing his face.

It came to him. Two figures, shadow-like against the brightness of the desert. The explosion that ripped apart the helicopter. Some kind of surface-to-air missile system. A Stinger perhaps. The pieces fell into a terrible order in his mind.

They were expendable, and they were loose ends. Brutus had done all he could to stay relevant and useful to Toth, but it appeared Toth found it imperative to eradicate all witnesses, anyone who could expose how much Toth was involved.

Brutus swore. The wreck billowed a dark smoke skyward, a clear beacon to their position. They would be coming, coming to make sure nobody survived.

Ash Gibbons moved to Brutus's side, his bulk blotting out the sun for a moment. He held basic medical dressings.

"Hold still, you've got a nasty gash to your head." He sprayed some saline and patted the bandage down. Fire burned at his forehead. Brutus gritted his teeth, ignoring the pain as best he could.

Ash strapped a clean gauze swab to the wound. "That'll have to do for now."

Brutus touched the dressing. "Daniel? Have you tended, Daniel?"

"He's unconscious. His leg's broken and he's got some busted some ribs. Probably internal bleeding. If we don't get him out of here he'll be dead in twenty-four hours." Everyone else is banged up pretty bad." He wiped his forehead. "What happened?"

"I think we outlived our usefulness."

"Toth?"

"That's my thinking. We're the pawns, expendable. I thought I was setting us up for something good. It was easy money, for all of us."

"If what you're saying is true, then we've more important things to worry about. The smoke from the wreck will give us away."

"My thoughts exactly." Brutus stretched out a hand and Ash hauled him to his feet. "What's the ammo situation?"

Ash shrugged. "We're down to a few mags each. Thirty or forty rounds for the sniper rifles. A few dozen shells for the shotgun. They'll send six to eight operators, heavily armed, and they'll come out shooting."

"We need to get eyes up high." All around were walls of sand, dunes rising up and falling away. "There." Brutus pointed to a particularly high dune, off to this right. "Have Roy take position there. Keep eyes north-east. We need to get everyone out of the helicopter. Can we move Daniel?"

"Do we have a choice?"

"Get him into shade, make him comfortable. Everyone else needs to grab their weapons. Pass out water rations. We've probably got an hour at most."

"What do you want to do with that infected in the bag?"

"You found it?"

Ash inclined his head toward a banged up rotor. Half buried by the desert lay the canvass bag. "Still moving. You want me to put it down?"

"No," answered Brutus.

Ash's hand tugged at his lengthy beard. "You know, when you first contacted me about this, I thought it was all crap. I didn't think we'd have done what we did. The money … the money we'll never see now."

"You'll get money. And more." Brutus would get something more. He would get revenge. "That canvass bag will get us something."

***

Roy held up both hands, indicating two vehicles approached, then crouched down into position tracking the movement with his rifle. Sinking down at the summit of the dune he disappeared from view. The dead and Daniel were moved into a makeshift shelter, hidden away and protected from the sun. The infected had been dragged a five-minute walk from the crash site and left. Brutus could not afford to leave any of the team as a guard. He needed everyone on point. The infected would likely never regain its footing. If it did, it would not be difficult to track.

Brutus concealed himself next to the ruined rotors. Lying flat on his stomach, he held the AK-47 ready. The other members of the team concealed themselves as best they could.

Three aging Land Rovers, their windows tinted dark and the number plates obscured by tape bounced over a dune and into the shallow at the crash site. They halted a short distance away. The doors opened and heavily armed men alighted. Brutus counted twelve in total, dressed in body armour and armed with AR-15s. The team leader directed them with hand signals. They spread into a well-practised line. Did a driver remain in each vehicle? Brutus doubted it.

They moved forward, slow and steady, moving weapons about searching for targets. Brutus knew Roy would be tracking the team leader. He would be the first to die. That would be the signal. He would be taken out and Brutus and his team would open up on the rest, emptying everything they had, avoiding damage to the Land Rovers in the process. The vehicles were their only method of leaving the Sinai alive. He almost pitied the newcomers. They probably knew as much about the mission as Brutus. Vague half-truths and golden promises. But they were obstacles Brutus needed to go through.

A high-powered sniper round blasted the team leader and sent him careering backwards. The whole crash site opened up on the new arrivals. Brutus fired controlled, single shots. The new operators returned fire, an undisciplined, unfocused move. They still hadn't located where the fire was coming from. Two went down to the left, and a third was taken by Roy. They scattered seeking the scant cover available to them. Bullets sprayed the helicopter carcass. Brutus ducked his head a moment, but kept firing.

One of the operators leapt back into the closet vehicle. Before Brutus could direct fire on him, the entire windscreen shattered, the operator slain in the driver's seat. Roy was in a perfect position. One operator leapt to his feet, and ran across the open ground, seeking to make it to the helicopter. His eyes went wide when he saw Brutus lying in its shadow. Brutus opened up on him, dropping the operator without a second thought. He changed to his last magazine.

Magnus stepped from behind his sand cover and lobbed a grenade at the cluster of the remaining enemy, then fired as he slid back to cover. The explosion felled three soldiers who lay too close to each other. Freddo took out another.

Gunfire continued, and it became obvious that nobody was shooting back. The crash site fell to silence. Brutus snuck forward on his belly, wriggling like a snake in the sand. Only two operators remained, both knelt, holding their AR-15s above their heads. Brutus stood and held his hand in the air, motioning for a cease fire. It made sense to question them before he killed them. And they had to die.

Freddo and Ash Gibbons joined Brutus. Freddo pulled his combat shotgun free. He kept the two surrendering enemies in his sights.

"Weapons down, five steps back. Hands on your heads."

They did as Brutus commanded. Freddo stepped up, pushing the barrel of his shotgun into one of the faces.

"Move, and you're dead," he said matter-of-factly.

Brutus let his AK go, resting it on the sling. He picked up one of the AR-15s, checked the weapon and sights before moving up to the two prisoners.

"You were sent here to kill us, to destroy the evidence of our mission?"

Neither man spoke. They kept their eyes to the ground. Freddo laid a meaty fist into the closet man's stomach, doubling him over.

"Answer his goddamned question, you bastards," he roared.

"No survivors," said the man doubled over. "We were told to leave no survivors and destroy the helicopter."

"What's your name?" asked Brutus.

"Fisayo," he said, with the accented style of a Nigerian national. He straightened, his dark skin beading with sweat.

"Who sent you? Tell us and I promise you won't be harmed."

Fisayo looked about him.

Freddo stepped forward. "Who sent you?" He pushed the shotgun close to his face. "Speak."

"Andor Toth."

Freddo sent Brutus a sideway glance.

"What happens once you've mopped up here?" said Brutus.

"Say nothing," said the other operator.

Brutus stepped up and smashed the butt of the AR-15 into the side of his head. He fell to the ground, unconscious. He rounded on Fisayo.

"I don't want any more bloodshed. Don't give my men or me an excuse. You were just following orders. We understand how it works. Andor Toth. You're meeting with him after this? Once the mission is complete?"

He nodded.

"When and where?"

Fisayo licked his lips. "I'll show you. I'll show you where and then you let me go."

Brutus weighed up his options. Would he be able to find Toth on his own? Unlikely. Fisayo was key to gaining access to Toth. Besides, he would suffice as a guide on the journey out of the desert and back to Cairo.

"When do you make contact with Toth?"

"Four days from now. In Cairo."

Brutus let a smile split his face. "Fisayo, you just saved your life. Get up."

"Freddo, keep an eye on him. He's not to be harmed."

"What about the other one?" He kicked at the unconscious operator.

"Leave him here."

It was a death sentence.

Brutus waved to Niall and the others. "We're driving out."

He checked the three Land Rovers. Fuel tanks close to full. The boots contained more ammunition and supplies, and canisters of drinkable water. It would take the rest of the day to get out of the Sinai and then another to Cairo. One day in Cairo to find somewhere to lie low. The fourth day, Brutus would arrange a reckoning with Toth. The puppet had just cut his own strings.

***

Chapter Six
Panopticon

Jane walked the corridors of the facility, her heart pounding. This was a prison by another name. Her movements were restricted.

Nobody gave the scrubs-clad woman a second glance, and she understood why. Everyone had a job to do. For her, she was Holden's assistant. The doctor slept off a raging hangover. If anyone asked, she would tell them he was under the weather.

Jane promised Holden they would form some kind of escape plan. Hyde held the key. He possessed a functioning satellite telephone. Jane needed to acquire it somehow and call for help.

Hyde's office was before her, the electronic lock blinked a red light. A bulky, black orb hung above the doorway, silently observing, no doubt broadcasting to a security station. How many guards watched her now on a monitor screen?

She snapped her attention away and moved off toward Holden's office. It was with some surprise that she found Holden sitting at his desk, head in hand. Two dissolvable tablets bubbled at the bottom of his glass of water.

"I didn't expect to see you up today, Eugene. How are you feeling?"

Holden looked up, his eyes narrowed as if the light burned. "Delicate. Take a seat. I feel as though I should apologise for last night. I tend not to drink so heavily. I fear I may have said some things I shouldn't have."

"We were speaking honestly for the first time, I think."

Holden nodded, squeezing his eyes closed. "We did."

Jane checked behind her. The work space was near empty. Even here, Christmas Day was observed. Someone would be tasked to check on the infected, feed them and keep them hydrated. The guards would still be on rotation, keeping everyone where they should be.

"What I don't understand is why the others working here accept that they can't leave, especially at this time of year."

"You have to understand, Jane, the medical staff and researchers believe themselves to be in a pivotal position to help combat the outbreak. Their egos are being stroked, and their pockets are being filled. Who knows what else they've been offered." Holden chugged back his drink.

"We're still getting out of here, Eugene."

"I don't see how we can."

Jane leaned closer. They were alone but she did not want to risk being overheard. "Hyde has a satellite telephone. If one of us manages to get a hand on it then we can make a call outside, and get some help."

"And who would we call?"

"Williamson?"

"I don't know how far his knowledge of this place goes. I get the feeling he is a good man, but it was under his advice that I came here. Yet, we can't call the police, so Williamson may be our only hope. He did leave me his personal number. But if it's the wrong decision we could be putting ourselves in danger."

"What choice do we have?"

Holden shrugged. "None. We can either act or remain."

"I'll get Hyde's phone. You'll need to distract him. We need his keycard to get into his office. There is a lot of security cameras in this facility. I'll need to find out if someone watches them all the time or if they're just recorded. It'll take a couple of days to check up on all these things."

"How will you get Hyde's card?"

Jane bit her lip. "I don't know. I don't have all the answers, or any for that matter. I just know we have to act. We can't let what's going on to continue."

Jane was not sure Holden agreed with her due to his moral compulsions or whether he was simply tired of wrestling with the herculean task of the virus and the infected. Whatever his motivations, their aims were the same.

The hydraulics of the door hissed. Both Jane and Holden turned. One of the research assistants entered. He waved a friendly greeting and wished them both a Merry Christmas. Holden smiled thinly while Jane returned the season's wishes with a more convincing smile. When he was far from ear shot, they returned to their conversation.

"You're too important to not be noticed if you weren't to go about your duties. I can move about far more freely. Over the next few days, I'll find out what I can."

Holden reached out and touched her arm. "Jane, what we're embarking on is dangerous. I want you to realise the gravity of the situation. It might be safer to remain here and let events run their course."

"Eugene, that's not an option."

"If we fail, the consequences could be dire. I only want you to go into action with your eyes open."

"My eyes are open," said Jane, resolutely. "This can't continue."

Holden rolled his glass in his hands. "I feel I should do more, most of this relies on you."

"I can move about more freely than you. Just be ready. If we have to leave suddenly, we won't have time to prepare."

Holden leaned back, a small groan escaping his lips. "When I think back to all that has transpired over the last few months, I see nothing but an entire world turned upside down." He shook his head. "I should have continued with my plans for retirement, I would have been sitting by my fire right now, reading *A Tale of Two Cities*. Instead, here I am, a fugitive, my academic and personal life in tatters, a refugee, hiding from the world, inflicting grievous wounds on ill people all in the name of progress. You and I are embroiled in an event that has changed the course of human history. If we're not careful, we'll be swallowed up and forgotten."

Holden looked nothing like the exceptionally gifted academic professor that he was, and more a tired and frightened old man. Jane wanted to reach out and offer some succour as was her nature, but no, she remained silent. Perhaps the situation was too far beyond words. Nothing was said for an inordinate amount of time.

Jane breathed in deeply. "You're thinking too much, Eugene. Try relax a little. We'll work this out together. A few days and we could be ready to act."

***

Jane moved between her duties as fluidly as she could, stopping to chat to a researcher here, making conversation with guards there, loitering in the corridor, eyes seemingly scanning the many bulletin boards. Over the past two days Jane counted twenty-five guards on duty at any given time. A quick peep into the control room at changeover discovered only one of the guards positioned at the monitors.

Holden went about his work as if on autopilot, with several researchers enquiring as to his welfare. The excuse of exhaustion was believable.

"Let's get some fresh air, Eugene. You look as though you need a break."

Holden grabbed his mug of coffee and followed without comment. They had agreed it was too dangerous to speak of their plans within the complex. Gaining access to outside the facility was not something that was encouraged, but even the guards knew they could not keep one-hundred or more people cooped up forever in the subterranean vault.

They walked in silence, their footfalls providing a lonely accompaniment. They reached the stairs and climbed, Holden grasping the rail, his breath laboured.

"Eugene?"

"I'm okay. Just a little unfit."

At the summit, a guard stood, weapon strapped to his chest. It had initially shocked Jane seeing so many armed men, but time acclimatised her thoughts. Weapons were her reality for now. Jane recognised the guard, having spoken to him a few times over the last couple of days. His name was lost in a jumble of faces.

The guard held up a hand, his ID badge being uncovered in the movement. "What can I do for you both?"

"Afternoon, Jon," Jane said, ripping her eyes from the guard's ID badge as quickly as she could. "Doctor Holden and I are just stepping out for a breath of fresh air."

Jon checked his watch. "You shouldn't be going out at this time."

"Jon, look at Doctor Holden. He looks dreadful. The ventilation system here is stifling. We'll only be ten minutes. It's too cold to be out longer."

Jon ran a hand through his red hair. "I guess, since it's you, Jane. Ten minutes. You know not to stray too far. It's dangerous out there, and the weather is getting worse, too."

"You're a star," said Jane, flashing one of her smiles.

He waved away the compliment and swiped his keycard to open the lock. The door swung inward.

"Ten minutes, Jane. No more."

She nodded. "We won't go far."

They stepped out into the winter world. The wind howled and snow blustered in every direction. The frigid air hurt as Jane took a breath. She wished she had dressed more appropriately. Holden pulled his coat tight about him. The snow that accumulated on the ground came almost to knee height. Narrow trenches had been shovelled through the drift, allowing easier access to the outer buildings and accommodation sites.

They walked a little from the doorway, out of earshot of the guard, not that he would have been able to hear them over the clamour of the storm. The narrow passages forced Jane to walk ahead of Holden. They made it to one of the outbuildings, a storage garage.

"I've got an idea," said Jane, checking they were alone.

"Go on."

"I can't get Hyde's phone unless I find a way into his office. Even if I make it in there, security will know I'm there."

"That's not necessarily an obstacle to everything," said Holden, his teeth beginning to chatter. "You said the guards rotate. Well, I wonder if they would know who has access to which rooms. Should we be able to acquire his keycard then you could simply walk in and get the phone, and walk out."

"And when Hyde discovers that his phone is missing, then what? They'll review the tapes and see me. Help won't reach us in time."

Holden flicked snowflakes from his glasses. "You have a point. Unless ... well ... unless Hyde isn't available to make anyone aware that his phone is missing. You said we needed a distraction.

What if I allow one of the infected to slip from some of its restraints? Not release it, but allow it some movement, enough to get their attention. In the confusion and panic we would find a window of opportunity to act, and Hyde would not be missed."

"I don't know, Eugene. That sounds too—"

"If you have a better suggestion, I'm willing to listen," said Holden curtly. "I understand your hesitation. I feel the same, but I see no other way."

The cold was becoming too much. Jane could only guess at the temperature, well below minus-ten. "If that's the only way?"

"It is."

"We should head back inside."

Jane could just make out Jon at the doorway. Was he waving them back? Possibly. They returned to their prison, the door closing with a bang of finality. They both shook the snow from their clothes. Holden removed his glasses and cleaned them off.

"Thank you for letting us out, Jon." Jane smiled her best smile again. She might need Jon's favour again.

"Are you feeling better, Doctor?"

"Oh, yes. Thank you. A brisk walk in the winter air does wonders."

***

Holden checked his watch. Jane was scheduled to attempt her part of the plan in fifteen minutes, and once successful, she would appear in his office. He would then put his part into action.

The chaos which would ensue would give them the opportunity to make a call and form some kind of escape. He pushed his foot against the bundle under his desk, a heavy winter coat and some snow-proof boots. He had the same ready for Jane.

He moved to one of the examination tables. The infected strapped and secured to it watched him, muscles bulging as it struggled against the restraints. Holden checked the chart. *Infected seventy-six.* They were experimenting on how cold affected the subject. It had been submerged in icy water for five hours, and its reaction times and resilience were measured and recorded. The virus was remarkable in a fashion. It provided a great deal of resilience against physical wounds and went some way to regenerating them, too. The Carrion Virus granted the infected abnormal strength. It certainly warranted more study under a controlled environment. That was the issue. With the infected, was there such a thing as control?

He checked his watch again. It was nearing time. Infected seventy-six would be his distraction, the one that he would allow a measure of freedom.

***

Jane kept a hand in her pocket, holding the thin syringe Holden provided. A plastic guard covered the needle. He had explained it would render Hyde unconscious within thirty seconds and would keep him that way for forty-eight hours.

She passed Hyde's office several times, without a real idea as to how to gain access. Knocking on the door would probably result in her being ignored or fobbed off. She had to wait for him to come out. Perhaps then she would have the opportunity to get him on his own.

Time dragged. Eugene would be waiting impatiently, ready to implement his part of the plan. She had to get to Hyde!

The door opened. Hyde stepped out and walked down the corridor, his nose buried in a report. Jane followed at a discreet distance, taking uncomfortably short steps to maintain the space. Hyde rounded the corner and moved out of sight. Jane rounded the same corner. The door to the male bathrooms swung shut.

Nobody else moved about the facility. If she waited longer there was bound to be a witness. Jane, heart racing, burst into the bathroom. Hyde stood at the urinal. He did not look up, but kept his eyes downcast. Jane pulled out the syringe, popping off the plastic guard, exposing the needle. Hyde turned toward her.

"What are you doing here? Get out!"

Jane lashed out, plunging the thin lance into his neck, and depressing the plunger.

Hyde snatched at his neck, as Jane stepped back. He pulled it free, looked down at it in his hands.

"You bitch!" He threw the syringe at her, took three fast steps and of a sudden his hands were on her throat. "What have you done to me?"

Those hands tightened. His eyes widened. "What? What have you done?"

Jane couldn't get air into her lungs. He squeezed tighter. She dug her nails into his wrists, scraping, pulling. He kept hold. Jane brought up a knee, her aim not quite right, hitting his considerable gut.

I'm going to die! I'm going to die!

Panic. Fear. Regret. She tried calling out, but no sound came. Sweat beaded on his forehead. The anger that distorted his face, fell away, so too, his hands.

Jane collapsed onto the ground, gasping, coughing, her hands at her chest encouraging air to flow.

Hyde's legs gave way. His head struck the tiled floor. His breathing grew rapid for a few moments but then settled to deep, long breaths.

Jane waited for something to happen, either Hyde to jump to his feet or someone to walk in and discover them both. Nothing happened. A tap dripped in the sink, rhythmic and steady.

Get up and move, she urged herself. Jane got to her feet, her neck burning. She patted Hyde's body, searching for his ID keycard. He usually wore it around his neck or clipped to his belt. She checked his trouser pockets and found what she was looking for. She pulled the small card free, and slipped it into her pocket. The disabled bathroom cubicle door was open. As far as she knew, there were no disabled staff working in the facility. It would do to store him out of sight for some time. Jane hauled his arms, dragging him only a few inches at a time. But each tug drew him closer. Finally, the fat body was in the confines of the cubicle. Jane pulled the door closed, and used a coin to lock it from the outside.

A part of her could not believe she had managed to do all this without something going wrong. Still nobody moved about the corridors. *Steady now, Jane. Normal movements. You can do this.* In the two days since Christmas, the operations at the facility ran on minimal staff. Jane confidently slipped through the maze of corridors, back to Hyde's office. She had walked the corridors more times than she cared to remember, the complicated layout no longer held any surprises for her.

The security cameras stood silent watch above her. Jane held the keycard to the reader and the blinking red light turned green. The door clicked open and she went inside. The office was modest in size, well-kept and organised. Jane found the satellite phone immediately. She tucked the device into the waistband of her trousers, pulling her top down to cover it. After a quick scan of the room, and finding nothing more of use, she slipped out.

***

The door to the office burst open and Jane entered. Holden stood, unsure if her rush was due to being pursued or if she bore other news. She pulled up her top and removed the bulky satellite phone, placing it into Holden's hand. He scarcely believed Jane managed to acquire it. Hope was all he had, confidence not entering into the equation of late.

"Hyde?"

"Unconscious. I've locked him in the disabled bathroom."

"And you weren't discovered?"

"No. Not as far as I know. Make the call, Eugene. If Williamson doesn't agree to help us then all this is for nothing."

"He'll help us, Jane. I know he will." Holden knew it was time confidence returned.

He began to dial.

***

Eric trudged into the familiar hotel in Aberdeen where Black Aquila was based. He had flown into the city an hour ago. Fires still raged, unchecked, sending black plumes of smoke into the air. A large flotilla of naval ships lay at anchor a short distance off the coast, large warships, an aircraft carrier group and a small cluster of commercial ships. The airport had been transformed into a military hub. Much of the open space was now taken over with temporary buildings, the runways and hangars clogged with all types of military aircraft.

Eric was shown to Williamson's room. When he entered, Williamson stood and shook his hand. He did not smile. Dark circles ringed his eyes. He appeared a man who carried the weight of the world on his shoulders.

"Eric, you've no idea how glad I am to see you. Grab a seat." Williamson moved to the sofa, eased himself back and cracked his neck. Laid out on the table before him were three laptops. He closed each in turn, snapping the lids down. Williamson rubbed his eyes. "How is the family?"

"Good. Great. Things are better. Thanks for allowing me those few days."

Williamson gave a genuine smile. Eric got the feeling it was not something he had done lately. The exchange was short-lived.

"Things seem different. The airport is crawling with military. There's an armada on the coast and still the snow falls. What's happening?"

"The situation has changed in the brief time you've been away. All Black Aquila operations have been suspended except for security of this building. Our men, my men refuse to work in the city. I've a list longer than my arm of casualties, the dead in the hundreds, so we've been suspended until further notice. There's been a sudden influx of American troops, not just at the airport but in the city. Elements are moving from the outskirts into the core of the city. There's been heavy losses. I don't even think they're attempting to subdue the infected. Shoot and kill. Damn it, can you imagine when it gets out that it's standard procedure? It'll drive people to ground, nobody will seek treatment for the first two stages. We're losing this, Eric. Losing badly. I've been excluded from high level security meetings. The Americans and some EU troops are filling in where we left. It's a shit storm."

It was much worse than what Eric believed would happen. He had been reasonably optimistic the outbreak would be under a level of control or that the CAF would be pushing further into the city, making it safe. It seemed all plans had stalled quite severely.

"So what do we do now? You wouldn't have brought me back here to sit in a room and wait for a call."

Williamson reached for a plastic water bottle. He turned it over in his hands while he talked. "You remember Gemma Findlay?

The reporter I commissioned to look into the outbreak and gather information on the ground?"

"Of course I do."

"She got herself to one of the displacement centres. A contingent of British Infantry, acting as CAF was stationed there. The centre, a hotel in the city centre was receiving some of the displaced, mostly women, children and families. Somehow the infected found it and overran the soldiers."

"Is Gemma okay?"

Williamson waved a hand. "She's okay. She got out and made it to Marischal College. It's the council headquarters, but the CAF are using it now. It's completely fortified. I need you to go there and bring her back. She got a message to me that she's discovered something vital regarding the outbreak."

"Like what?"

Williamson shrugged. "She wasn't clear. Whatever it is, I need her back here."

"How do I get there?"

"There's an airlift flying out in a few hours. They're bringing in supplies, I can get you on there and a return trip not too long after."

"Our bird?"

"Our Chinook has been grounded for the foreseeable. Mind your Ps and Qs. We're skating on the thin ice of their goodwill. You won't be able to carry any kind of armament."

Eric scoffed. "Nothing? I don't like this, Ben. I'm being flown into the most dangerous city in the world and I've got nothing?"

"You'll be safe, Eric. There's enough soldiers and guns around to keep things in order."

Guns in other people's hands always seemed to lead to disaster, and more so if the CAF forces were trigger happy. Nervous soldiers and Eric walking around empty-handed did not fill him with confidence.

"Someone will call you when it's time for the chopper. You've got an hour or so to get your things stowed away and gear up. You'll have your own room this time."

Eric knew the reason. Losses thinned the ranks of Black Aquila. How many friends died? Eric forced the thought from his mind. He needed to bring Gemma back to safety.

***

Gemma pulled one of the office chairs to the windowsill. Since being taken inside Marischal College she and George were interrogated, medically examined and eventually allowed to remain mostly at liberty. They were fed soup and slabs of bread more stale than fresh. Gemma was granted a phone call. She called Williamson's people and told them where she was and that she may have some vital information. They were noncommittal about a rescue. She hoped that someone would come for her and that she would not just become a forgotten name on a report. It was not all about self-preservation, she finally had a lead, a lead that would possibly shine a light on the source of the outbreak.

The office had tall windows, ornate and gothic in style that looked over an inner quadrant of the building. The sill started above her eye line. Gemma clambered on top of the chair, balancing as best she could to avoid the chair slipping out from beneath her.

"What are you doing?" George lifted his head from a desk he had slumped at too long.

"I think something's happening."

The bottom of the window was obscured by the accumulating snow. Large floodlights flashed, their brightness forcing Gemma to close her eyes for a moment. The sound of aircraft grew louder and louder and the windowpane rattled. The Chinook hovered above the inner courtyard, strong crosswinds rocking the aircraft from side to side. It dropped down, controlled for the most past. The downdraft cast snow in every direction. It touched the ground.

The floodlights went out as the powerful engines came to a stop. Gemma climbed from the chair gingerly. George went back to resting his head on his arms on the desk. Since arriving he had been despondent, not speaking much, even to the military who questioned him over and again. Gemma spoke in his defence, as much to protect the lead in the outbreak as of genuine care for him.

She thought of Dylan and his unfortunate death by friendly fire that almost claimed all their lives, too. Gemma felt the need to cry, but no tears would come. It was not safe to show emotion, not anywhere in the city. The tears would have to wait for the day she returned home to her parents.

"They must be flying in more people or supplies. A big helicopter just landed, could be our ticket out of here."

"You really think so?" George mumbled, no hope in his monotone voice.

Gemma nodded. Not until you've taken me to that club and retrieved the artefact that linked the Carrion Virus to a deliberate act, she said silently to herself. She sat down at a desk and moved a mouse connected to a powerless computer. Gemma wondered what happened to the person who sat there each day. Were they dead? In containment? Or hiding somewhere in the city?

Her cameras were taken from her, with a promise they would be returned when it came time to leave. The pictures and film she captured offered a unique insight into life inside the quarantined city. Bringing Williamson the container that George spoke of would solidify her usefulness to Black Aquila. As long as she did her job, and well, she would be safe and under their protection.

The security door beeped and opened. Two soldiers stood in the office and a familiar face entered.

"Eric!" Gemma flew into his arms, soaking up his reassuring presence. Those tears threatened to come, but she allowed herself to smile.

"I heard you got into a spot of bother out there."

Gemma moved from his arms. "You could say that."

"You want the good news? That Chinook out there is to take you back to the airport. It's making a supply drop and collecting the wounded from here. We'll be back at the hotel in several hours."

"We can't go," said Gemma, flatly.

"I'm sorry?"

"We can't go, Eric, at least not right now."

"Why not?"

Gemma hiked a thumb over her shoulder. "Because of him. George Reign."

"And he is?"

"Nobody, it appears." George was upright.

Emma began in a hushed voice. "I didn't want to talk about this in my message back to Williamson's people. I made mention of something. He's it. He was working in a club on Belmont Street here in Aberdeen. He thinks the outbreak started there. He can tell us the day, and can list the people initially infected. More than that, he thinks he knows what kind of device was used to release the infection."

Eric blew out his cheeks and rubbed his chin. "My orders are to bring you home."

"Eric, we can't let this opportunity go. This is what Williamson wanted me to do, to investigate, to dig deep and find things that normal investigations wouldn't."

"So what is it that you want of me?"

"Get us to Belmont Street. Help us to get the device and get us back to the airport in once piece."

"What you're asking I can't do. It's just me on my own, and I don't have weapons."

Gemma's eyes were full of pleading.

"Damn it, Gemma, this isn't like a stroll in the park. You're talking about the most dangerous place in the world. You can't just saunter down the street with your headphones in."

Her volume increased. "Five minutes down the road. No longer."

"On a normal day. Not today with the storm and the infected. Not today. I need to bring you back to the airport."

"I won't go."

"Gemma, just think about what you're asking."

George left his desk. "If it means I can get out of the city, I'll take you to the club and get you what I want."

"No," said Eric, and pointed back to his seat. "You're not going anywhere."

"I promised him that if he helped us get what we needed then we would get him out of the city."

"You can't make those types of promises."

"Well, I did. He's important."

"She's the only one who thinks I'm important." George returned to his desk.

"Don't make me go on my own, Eric. Please."

Eric leaned in closer. "You're asking me to risk our lives for something that might not even be there anymore. Pass the intel over to the CAF and let them deal with it."

"No one's listened to us so far, and every minute we waste might mean it gets lost or broken." Gemma wanted to grab the story for herself, not leave it to some military or government group, no matter the dangers. "I'll do it alone."

"That ID badge you've got there won't protect you anymore. The CAF forces are shooting on sight. You and I are going back to the airport." Eric turned on his heel and marched out.

"I'm not leaving you here, George. One way or another we're getting that container."

"How? You heard him as well as I did."

She gave him her best look of confidence.

"I thought I was going to die out there, and you're suggesting we go back out, with no protection, just us?"

When Gemma tried to protest, he shushed her to silence.

"I know, I know. I give you what you want and you make sure I get out of the city."

"George. I …"

There was nothing to say. She was using him to get what she wanted, what she needed. *Jeez, Gemma. When did you become such a ruthless asshole?*

***

Stubborn girl. Eric knew she would not give up. Gemma and George stood by the doors, behind the sandbag and machine gun placements.

Boots, jeans, a shirt and a leather jacket did not make Eric adequately dressed for venturing out into the city, but they'd have to suffice. He acquired a stun rod and a short range radio from the supplies. Nobody seemed to challenge him. Walking with purpose seemed to open many doors for Eric.

Eric joined the two. Gemma was wrapped in a thick coat and armed with an array of cameras, more digital equipment than one person could possibly need.

"We're doing this then?"

She turned with a knowing smile. "I knew you wouldn't let us go alone."

"I should have thrown you over my shoulder and carried you to the chopper. But, Williamson will want evidence of this lead of yours. We've two hours before the chopper lifts off. We need to be on it. There won't be another."

Gemma looked him up and down. "You're going out in that?"

"Your memo didn't reach me," he joked. He anticipated nothing more than a quick flight over the city, collecting Gemma and returning.

"Pray we don't need that," said Gemma, indicating the stun rod tucked under his arm.

"Let's get this over with. Stay close to me."

They stepped out into the winter-clad city.

***

The first part of the journey was uneventful. The only difficult encounter was forging a pass through the snow. *X* was spray-painted in red on the club's damaged doors.

"That means it's clear," shouted Eric above the wind.

Gemma nodded, her scarf over her mouth.

"We still need to be cautious. You both stay here until I say to move." Eric was cold. Brutally cold.

George nodded, blinking heavily as snowflakes fell on his face.

Eric stepped inside. The walls gave him a brief respite from the extreme cold the wind whipped up outside. Broken glass, hidden by the snow, crunched under his boots. He held the stun rod at the ready. The club was in ruins, everything broken. Dead bodies covered the dancefloor. Some were in black body bags, others were covered with thin white sheets. Arms and legs poked from the sides of makeshift covers. He halted, a sudden thought that the sound of his footfalls would somehow wake the dead.

"My God," said Gemma.

"You should be outside."

She ignored him. "Who are these people? There are hundreds of them."

George paled. "The club," he stammered. "What has happened?"

A blue flash lit up the building. Eric slapped the camera from Gemma's hands.

"Hey!" she complained.

"You want to announce to any infected that we're here?"

The look of annoyance dropped from her face. "Sorry, I should've thought."

"George." Eric waved him over. "Lead us to the room."

George paled, pointed to the other end of the building, across the dancefloor and sea of bodies. "It's over there."

"I need you to show us. Lead on and I'll follow. I'll be right behind you."

"I can't. I can't do it. It's over there, through the double doors and to the right, in the staff room."

Eric stepped closer to George. "Each minute we're out here in the city, cut off from anyone who can help us, puts us at serious risk. You can do this, I'll be right behind you."

"Me too," said Gemma.

"I can't."

"You want out of the city?" prompted Eric.

George licked his lips. "Out of the city? Yes."

"Then you have my word. This one task, and then I'll get you out." Eric knew it was a promise he may not be able to keep. "Stay close to me."

They took their first tentative steps. Behind, snow blew in the door. The bodies did not smell. Perhaps the plan was to use the building as cold storage for the dead until the security situation in the city improved. Or perhaps it was something much worse. A massacre.

Gemma whispered encouragement to George as they picked their way through the press of bodies. Gemma did her best to ignore the squelch as they stepped. George winced with each step. He held a hand over his mouth and nose. His eyes narrowed. He struggled on.

They cleared the dancefloor, George giving over a nervous smile, as if he had successfully negotiated a minefield without being blown to pieces.

"Past here and to the right." He pointed to a door which Eric assumed lead to the rear section of the building, a place where perhaps a bouncer once stood, preventing wayward patrons finding their way to the staff areas.

Eric turned the handle. The hinges creaked with such volume that all three checked behind them in case it acted as a beacon to the infected. Nothing moved. It was a house of the dead. Eric heaved the door inward, stepped inside, stun rod up. The corridor beyond the door was empty, dingy and smelled of mould. George pointed to the right and to another door, smaller and with a sign, *keep out, staff only*. Eric tried the door. Locked.

"Key?"

"My boss probably has it."

"And your boss is where?"

George shrugged.

"Gemma, watch for movement." Eric said impatiently.

Eric passed the stun rod to George and threw his shoulder into the obstacle. The door heaved inward but held on.

"Anything?" he asked of Gemma.

"Nothing."

The door had rattled on its latch. One more sturdy bash, thought Eric. He stepped back a few steps and again drove his shoulder into the door. It broke inward, shattering the lock. He fell to his knees, but quickly regained his footing, scanning the room for the enemy. The staffroom was empty of bodies. The cramped room sported a garish sofa, duct tape concealing the many rips in the material. A tea-stained table, a few chairs. A TV mounted in the corner. A kitchen area, sink, microwave and small fridge.

Eric beckoned them both in. George returned the stun rod. He needed no urging. He went straight to the kitchen area, opened one of the cupboards and removed a large square box. Someone had written *Lost Property* on the side with a black marker. He laid the box on the ground and rummaged around some before pulling an object free. He passed it to Eric who turned it over in his hands. It looked very similar to a flask, one his dad used when working nightshifts. The stainless steel exterior was flawless, no marks or scuffs, the surface free of abrasions. In the lid sat a clock face. Maybe a small wristwatch was embedded.

"This is your lead?"

"Yes."

"It could be nothing, Eric," said George. "But then …"

Eric watched his distorted reflection in the steel for a second. "I don't think it's nothing, George. It's something out of the ordinary. We were right to come after it." He passed the device to Gemma, who snapped a quick picture of it before securing it in her messenger bag.

"Now, we get back to the CAF and fly the hell out of this city."

"What about the bodies out there?" asked George.

"I'll tell Williamson. Aside from that we say nothing. Until you know who you're speaking with and why they're asking, play ignorant. Understand? Okay, let's go."

***

Gemma quickened her pace and reached Williamson before Eric.

"Ben, we've found something you need to see!" She reached into her knapsack.

Williamson looked directly to Eric, his expression neutral, and if Eric guessed correctly, it was a face full of worry.

"Eric, a word." Williamson did not break his pace, instead marched out the front door tugging at his ill-fitted coat.

Gemma stood with hands on hips. "I don't believe it."

"Make sure George's allocated a room," instructed Eric. "I'll catch up with you when we're done."

He ventured after Williamson. For a moment, he could not find his boss, but fresh tracks in the snow led him to the far side of the car park, away from anyone, alone in the white. The lights of the airport flickered through the snow. A small fleet of ploughs worked tirelessly to keep the runways clear. The wind died down, bringing a late afternoon calm despite the snowfall.

"Was it really necessary to come out in the snow? I've just got back."

Williamson did not turn to look at Eric. "I've spent more days than I care to remember glued to computers and telephones, meals taken at a desk, sleep snatched when I can. Sometimes it's just pleasant to take some fresh air and remind yourself that the world is still turning."

"Even when it's below freezing?"

"Eric, just when I thought things couldn't get worse, another worry is heaped upon me."

"What's happened?"

Williamson said nothing for a time.

"I've brought the girl back. She found something in the city she thinks could be linked to the outbreak."

Williamson turned to Eric, breaking his reflective mood. "I'll review it soon. But our problems don't directly concern the events here in Aberdeen. About an hour after you left I received a call from Doctor Eugene Holden."

"I've not seen or heard of him since we pulled him out of here. Where did you send him?"

Williamson blew out a sigh. "I didn't tell you where I put him because you didn't need to know. Eric, I find myself in the unfortunate situation where the number of people I trust has shrunk to a handful. You're one of them. Holden was moved to one of our facilities, a research centre specifically converted to tackle the Carrion Virus. He painted a bleak picture of the work that's going on there, the conditions they're working in. He expressed a fear for his safety. He suggested the research there is immoral, even evil."

"You believe him?"

"The doctor is beyond reproach. A few weeks ago I was made aware of a group called The Owls of Athena. I don't know who they are, or what they do, but I know they exist."

"How?"

"You don't need to know that."

"Are you sure I'm one of the few people you trust?"

"My apologies. I'm facing the very real situation that I've lost elements of my company to these people. I no longer know what's happening. I remain the majority owner of Black Aquila, but I can't trust what our branches are doing."

Williamson was full of emotion. Eric understood. Williamson was the king on the mountain who realised everything in his kingdom was not as it should be.

"What does Holden want?"

"He wants to be extracted, he and a few others."

"So I go get him?"

"Eric to do that …" he pinched the bridge of his nose, "… to do that we may have to break some rules. The guards stationed there are Black Aquila."

"And you can't or won't trust them?"

"I can order them to stand down, but if the order doesn't get through …"

"We'll be dropping into a battle?"

"Potentially, yes. We've slipped from the understood world of black and white, into the murky beyond. Whatever follows will be dangerous and illegal."

"Worse than what we've dealt with already? Ben, what happened in Aberdeen was nothing short of murder. When the infected became too much to control they were exterminated. We're all damned already. Holden might be the key to unlocking the virus. We can't abandon him."

"I've always held the reins of the company tight, Eric. I've managed everything myself, held investors at arm's length. I don't know what's next for Black Aquila."

Eric placed a hand on Williamson's shoulder. The man was trembling.

"We should head inside, Ben. We need to prepare."

"I'll organise clearance for our bird. Bring back Holden and any of his staff he deems worthy. Follow me. You should see this."

They returned to the hotel, and made their way through the busy reception, toward the rear of the hotel, out of sight of the public area. Williamson pulled a key from his pocket and unlocked a sturdy door.

"Close it behind you," he said, stepping into the room beyond.

Eric did as instructed. The room was some kind of secure lockup, perhaps for valued goods. On the floor sat two equipment crates. Williamson popped the lid of the first one letting it slip to the floor. Inside a supply of ten MP5s, a stock of magazines for each weapon and spare ammunition.

Eric took a step closer. Williamson stocking lethal weapons? They were not in a war zone, it was the streets of the United Kingdom. "How can this be?"

"We needed to be prepared for all eventualities. You knew it could come to this. Either the infected would grow so dangerous or resilient that they would need to be tackled with lethal force."

As much as Eric wanted to argue, he knew a dog should not question his master.

"Wheels up in thirty minutes. Get your team ready, brief them en route. Bring Holden back, then we'll talk."

***

Holden placed the satellite phone on his desk. Jane looked up from where she sat, alert at the suddenness of the noise. The second call to Williamson went better than the first. Two and a half hours was the ETA of their rescue.

"He's sending a team led by a very competent soldier, Eric Mann. He agrees that we need to be outside the perimeter to be rescued."

"We go through with the plan then. Have you selected one of the infected?"

Holden nodded. "Infected seventy-six. As much as I wish we had an alternative, we'll release some of his restraints. That gives us thirty minutes to get outside and find Eric. Williamson said to move east."

"We're doing this then. For real?"

"Yes, Jane. We are." Their plan burned at his moral core, but he only needed time for Jane and him to escape. Nobody needed to get hurt, just scared into distraction.

***

Jane supervised Holden loosening the wrist restraints of Infected seventy-six. He was once a man, probably quite handsome before the infection took hold. The infected's legs were still held tight. Jane pulled the mouth guard free, its teeth snapped after her hand.

They made their way to Hyde's office, the only place they were sure nobody would look for them, and pulled on their winter layers.

This was a final throw of the dice, a desperate gamble that would either liberate them, or … well, the consequences did not bear thought.

"I'll check the door." She opened the door a fraction, knelt down and watched through the crack. "How much time do we have?"

"It's only a matter of moments before someone realises his arms are free."

"If nothing happens in the next three minutes then—"

A blaring alarm sounded. A wailing siren.

"That's it!" Jane leapt to her feet. She was about to step through the door when Holden took hold of her arm.

"Not yet," he warned.

As if Holden was blessed with the gift of foresight, a group of Black Aquila guards ran past, weapons ready. It would take a few minutes to run from Hyde's office to the exit. Once free of the door, all they had to do was keep running east until salvation appeared.

Screams came from further down the corridor. Gunfire now, echoing through the narrow corridors. A few shots, followed by shouting.

"Eugene, we should go now."

More gunfire came. Holden pushed his glasses up to his forehead.

"Now! Go! Go!"

Holden swept out of the room, his boots clomping on the floor. Jane followed pulling closed Hyde's office door. The doctor was slow. Jane grabbed for his arm to support his dash to the exit, but he pulled away.

They rounded the corner and up the few steps that took them to the exit. A figure, clad in black and rifle drawn stood before the door. Jon!

"Jane! Doctor Holden!"

Jane slowed her run, as did Holden, breathing hard.

"What are you doing? Why are you dressed like that?"

"Jon! You've got to help us. One of the infected broke its restraints," said Jane. "It's not safe for us to be here."

"Some of the guards were sent to take it down. Wait here, and everything will be okay."

More gunshots and shouting, this time closer. Jon pushed a finger to the earpiece he wore.

"There's infected loose," said Jon.

"What?" Holden shook his head. "That's impossible. It must be a mistake."

Jane pleaded, "You know we're losing control, Jon. What are they saying? Every second we waste discussing this puts people in danger, innocent people. Please."

He looked directly at Jane. "They've brought down one, but there's more on the loose. They're falling back from the labs."

"You need to let us out, Jon. It's not safe."

Jon's focus darted between Jane and Holden, and then down the hallway as if willing someone more senior than himself to appear and solve the issue.

"Jon," said Holden, taking a step forward. "You know me, yes? You know what we're doing here, the danger we have with the infected that are incarcerated here? If one of them has broken free, it won't stay just one for long. The infection passes from infected to victim in a matter of minutes. If there was one, there could be dozens by now. You and your fellow guards don't have the strength to contain this outbreak. You need to open the doors and allow the staff to exit. It's the only way."

"That's not my orders, Doctor." Perspiration gathered at Jon's forehead.

"If you don't open this door, Jon, the death of everyone in this facility will be on your hands. The clock is ticking."

Jane took a step closer to Jon, her focus on his holstered sidearm. The time negotiating with him brought the chance of discovery or the infected reaching them ever closer. She would make a grab for it, if no other options were open to her.

"I should ask someone, make sure we're doing the right thing."

"Ask who, Jon? They're all in there fighting. Open the door or we all die in the most horrible way."

Jane reached out. The handgun was no more than a foot from her hand. "Jon, help us save lives."

Jon took a step back, lowering his rifle. He clicked the button on his radio to transmit. "This is Jon. I'm opening the secure door to let survivors out of the facility."

He waited for the response but none came.

"Screw this," he muttered. "I didn't sign up to keep people locked up like animals."

He scanned his ID badge on the door opening the lock. The great hydraulics hissed into life. Jon pushed the door outwards, opening the facility to the winter.

"Go." He pointed with the rifle out into the white.

"Come with us," insisted Holden.

"I can't. My place is here."

"Don't be so noble, Jon. Come with us. They know where the exit is."

"My place is here. Now go, you're wasting time."

Jane embraced the guard. "Thank you."

Holden and Jane started out into the snow, their hands raised to ward off the drift.

"One more thing," called Jon. "There's a second team of guards who operate on the outside, securing the perimeter. We don't know them or how they operate."

"What does that mean?"

"Keep your wits about you."

Watchmen watching the watchmen? Holden paused in the drift, checking from side to side. He pointed to the left of the accommodation units.

"East!"

Jane waved her understanding and pulled her hood up, drawing the sides close. There was no path cut into the snow to guide them. They were left to trek through the banks of snow. Each step sank them down into the freezing depths. Jane, struggling enough aided Holden through the snow.

They passed the accommodation units, all windows dark, the buildings empty. To the rear of the buildings stood a large, chain fence topped with razor wire, taller than Holden by half. Jane reached out, grasping the cold metal in her hands and shook it. It rattled dislodging a dusting of snow.

"We need to find a way round, Eugene."

Holden shook his head. "There's no time for that. We need to go up and over."

"It must be at least ten feet high. There's no way we can go over."

"There!" Holden pointed to a stack of empty pallets. "Drag them over, we can use them to climb up."

Jane ran, taking long strides through the snow. She grappled with the wooden frames, pulling two of them to the base of the fence. Holden helped prop the pallets against the fence. Jane kicked out, the fence unyielding, moving inward only a fraction. Holden stripped off his coat, and with a throw like a fisherman casting a net, he launched the garment up and over a portion of the razor wire. The sharp blades snagged the material, holding it in place.

"You go first, Jane. Up and over."

"You won't get up without my help. Go first. And don't give me any of that *I'm a man, you're a woman* crap." Jane looked behind. "Now, get up there."

Holden also peered into the white. He nodded and scaled up the pallets. Jane moved behind, placing her hands on his rear, steadying the doctor in his ascent. Great gouts of steam rose on his breath. He pulled himself up, his body shaking. A groan of relief escaped as one leg headed over the razor wire. The coat protected him from serious laceration.

"Take my hand. I'll pull you up. Quickly now, we've lingered here too long."

Jane clambered up the pallets, one hand holding the fence for balance, the other grasping Holden's offered hand. The doctor heaved, his arm shaking, hand as cold as the snow. Jane managed to drag herself to the summit. The addition of another body, caused the fence to wobble, and balance lost, they fell, Holden plummeting face first. Jane fell next, landing heavily.

The fall and the suddenness of the cold robbed her of breath. She pushed herself up, wiping snow from her face. Holden lay a few feet away, on his back, eyes cast to the colourless sky. The fence was on the boundaries of a forest, not particularly dense, but the trees were ancient, thick branches, devoid of foliage.

Jane pulled herself across to Holden. "Eugene? Are you alright? Are you hurt?"

"Just my pride," said the doctor, wincing. "And my ribs."

"Can you move?"

Holden held a hand to his side, his glasses slightly bent.

"I think so. Help me up, Jane."

Someway off, dogs barked.

"You hear that?"

"Dogs," agreed Holden.

"Maybe it's a dog lost in the woods or something."

They listened.

"No. There's more than one. I think we're being hunted by the other security team."

"Why? How do they know we're here?"

Holden checked his watch. "Eric and his men are due to arrive in less than ten minutes. We need to move."

"You'll have to do it without your coat. It's stuck up there."

"Then the faster I move, the warmer I'll be."

They ran as best as they could, feet sinking, injuries slowing the progress. The snow by the trees became less deep, the forest providing the earth some shelter. Holden's breathing became more audible, labouring to keep the pace Jane set. They moved on, not daring to halt. They cleared the small forest, and into open countryside finally. Holden stopped, his chest heaving, his entire body shivering uncontrollably.

Jane unzipped her own, pulled it off and wrapped it around Holden.

"I ... can't go on," he gasped. "My chest feels like it's about to burst."

"Not much further. We can do it. I'll help you. Together."

"I'm slowing you down, Jane. There's no sign of Eric yet. You can still make it. Go!"

The scene beyond would have been picturesque, Christmas card material. She had no idea where in Scotland she stood, or how close the nearest, populated centre was. If Eric was delayed and she took off into the unknown countryside it could be thaw until anyone found her body. If she stayed with Holden … well, the guards were an unknown factor.

"I'm not leaving you here to die, Eugene. We go together or we stay together."

The cold whipped blades of ice into Jane, making her feel naked to the elements. The dogs were getting closer. Gruff voices carried on the wind.

Holden was done, in pain. Moving him could end him. Holden looked on the verge of passing out.

They rolled the dice and gotten double ones.

Holden sank down, rambling off apologies, when the roar of a low-flying aircraft ripped through the air. A black painted Chinook, the red emblem of Black Aquila blazing on the side.

Eric had come.

***

Ten men including himself, was all Eric could scrounge up. Carter, his first choice was not an option. Carter's war on the Carrion Virus was over. He may very well have been one of the lucky ones, his ankle snapped to such a degree he would probably walk with a limp for the rest of his life. The entire team welcomed the instruction to be armed with live fire, MP5s and grenades, eager to be equipped with the better means.

Speeding over the frozen land in the Chinook felt like sitting in a meat freezer. With fingerless gloves, Eric rubbed his hands together, keeping his weapon tight between his knees. The Chinook dropped, a sudden movement. Eric grasped the sides of his seat. The ground raced up to meet them, the helicopter landing in a jarring motion. The great engines powered down. Eric unclipped his safety belt, moved to the controls and lowered the ramp. His team formed up behind, checking their weapons. All were dressed in thermal combat clothing, white to blend with the conditions.

"Identify your targets before firing," Eric instructed. "There could be civilians lost in the forest. We need to clear the treeline before we make the facility. Spread out, and shout out anything you see."

Eric led his men onto the frozen landscape. His team spread into a single line, a space of ten to fifteen feet between each man. They all held their weapons ready. Each one had endured a spell in the city, battling the infected, and had returned unharmed. They knew what to expect, and that made each man even more prepared. He waved them forward. They moved in a controlled manner, keeping the line. The snow obscured his vision. He could make out the height of the trees ahead but little else.

Holden had to be somewhere out there. Williamson had informed Eric the doctor would be free of the facility, and if they didn't find him soon, he'd die.

They pushed on through the drifts. Would the winter storms ever end? The first trees of the forest revealed themselves. Progress became easier, the snow lighter on the ground from the shelter the trees provided.

From his ear piece, Richards transmitted, "Contact left."

"Hold the line," replied Eric.

He broke formation, and ran, taking long looping strides through the snow. Eric reached the outer most member of his team, who pointed directly before him. Among the trees, two figures, dark against the snow, made slow progress toward them. Eric raised his weapon anticipating nothing but trouble.

"Be ready," said Eric.

"Always am," said Richards.

The snow made it impossible to identify the figures at that range. Eric was ready to drop the targets at the first indication of danger. They drew closer. One wore a thick winter coat, the other had hair untied and blowing in the wind. The figure in the coat revealed itself to be Dr. Holden. Eric lowered his weapon and raised his hand.

"Secure the assets."

He raced toward the two. Holden leaned heavily on his companion, a pretty girl dressed in medical scrubs.

"Doctor Holden, we've been expecting you."

Holden breathed hard, close to exhaustion. "And we've been expecting you. This is my companion, Jane."

"Is there anyone else?"

Jane answered, "There's been an outbreak at the facility, I don't know who else got out. And we're being followed."

"Black Aquila?"

Jane shook her head. "No, another group, whoever is responsible for the exterior."

"How many?"

"I don't know. They've got dogs." Jane shivered almost uncontrollably, her skin painfully pale.

"I'll get you back to the chopper."

"You're a good man, Eric," wheezed Holden.

Gunfire rang out in the forest. Eric instinctively pushed between the two positioning himself in the line of fire.

"Get them back to the chopper, Richards!"

Richards moved up, grasped Holden and Jane by the arms and they were gone.

Eric sank to his knees, the snow freezing his kneecaps. His mission was never to eliminate the threats at the facility, only to extract Holden and his companion. There was no way to disengage from the new threat without taking losses.

Eric's team moved to deal with the new enemy. Figures, clad in winter camouflage moved between the trees. Sudden bursts of gunfire erupted, spraying snow around Eric. He dropped to this stomach, and returned fire.

Eric fired short, controlled rounds. His men followed suit. If nothing else, they were keeping their enemy pinned down.

Rounds whizzed past, striking the trees and snow. More intense now and more accurate. Eric fired again, emptying a magazine. A crimson cloud exploded from one of the white ghosts. It fell with an audible scream. Eric reloaded, slotting a fresh magazine into the weapon.

His team, all now on their stomachs, crawled forward, elbows digging in and clawing. The fired as they moved. They were only a hundred-and-fifty feet away. He had no idea how many they faced. There was no real way to advance, if any of his men got to their feet, they would be picked off quickly. If they were to retreat, they risked being overrun.

Eric patted down his tac vest and pulled three grenades from one of the pockets. He clicked the radio to transmit. "Grenades. Then we move up."

Eric pushed himself from his stomach to his feet. He pulled the pin from the first, and tossed it forward, into the trees where his quarry waited. A hail of firing came. Eric dropped back onto the snow. The explosion rocked the forest. A moment of calm fell. Confused shouts came from the far side. Another explosion, followed by another. Eric's team lobbed their grenades, one after the other, the explosions booming one after the other, clouds of snow rising and falling. Ten. Eleven. Twelve. Eric fired more rounds. He slipped his two remaining grenades back into his pocket.

"Up and at them. Take them now!"

Eric got to his feet. They fired as they advanced. Anything that moved became a target, even those that fled. Eric reached the first white ghost, dead in the snow, his chest and neck ripped open from the shrapnel of the grenades. Eric searched the man's face, fearing that he would recognise him from the ranks of Black Aquila. Nothing. An unknown.

They were armed with modern military small arms, AR-15s. No markings on their uniforms or any personal effects. The white ghosts were just that. Ghosts.

Eric's team shouted that the area was clear and secured. All enemies either dead or retreated. The mission objectives were met. Holden was safe and Eric's team unhurt. They were lucky.

"Eric, weapons have been collected. Should we press onto the facility?" asked Richards.

A quiet descended on the forest. The battle lasted less than ten minutes but the noise was incredible. The pregnant silence, so full of mystery and potential, gave Eric an uneasy feeling. The facility, a secret Black Aquila research centre was someone else's problem. Eric could have pressed on, rescued any other staff who may have fled, but that risked more lives and ensured an encounter with the infected.

"We've got what we came for. Take the weapons and ammunition and head back."

A smile, perhaps one of relief passed over Richards' face.

"We're done here."

His team stripped the dead of their weapons and ammunition. Williamson had a long arm and deep pockets but realistically he could not accumulate so many firearms. Not in Britain. Improvised security for the days to come.

The team cleared away first. Eric stood alone with the dead. *No infected here, only the dead.* Perhaps there was a solution after all.

Eric trudged back to the Chinook. It looked out of place against the white. Two of his team kept a perimeter, waving him toward them. He picked up the pace, kicking up snow as he ran. The engines powered up, the rotors turned creating a downdraft, throwing powdered snow into a whirlwind.

Eric climbed aboard, closing the ramp behind. Holden sat on the far side of the hold, wrapped in a heavy blanket. Jane lay next to him, also wrapped in a blanket, slumped to the side, resting her head in the doctor's lap.

Holden's face was ashen, drooping on one side. Fear or exhaustion. Eric gave him the thumbs up. The Chinook lifted up, the ground fell away. Two and a half hours and they would be back in Aberdeen.

***

Like a bullet fired straight at a target Gemma made for Williamson's suite at the airport hotel. A Black Aquila guard lounged in a chair in the corridor Williamson had taken for his own. Gemma held out her Black Aquila ID badge. He looked up from his battered paperback and waved her through.

She knocked firmly twice then opened the doors without waiting for an invitation.

Williamson's feet were crossed on the coffee table, satellite phone in his hand, turning it around, over and over. He didn't look up, perhaps lost in thought and not recognising an intrusion to the room.

"Ben, it's time you listen to what I have to say."

The phone stopped spinning.

"Gemma I don't know what you think—"

"You were rude to me downstairs earlier. I've risked my life to go back out into the city to investigate, to get you the information you need. And when I finally find something you brush me off like I'm a nuisance. I'll be heard, Ben. And now."

"You can't just barge in here."

The owner of Black Aquila, astute businessman and former soldier, looked ready to erupt. Perhaps had she been one of his staff, he would have. Instead, he sniffed heavily, removed his feet from the coffee table and waved Gemma to the seat across from him. She pulled her knapsack onto her knees.

"So," said Williamson spreading his hands, "what must I hear?"

"This."

Gemma undid the clasps of the knapsack, and pulled out the device. She placed it on the table.

"And this is?"

"I … I don't know for sure, but this may have been the device that was used to create the original infection."

"It looks like a flask." Williamson dropped the satellite phone and picked up the device.

"The boy I brought back with me, George Reign, he worked at the club on Belmont Street, and he believes his work colleagues were some of the first to be infected, or at least fall ill. When they were cleaning the club this was found under one of the seats. Nobody thought much of it, other than George."

Williamson stroked his stubble-darkened chin.

"This indicates a deliberate infection of a civilian population."

"If you're correct."

"It's always been the most likely origin. Or that's what most academics studying this believe. You don't seem shocked."

"Like you said, it was always the most likely outcome. Someone has gone to a lot of trouble to make this seem like something very ordinary, and it's far from that."

"There's something else, a rumour perhaps, nothing more. We weren't able to substantiate."

"Go on."

"At the displacement centre, the one that was being opened up, the hotel, I heard that someone in the guise of a medic or doctor was injecting people. Whatever the injection was, it caused the sudden onset of the Carrion Virus."

Williamson returned the device to the table. "How credible do you find this to be?"

Circumstances robbed her of the chance to fully investigate. "I think there's truth to the accusation. A woman, in the early stages of the infection ranted about a medic injecting her family and the virus followed quickly after."

"Hardly grounds to make a decision."

"A credible theory, I would say."

Williamson nodded. "What happened at the displacement centre, you were lucky, yes?"

"I was lucky. I escaped with a soldier and George. We made the short journey to the CAF outpost to raise the alarm. The soldier didn't make it. We did. We were lucky."

"You put yourself at great risk, Gemma."

"You want to know why? I know the answer to all of this is out there in the city. We're a few steps behind but we're catching up fast."

"We'll get the device to our labs, get it tested."

"So what now?" Gemma leaned back in her seat. "Where's Eric?"

"Eric is running an errand for me. Once he's back we need to take stock of the situation."

Williamson's gazed altered. It made her uncomfortable. She looked away.

"I'm finding the number of people I can genuinely trust to be shrinking. Those I once thought to be most loyal have given me cause to think otherwise."

"Me? I've gone out of my way to bring you evidence, clues. Anything I've thought of value I've documented and catalogued."

Williamson tweaked his eyebrows.

"I didn't have to be here. I could have gotten out of the city, celebrated Christmas with my family and pretended all this was just a bloody nightmare. But I came here, to help you."

Williamson still watched her, but his expression softened. "Okay. Listen and listen well. Black Aquila isn't just a security company. We have data experts and analysts, research and development facilities. Doctor Holden, you've heard me speak of him before, for his protection I moved him to a research station to continue his work on the Carrion Virus. Had he remained here, he would have been arrested for something he played no part in. I felt he was the most likely candidate to break the secrets of this outbreak. Elements of Black Aquila were not following orders. They introduced immoral research and kept the research teams locked up. Holden feared for his safety and that of the people in the facility. Eric was dispatched to bring him and a few others back. My initial report is that they have Holden and one other, but the facility suffered a catastrophic outbreak. We've dispatched a second team to bring the facility back to compliance. You're probably asking yourself why I'm telling you all this, something that many of my inner circle may not know. The truth is you're with us now, there's no choice in that. You rise and you fall with us. Do you understand?"

Gemma nodded. "Our fates are linked. If parts of your company aren't reporting to you, then who are they reporting to?"

Williamson looked out the window. "The Owls of Athena."

"The what of what?"

He returned his gaze to Gemma. "The Owls of Athena. I suspect an unknown organisation has engineered this outbreak. I don't know why, but we're starting to understand how. They couldn't do it without having assets in the government, in my company, and God knows where else."

"How did you become aware of them?"

Williamson stood and moved slowly to the window, the one that faced out into the snow covered fields past the city limits. "That is a conversation for another time. Perhaps when Eric returns. Go back to your room. When Eric returns with Holden, I'll have someone fetch you."

Williamson fell to silence. She gave the device a final look before leaving the room, then paused a moment on the other side of the door. The situation opened up new terrifying dimensions. A shadow agency, who deliberately infected a city in the United Kingdom, with resources to keep their actions secret? Gemma felt a panic threaten to rise. She wished she could pass the burden to someone more capable than herself. But that was an impossibility.

Whatever happened now, Gemma's fate was interlinked with that of the Carrion Virus. It would either fling her to new heights in her career, or it would bury her. She never thought her career might be built on the foundations of so many dead.

Williamson is hiding something. It did not make sense how he would know of the existence of The Owls of Athena yet say nothing. What if he was part of the conspiracy? What if he merely tested the waters to see who he could trust going forward?

Relax, girl, she thought. Wait and speak to Eric when he returns. He was someone who she could bounce thoughts off, without risk of betrayal. Where was Eric?

***

Chapter Seven
Time's Winged Chariot

For the first time, Ryan was allowed to leave The Owls' Nest. Not alone. Hector Crispin escorted him. Ryan chose from his new array of clothing, all gifted. A dark suit, a white shirt and a bright tie. His shoes were shined to perfection. Ryan had arrived at The Nest dressed not unlike a pauper, but now looked very similar to Hector. He pulled at the collar, the high button annoying his neck. A third man joined them. Hector introduced him as Mr. Rennie. Steven, if he remembered rightly. Not a tall man, but well-built, with a knowing look of danger.

Although allowed a measure of freedom, Tokyo was still a mystery to Ryan. Hector revealed little as to his motives, yet maintained the threat of tacit violence should Ryan not provide answers to his questions. Hector was amiable until presented with a piece of information that differed with his beliefs. Then the ranting tyrant appeared. Ryan decided he preferred the pleasant side of Hector Crispin and resolved to keep him as such.

"Are you excited to get out and about the city, Ryan?"

"Yes. It'll be nice to be out for a while." He wanted to ask where they were going but knew better.

"Regrettably my work keeps me indoors. Precious are the times I manage to schedule for myself. Shall we?"

Mr. Rennie stepped before Hector and opened the glass doors. Ryan followed after. No car waited.

"I find if you become over reliant on vehicles, you rob yourself of the ability to enjoy a simple walk."

Hector lead on, walking through the large car park toward the gate. The entire building was ringed by a high wall, looking like a castle's curtain wall. They stepped out into the street, and into the bustle of Tokyo. Hector set a steady pace. Rennie walked behind at a respectful distance, yet close enough to act if anything untoward threatened.

Floods of people walked in every direction, so much so that Ryan troubled to avoid colliding with pedestrians, until he found an eye for momentum and dodging. Cars clogged the streets. Ryan knew the scene, much like back home in Seattle, but the buildings were different, tinged with an Eastern flair. Bright billboards with overly smiley females selling products that Ryan could not make out covered much of the cityscape.

"What do you think of our building, Ryan? Black and reaching to the sky. Modern and sleek. It certainly stands out from the surrounding architecture, don't you think?"

Ryan skipped to bring him in sync next to Hector. "It's a fine building, Mr. Crispin."

"It was the prototype, the first. Your father had a hand in its design. Not an architect by trade, but he could turn his hand to many things and forge success."

He was? He could? Ryan's father had been brought up in conversation frequently. Ryan was bursting with the need to ask so many questions. What could the man who remained much of a mystery have gotten himself involved in? Was he a part of the foundations of this group? Or was his academic brilliance key to ushering in the Carrion Virus? But asking questions was not appreciated.

"There are now many buildings like it. Our energy requirements are mostly met through clean resources. It's years before its time."

"You're lucky to live there, Mr. Crispin."

"Luck had nothing to do with it, Ryan. Planning and strategy breed success. I suppose you're curious as to where we are going. We'll, it's a small eatery which I like to frequent. Very expensive, popular with those who work in the financial sector. Mr. Rennie back there, doesn't think I should be walking the streets like this. If he had his way, I'd be wrapped in blankets, kept under lock and key. Ah, here we are."

The windows of the small restaurant were blacked out. Rennie moved ahead and pushed the door, holding it open for Hector and Ryan. His face was so serious, so bleak. A bell jingled and an immaculately dressed man, his hair well-oiled and slicked back appeared as if from nowhere. He conversed with Hector in hurried Japanese before showing the two to a rear room. The restaurant smelt of delicious spices and oils.

Hector indicated that Ryan should sit.

"We have water, Ryan, or would you prefer something else? Diet Coke? I would not suggest the latter."

"I don't like Diet Coke. Water will be fine."

He poured water from a jug for the both of them. Ryan sipped. Rennie remained outside the door.

"Do you know why I chose here, Ryan? It's because I have an understanding with the owner. He ensures that this room remains free from unwanted attention and surveillance, and I enjoy some of the best oriental food in the city as well as making a sizable donation to Mr. Goto. It's a useful arrangement and suits my purpose."

"It's nice. Really nice."

Hector held up a finger. "This is about what I want and can have, rather than what is necessity. I afford myself luxury. I've ordered for you. The food shall arrive shortly. What did you notice as we walked here, Ryan?"

"Mr. Crispin?"

"It's a simple question, Ryan," he said, hands spread. "What did you notice?"

What had he noticed? He had focused on Hector. The press of people, felt like a current trying to flush them back. "The streets were busy, very busy."

"Good. Good, Ryan. Yes. The people. What do you believe they were thinking as they went about their business? I'll tell you, Ryan. Each and every one, consumed by the pettiness of their lives. Sheep herded along by government. They sicken me, content to float along in life so long as they can achieve low level goals. Sickening really."

Ryan put his glass down.

"Your father, Ryan, he was one of the founding members of The Owls of Athena. What I'm telling you now, is a result of the foundation of trust we've built. Partly due to the link you have through your father, partly due to the work you've done. I will reveal to you what few know, the aims that we have."

No please, I don't want to be involved in this anymore. I want to go back to my old life, knowing nothing and just existing on the fringe of society. "Certainly, Mr. Crispin."

"Not too long ago, the world balanced on a knife edge, a moment of sheer cataclysmic potential, so much so we may all have woken to nuclear war."

"You're talking about the Cold War?" Ryan assumed, venturing that one question harmless.

Hector nodded, tilting his glass. "I am indeed. On one side the USSR, on the other NATO. The world held its breath. The Owls of Athena trace their origins back in the annals of history. We're not quite sure of our original founding member but this is not important. Our goal has always been to safeguard this world, to watch for the moment the nations of the world become so dangerous, so unpredictable that intervention must be staged to pull the world back from the brink."

"The Carrion Virus? That's the start?" Ryan shifted in his seat. Too many questions.

Hector smiled, placing his glass on the table. "Indeed. Would you like to know how we acquired the virus?"

Ryan nodded. He wanted to know, but didn't want to hear.

"The Carrion Virus was created at a time when billions of dollars were being pumped into non-conventional methods of warfare. The United States conducted research into biological warfare. The result was the creation of the virus. Now, here is where events become murky and the exact details are lost. The virus was created, tested and deemed too dangerous to ever become viable. It was stockpiled to be destroyed. Some of our number, high ranking military members, secured the stockpile for our use. As far as the United States military knows, the virus was destroyed, the evidence classified above top secret and forgotten. Nations may control an awesome arsenal of nuclear weapons but imagine a weapon that turns a nation's strength, its own people against that country. Eaten from the inside. The Owls of Athena have carried the heavy burden of this responsibility for several decades. Until now." Hector leaned back in his seat, the padded wood creaking with the movement. "And I'm sure you're asking, why now?"

"Yes, Hector." He tugged at his tight collar.

"The world is slipping into an abyss. People don't realise this simple yet undeniable fact. State-run media propagates the idea that everything is okay. All the bad things in the world are happening elsewhere. The truth is much worse. Governments are no longer accountable to the people. Tyrants, hidden in the shadows rule corrupted bureaucracy. People are reverting to an almost medieval level of barbarism. We are losing ourselves to the point that it is necessary to act. Your father when he was alive voted for action. He understood the importance of what we are about to achieve."

Ryan's mouth flapped open and closed.

"You look surprised. The outbreak you orchestrated in Aberdeen was the first step. We're in preparation to unleash the virus globally within the next few years. You see, in order to safeguard the survival of this world, we need to tear down the established and corrupt governments. The Carrion Virus is a perfect weapon. We can cripple or destroy a population and yet keep damage to infrastructure to a minimum. When the time is right, we can emerge and retake the remnants and shape what's left to a more structured ideology. You see, Ryan, what we're doing is changing the world. Not just changing it but ensuring our continued survival and flourishing. In time, of course."

The old man seemed to be enjoying their conversation. How could he sit there spewing such horror from his mouth, without needing to adjust his top button? What scared Ryan most was the absolute conviction he detected. The Owls had the means to escalate the outbreak, and intended to do just that.

"Well, shall we eat?"

Hector pressed a small buzzer at the side of the table. A hidden door, undetectable in the wall, opened and staff entered carrying steaming platters of food. The world had turned to a place Ryan did not understand, a place of dark potential and horror. He yanked at his collar again, and hoed into the food.

***

"You're not thinking clearly, Eugene! You can't just throw your hands in the air and walk away from this!"

"I've given more than most when it comes to combating this outbreak! What more can I give, Ben? What more?"

Both men shouted, Holden from sorrow and frustration more than anything else.

"When the allegations were made against me you promised to keep me safe. There was nothing safe about that place. And to escape, we nearly died. Jane is being treated for hypothermia. I, only for good luck, am here before you." The truth brought more pain than those revelations. While the doctor was wrongly accused of the first outbreak, he could be rightly accused of the second. It was never supposed to end like that. *Stupid! I am so stupid!* The guilt weighed heavily, a noose of metal around his neck. "Good, innocent folk died back there. Good folk, wanting to fight the outbreak. It's too much."

"It's not your fault, Eugene." Williamson's face softened. He turned to Eric who stood in the corner, leaning against the wall. "What of the facility?"

"We never pushed on to the facility. We secured the doctor and Jane and retreated. We eliminated those trying to stop us."

"Losses?"

"None. None of ours."

"And we don't know who *they* were?"

"Nothing to identify them, but well-armed and well-funded."

Williamson crossed to Holden. "You're tired, Doctor. You've endured a traumatic experience. More than one. Don't make any rash decisions on the strength of recent events."

The words were hollow and meaningless. Holden suffered a crushing fatigue that would not leave him.

"Yes, I'm tired, Ben. You have no idea how tired. There will be no more research from me."

"Eugene, you are the eminent researcher in this field. Think about that."

"I believe I've made my feelings painfully clear."

"And what will you do without my protection?"

"I won't be threatened into submission."

Eric stepped forward. "Perhaps what we need is to have a break, and talk about things tomorrow. It's late. Many things have happened."

Williamson stormed to the window, his back to the two men.

"Get him out of here, Eric."

Holden stood, a great effort, his weary bones almost betraying him. They left the room and walked down the long corridor.

"Don't judge him too harshly, Doc. He's in a tough position. We all are."

"I've been a commodity to be used. I've had enough. I've seen enough. Too much death and sorrow. Too much for one man to take."

Eric made a sound of understanding. "Williamson is a military man at heart, he sees us all as strategic pieces. He's a realist, he knows that you're important, probably our best chance of beating this thing."

"He'll have to look elsewhere. My endurance has dissipated."

"Does the phrase The Owls of Athena mean anything to you?"

"No, and I have no interest in any owl, or wherever the thing is from. No interest in anything related to this place from here on in. Now, if you'll excuse me."

"The girl, Jane. Do I know her? She seemed familiar."

Holden smiled. "She should seem familiar, you rescued her from the hospital in Aberdeen. You helped evacuate some of the medical staff and patients."

"The police officer?"

"Yes, he did not survive. Now, I must find some sleep."

Holden walked away, not looking back.

***

Brutus watched the building from the street corner. It was used as a safe house before the mission. Now, Andor Toth and a few of his men, bodyguards probably, waited for the second team to return. Only all members of the second team were dead, and Brutus would return bringing hell with him. Tomorrow, he would use Toth as a bargaining chip.

Brutus checked his watch. He had more pressing matters. He got into the vehicle he'd liberated from the desert, his destination a bar far from the tourist areas of the city. He had been there once when doing freelance work. Unofficially, the bar was a kind of mercenary exchange. Business was agreed and traded on the dirty floor of the stained beer hall. The environment, while not pleasant was one that Brutus felt comfortable in.

The bar was quiet, only a few of the tables occupied. Nobody paid much attention to Brutus when he entered. The rule of the bar was simple. No weapons. No violence.

"Brutus! Over here."

When they returned from the Sinai, Brutus called one of his former associates, Artyom Vetrov. Vetrov had worked for the Kremlin many years ago. Now, he was freelance and with a healthy remnant of connections. They became friends one night in Afghanistan, sharing some awful whiskey, huddled by a fire under the stars.

"Two." Vetrov held up two fingers to the barman.

"Brutus, good to see you," said Artyom, his Russian accent thick. He reached out and brought Brutus into a tight embrace, slapping his back before releasing him. He pointed to the scar on his face. "That is a new one, yes?"

They sat. Two glasses of whiskey arrived. They touched glasses and both men drained their drink and thumped the empty tumblers on the table. The whiskey was cheap, like the kind they shared in Afghanistan. It was a tradition. Vetrov raised another two fingers.

"How's business, Artyom?"

"Things were good until all that craziness in Scotland. People are nervous. People need hired guns to reassure them. I sell guns, and men to use them, and reassurance." He smiled revealing a gleaming gold tooth.

The waiter leaned over and poured.

"Yourself?"

"Busy here and there. Business has been interesting if not good."

"Are you still with Black Aquila?" asked Artyom.

"Not as such, no."

"I must admit, I did not expect to hear from you. Since your call I've been wondering what would bring my friend to call at my door."

Brutus decided long before entering that honesty, for the first time in a while, seemed to be the best option. "I came to you for help, and with a business proposition."

"Making money? You have my attention."

"How long has it been since you worked for the Kremlin? Officially and unofficially."

"Officially, it is coming up to ten years." He picked up his glass, and swished the gold liquid about. "Unofficially, you never fully stop working for them."

"What do you know of the virus outbreak back in the UK?"

"Enough to know that the rest of the world should be wary and watching with great concern."

Brutus leaned in close. "And what would you say if I told you I had a live sample, fully infected, restrained and ready to be transported within twenty-four hours?"

Artyom leaned back in his chair, wiping sweat from his forehead. The heat was stifling. He retained a neutral expression, a tactic he no doubt employed for all business negotiations.

"And where did you acquire this sample?"

"Here, Egypt. And she won't be missed. Untraceable. Nobody will be looking for her. I imagine that every functioning government would love to get their hands on a subject infected with the Carrion Virus. As far as I know, Russia nor its allies don't have access to this."

"What do you want from me?"

"For the moment, what I want is cooperation, help to move from nation to nation since there's so much travel restriction. Not just me, but my team and some equipment, too. Perhaps money, or further equipment."

"To what end?"

Brutus leaned back, matching his companion's posture. "Now, Artyom, you know not to ask questions you can be sure I won't answer. Can you facilitate this for me? You've still got the contacts, I assume?"

Artyom drained his drink. "I'll need to see the asset."

Brutus drained his. "Outside."

The two men made their way out and across the street. Late evening and the street was almost deserted. Some distance away, car horns blared. Somewhere in the night, a cat mewed its mating call. Brutus unlocked the vehicle and opened the boot compartment.

One final check to ensure they were not followed, and Brutus pulled at the hessian sack. The infected rocked back and forth, rolling roughly. Brutus held it in place and peeled the bag back. She was restrained to the maximum. Arms tied behind her back at the wrists, ankles tied together, as were her knees, and a spit-guard covered her head.

Artyom stepped back, his hands raised in fists.

"She's secure," reassured Brutus.

The infected thrashed and fought her restraints, her eyes fixed on her two captors. Her bloodshot eyes bulged. A thick vein pulsed down the centre of her forehead. Dried blood coloured her face, like some savage painted for war. Beneath the gag, she chewed on her restraints. A low rumble built in her throat. Remarkable in a way, considering how much punishment she received during her subjection. Her body displayed little signs of injuries other than the original sores from the virus.

Artyom said something in Russian. A little colour dropped from his weather-beaten face.

"So, what do you think?" asked Brutus nonchalantly, not wanting to draw attention to them. Even quiet streets bristled with eyes and ears.

"Can this be real?" he muttered.

Brutus pulled the sack back up, tightened the ends and pushed her out of view. He closed the boot and stepped back. "It's real. That's what we're dealing with back home. They're fast, deadly and ruthless. Your country needs to be ready to meet this threat. No matter how prepared they are, the infection will spread past the borders of Britain. This could be the difference between a crisis and a disaster."

Artyom nodded, though his mind seemed elsewhere. He nodded, over and again. "Keep it secured. I need to make some calls. Tomorrow, how do I contact you?"

"You don't. I'll contact you. Twenty-two-hundred-hours. You can meet me at my location. By then, I'll have a better understanding of what it is that I require."

Artyom banged the vehicle door twice. The infected thrashed harder.

"You know, Brutus, had it been anyone but you I would have taken this infected and sold it myself. Anyone but you." It was not a menacing statement, more matter-of-fact. "I'll get in touch with my contacts back home, see if we can come to an arrangement. Either you have just made us both incredibly rich, or we are dead men walking. Tomorrow, at twenty-two-hundred. I need some more of that rotten whiskey."

Brutus held all the aces. Artyom was scared and intrigued. Brutus had broken the barriers between fiction and reality. The Carrion Virus had arrived in Artyom Vetrov's life.

***

It was on Magnus's watch that a visual of Toth was confirmed. Toth had returned to the safe house. It was time to strike. This was the time that Fisayo and his comrades were to report back. Brutus's men were positioned on all street corners, weapons hidden in a carry bags. Brutus himself crouched directly across the street, in the cover of a derelict car, long ago rusted to its bare bones. The street masking the safe house had been selected wisely. Passers-by were a rarity, almost like the locals knew not to attempt to come close.

Affixed above the door and to the left was a newly installed security camera watching approaches from the right.

"That's new," said Gibbons, his hand on the back of Fisayo's neck, keeping his head down and out of view. So far, Fisayo had been nothing but compliant.

"It makes getting in there more difficult. They'll spot us before we even reach the door," said Roy. He abandoned his sniper rifle. It would be of no use for what lay ahead.

"The wire from the camera unit is exposed. Maybe it's not hooked up yet. To the left is a blind spot. We can cut the wire from that approach."

Roy's face was damp with sweat. "If they don't spot us from some other angle. We could be dead in seconds."

"We cut the wire, and go in hard. I'll take the lead. I need Toth alive."

Roy blew out his cheeks, then pulled a combat knife from his belt. "I'll take the wire, just be ready to move when I give the signal." He nudged Ash Gibbons. "Ash, you're with me. The camera looks too high for me to reach."

The two men took off across the street, their light, quick steps kicking up small clouds of dust from the road, the gravel crunching underfoot. They gave the perceived arc of surveillance a wide berth, and reached the building's wall, throwing themselves heavily against it.

Gibbons linked his fingers and in a fluid motion provided a step up for Roy. It must have been eight feet from the ground, yet Gibbons heaved Roy up like he weighed little. Roy grasped the wire, tugged at it once then slipped a blade beneath the black cord. He sawed, short fast motions, and severed the wire. They retreated, breathing heavily as they slumped down next to Brutus.

"Good job."

"If they've realised something is wrong they'll be preparing for an attack," offered Roy.

"Or they'll send someone out to fix the feed."

"If they do nothing we can't just blow the door and walk in, guns blazing. We create too much commotion and we'll have the Egyptian Army here, closing us down. They can wait us out," said Ash Gibbons.

Brutus watched, waited for any sign that something was in motion. Nothing. Could they have been that lucky? Brutus was not a man to believe in luck. He made his own way in life, fate moved aside for him.

"Arm yourselves." Brutus got to his feet.

"Where are you going?" asked Roy.

"To get us an invite. Form up on the door. Remember Toth is to be kept alive. Fisayo, you're up."

Brutus led Fisayo around the side of the rusted car. They crossed the street, to all appearances two friends making their way home.

"This is what is going to happen. You'll approach that door, they know you, and they're expecting you to return. They'll open the viewing slot and you'll tell them to let you in so you can make your report. Once the door is unlocked, you crouch down and keep out of the way. Understand?"

"Yes. I understand."

"Do you have family, Fisayo?"

"One sister back home."

Brutus smiled, nothing generous. "You'll see her again soon if you do this for us."

They reached the safe house. Brutus grasped his handgun, but kept it within the recess of his shirt. He pushed himself to the wall of the building, directly under the camera. The cut wire dangled above his head.

Past Fisayo and to the right, Freddo McLeod moved forward, shotgun held ready. He would be second in, wielding his weapon in the close-quartered environment.

Freddo nodded, ten feet away from Fisayo. They all crouched, waiting for the signal to move.

Fisayo licked his lips and knocked on the door, three loud raps. He stepped back, Brutus expected him to run but he held fast. The bolt of the latch clicked open and the viewing visor opened.

'Fisayo?" came a voice through the door. "Where is everyone else?"

"Parking. They've sent me along first to make sure everything is in order."

"Hold on."

Brutus waved a hand. Fisayo turned his attention only for a second.

"Is it Toth?" mouthed Brutus.

Fisayo gave a tiny shake of his head. Good, thought Brutus. He did not think that Toth would be the one to open the door. He was not the type to get his hands dirty. *Bastard.*

The lock of the door disengaged, the heavy bolt pulled back. Brutus was moving before the sound fully registered, before Fisayo had time to duck. Brutus kicked Fisayo out of the way, no time to be gentle. Freddo was up. Brutus pushed the barrel of his handgun through the viewing slot, and fired three quick rounds. The heavy metal of the door muffled the shots. Brutus kicked open the door. A man on the other side lay dead on the floor. Brutus stepped over the corpse pressing onward toward the rear room.

Freddo entered behind, kicking the Glock from the dead man's hands.

The door between the front room and the rear opened. A soldier, packing an AR-15 stepped through. Brutus threw himself forward, grabbed hold of the barrel and forced it upward. The unprepared soldier grunted his surprise. Brutus unloaded the remainder of the clip into his chest.

Brutus dropped the empty handgun, flipped the assault rifle round and made ready. Gunfire from the back room splintered the door and frame. Brutus ducked out of the line of fire. Freddo, moved forward, blasting shot after shot into the room, then darted to the side as more fire burst from the room and reloaded. Brutus motioned his intention to breach the room. Freddo gave a thumbs up, then pumped his weapon ready. Brutus unloaded into the open doorway, suppressing enemy fire. Freddo dashed to the door, shotgun raised. Brutus moved also, right behind Freddo.

Toth cowered in the corner of the room, as far away from the gunfight as he could physical squeeze. A third mercenary, the only one putting up resistance, clung to flimsy cover behind an overturned table. He knew the situation was hopeless, threw his assault rifle down and raised his hands. Freddo secured him, keeping him covered.

Brutus walked slowly to Andor Toth, enjoying each step as Toth's eyes burned a hole into his middle. He held the rifle casually, reached into his shirt pocket and removed a cigar.

"Surprised to see me, Andor?" Brutus placed the cigar in his mouth. "You didn't think you'd be seeing me again, right?"

Toth said nothing. Brutus crouched down, close to him. Whatever Toth was, he was not a fighter, others would fight for him. Brutus was in no danger.

"I know you expected me to be rotting in the desert. You made me lose good men out there. That isn't something I'll forget. You know the screwed up part of it all? I actually understand why you did it, why you'd have me killed. I'm a liability, I've done enough and know enough, and you feared if I talked I'd cause," Brutus lit the cigar, "problems. That's the thing about me, I've a nasty habit of surviving when I shouldn't."

"You've no idea who you're dealing with, Brutus. You're a dead man for this."

Brutus surveyed the scene. His men had done their job. The place was secured.

"Perhaps. Then again, perhaps not. That's your problem, see, you assume that all your plans will be completed flawlessly. Foolish really. Now, listen to me, Toth. You're going to tell me who you work for, what your plans are with the virus and with any other assets you have here in Egypt."

Toth laughed, a forced laughter betrayed by the fear narrowing his eyes.

Brutus lashed out with the speed of a cobra. He grabbed Toth by the neck and squeezed. Toth's pulse, fast, travelled up Brutus's fingers. All it would take was a little more pressure and he would break Toth's neck. He puffed on the cigar, then spat it to the ground. With his face inches from his victim, he exhaled.

Toth coughed roughly.

"You mean nothing to me. Killing you means nothing to me. Killing you slowly will mean a great deal to you. Tell me what I want to know or—"

Toth spat into Brutus's face.

He thrust him backward, smashing his back and head into the wall with enough force to crack the plaster behind. Toth slumped down, unconscious. Brutus wiped the spittle from his face with the back of his hand, and stood.

Niall stood behind him. "What do we do now?"

"Set a watch to the front, make sure we've not been discovered. I want you and Freddo to stay here with me and him," he said indicating Toth. "Everyone else is to stand down and return to the hotel. Bring the infected girl here, too."

"What about the mercenary and Fisayo?"

"Secure them here. They might be a problem that we have to deal with soon enough."

"What about him?" asked Niall with a nod of his head to Toth.

"All through this, Andor Toth has been in the centre of things. It was always him that I met with. Always him who provided missions and payments. Mr. Toth has a lot of beans to spill. He's tight-lipped right now. I need to know what's coming next."

***

Brutus threw a cup of water into Toth's face.

Realisation dawned. Toth struggled against the restraints, holding his hands tight to the rear two legs of the chair he sat on. His legs likewise were lashed to the legs of the chair. A trickle of blood ran from the corner of his mouth.

"Where are my men?"

"Your men? They're dead, Andor."

Brutus stepped aside to give Toth an unrestricted view of the room. Splatters of blood, marred the floor and walls. Bullet holes scarred the walls.

"So now what, Brutus? What do you do now? I know you, know your type. Men like you don't think, they do. They follow orders. Yes sir, no sir. That's what you're good at."

That was probably a fair assessment. But things, like the world, change.

"I can make you a very wealthy man, Brutus. Very wealthy. All you need to do is let me walk out of here and you'll never hear from me again. We won't look for you. We've got more important things to focus on, trust me."

"I've already got money."

"I can get you ten times what we paid you previously, let you disappear and live like a king. I don't matter to you. Think about it."

Brutus stepped forward. "You see, that's where you're wrong, Andor. You do matter to me." Brutus dragged a chair over and sat down right in front of Toth. "You made me care what happens to you the moment you ordered my team and me be taken out. It was that moment that I decided I needed to take an express interest in you."

Toth's eyes darted about. "Brutus, you have to understand, I didn't decide anything. Orders came down. I was just following orders. Like you. It was nothing personal."

"You know that interests me a great deal. Orders to you. For a while I assumed you were the one giving the orders, but then I realised someone giving orders wouldn't be doing so much of the leg work, or placing themselves in such danger. For a while I thought *you* were The Owls of Athena, or at least part of them. I'm curious, tell me about them."

Toth's face slunk to an expression of panic. "I can't, Brutus."

"Can't or won't?"

"I can't."

Brutus mocked a gameshow buzzer. "Wrong answer, Andor. Wrong answer."

Brutus stood, and knocked the seat aside. He grabbed Toth by his already bruised neck. "You see, Andor, I'm guessing that Aberdeen and that business in the Sinai aren't the end of all this. If you're eliminating assets who know too much, it sounds like you're tidying up loose ends, moving onto a new phase."

"Think of the money, Brutus, please."

"I'm thinking of survival. The Carrion Virus, what we unleashed, it'll never go away. If The Owls are planning more intentional outbreaks then that changes things. All I wanted was to be filthy, stinking rich, to surround myself with beautiful women and drink whiskey on the beach, good whiskey. Now, all I'm seeing is the possibility of that not happening and I want to be prepared."

Brutus pushed at Toth's head. The frightened man tipped back in his chair.

"So you see, Toth, you'll tell me everything about The Owls of Athena and their plans. And you might just live at the end of it all."

"I can't, Richard, please, you have to believe me."

Brutus grinned at the use of his real name. "I'm a violent man, Andor, you know this, that's why I was hired. I'm not afraid to get the job done no matter the consequences."

"You'll torture me?"

"Yes. But not your body. Behind that snivelling act you project I sense some resolve. I could break your body so many ways, cripple you for life and you might not tell me a goddamned thing. That's why what I've got planned for you is much, much worse."

"So that's your grand plan, Brutus? You tie me up and threaten me with what? Scare stories? You don't think that we've got people in this city, people who won't come looking for me if I don't call in? You think we're stupid, Brutus? We plan for these types of events all the time. You are a dead man, Brutus. Untie me, walk out of here and disappear. You need never hear from us again."

Brutus took a step back. He proved more resilient to threats than Brutus credited. Toth was the locked door to the information contained behind. He needed to access it and was prepared to smash down the barrier if required.

"Let me go, Brutus. It's your only option."

"I disagree, Andor. You think I would've gone to all this trouble to get you here, just to let you walk out the door? Nope. I told you. I want information and you'll give it to me."

Brutus left the back room, moving to the front room. Niall sat on the edge of the table, his assault rifle resting on his lap. The two prisoners sat on the floor, their hands tied together. Freddo stood over the wriggling hessian sack, shotgun pointed down.

"What's going on?" he asked.

Brutus moved his shotgun aside. "I'm borrowing this." He picked up the edge of the sack and began dragging it back toward Toth. "You'll hear screams. Don't come running."

"What are you doing with it?"

Brutus waved away the question. "Unless it's my screams."

He pulled the sack through the door, kicking it closed behind him. The infected inside rolled and growled. The infected had not eaten since it was bagged. Whatever food Brutus and his men tried to feed her, she rejected. They threw a cup of water in its face several times a day not knowing if it needed any form of hydration. Brutus reckoned he knew what it would eat, but so far resisted pushing raw meat at it.

"What the hell is that, Brutus? Answer me."

Brutus ignored Toth, ripped open the ends of the bag and dragged the infected out by the ankles. "You know, it occurred to me that I don't suppose you've ever come face to face with what you've unleashed. Sure, you've probably seen these monsters in a cage, but in your face? I doubt it."

He pulled the infected to its feet, its roars muffled by the gag at its mouth. Brutus kept his back to Toth, ignoring his cries of fear. "It's quite something to look into the face of someone riddled with this virus and know all they ever were is gone and replaced with hatred and fury and an unending need to kill. Would you like to see what The Owls and yourself have wrought, Mr. Toth?"

Brutus turned, swinging the infected around like a dance partner. He adjusted his grip, taking hold of its neck from behind, his other hand holding the restraints at its wrists. Toth screamed, pulling himself away the scant inches he could. Brutus whipped off the mouth guard and threw it aside.

"Tell me what I want to know!"

Brutus allowed the snapping jaws to almost touch Toth's face. It wasn't easy going, the thing was a cyclone of strength. Toth begged Brutus through tears and curses to let him go. He screamed from a fear he undoubtedly did not know could exist.

Brutus screamed, too. Over and over. "Tell me! Tell me! Tell me!"

Toth cried, threw his head back, his mouth growing wider and wider. The infected's legs touched Toth's and only Brutus's strength kept it from falling on top of him and sinking teeth into his flesh.

"Okay! Alright! Brutus, please. I'll talk."

"I can't hear you over the noise," Brutus lied.

"I'll talk! I'll talk."

Brutus threw the infected to the left, a giant ragdoll cast aside, then sprang after it, planting a knee into its back and securing the mouth guard again.

"You tell me what I want to know now. There won't be a second chance, Andor. You delay or try to fob me off, I'll let the bitch chew you up. Whatever happens next is up to you."

Toth regained a measure of composure, and rubbed his snotty nose on his shoulder.

"Everything. Tell me now, Andor."

"What happened in Aberdeen? What you helped to create, Brutus, was the first step. That was our testing, to see how effective the Carrion Virus would be to our purpose. The events are being observed, and our agents have infiltrated the city, and CAF forces alter situations to extend the outbreak. So far, it has exceeded our expectations."

"In the Sinai?"

"We needed to see how a small infected population would behave in their natural environment. Your combat data and that from our drone shed a great deal of light. A population of one-hundred, not terribly dangerous to a fully equipped military team, but against an unprepared force or civilians, quite deadly I imagine."

"Tell me about The Owls."

"Brutus, if I tell you, if I betray them, we're both dead. Their reach is long, and they won't stop until we're both dead."

He crossed his arms. "We're all dead, Andor, it just depends on when we draw that final breath. Tell me."

"The Owls' sole purpose in creation was to impose an intervention in world events when they felt it necessary to avert some kind of cataclysmic misadventure. Something happened, and I'm not sure what it was that caused them to act. The result is the Carrion Virus outbreak."

"Who are they?"

"I don't know. Only those in the top echelons know the names of others. You could be one for all I know."

"So what do they want?"

"Want?" asked Toth with a humourless laugh. "They don't want anything. They have everything. Money. Influence. A deadly weapon. They don't want anything. Their agenda is something quite different. They're going to seek to alter the course of human history. You're seeing the early stages of the destabilisation of a nation with a deliberate infection. Imagine this happening in every major city in the world and you have an idea of the scare we're looking at."

Brutus said nothing for a moment. There was a chance Toth lied, but the man feared for his life. Brutus looked to infected and back to Toth.

As if reading his thoughts, Toth said, "It's the truth, Brutus. I swear."

"They're going to screw the world, then what? They rule over the cinders?"

"You might think that The Owls sound foolish or short sighted with their plan, but that's not the case, I can assure you. They have contingency plans for when the pandemic occurs. The Owls and those they deem important will go into hiding in holdings called bastions, refuges against the virus where they can survive until it's time to emerge and guide the remnants of the world. Brutus, they can do this. Years of planning, many billions of dollars and a diehard commitment. You can't fight them. You can't stop them. The best thing to do is disappear, find a quiet corner of the world and weather the coming storm."

"How long until they release more of the virus?"

Toth remained silent.

"How long?" Brutus pulled his assault rifle to his hands and drove the stock into Toth's stomach.

Air rushed from Toth.

"How long?"

"A few years, maybe less. Plans are fluid. It depends on how this current test resolves."

"These bastions, how many are there in the UK?"

"Three," said Toth spitting. "One in Scotland, two in England."

"How many people can live there? How many people are required to run the operation?"

"Please, Brutus, let me go."

Brutus raised the weapon a second time.

"A few thousand. With supplies for that much to last a year and a half.'

"Good. Good, Andor. Have a break. I'll get you some water and then we'll continue this conversation. You see, I wanted to disappear and live a quiet, wealthy life. Now, The Owls of Athena have reduced the chances of me achieving this to nil. I need to make provisions to survive what's coming. If the world is to die, I'll cling onto its corpse."

***

Brutus walked from the back room, blood smeared across his knuckles. Andor's blood. After the first pause in their talks he grew reluctant again.

Niall checked his watch. "You were in there for two hours. What's happening?" He seemed nervous, probably aware they lingered somewhere not safe.

"We're bugging out. Pack up. Get the angry bitch and the scared little mouse ready to travel."

"What about Toth?" asked Freddo.

Brutus wiped his hands on his trousers. "Bring him, too. I'll bring the car round. We're going back to the hotel."

***

Artyom Vetrov opened the vehicle's door and slipped inside. He wore a shirt more unbuttoned than fastened. Large aviator glasses hid his eyes.

"You were right, Brutus. My associates back home are interested and keen to negotiate."

Brutus shook his head. "No negotiation, Artyom. I tell you what I need and you agree. Simple."

"That is not how business is done, my friend."

"It's how I'm doing business. Listen well. I know your associates have resources which I need to tap into. I need a way to return myself and my team, less than ten of us, to the UK unannounced, bypassing quarantine control. Once there, I need weapons, enough for twenty men, several hundred rounds for each weapon, and grenades and equipment to live off the radar for a year. We need to be back in the UK within three weeks. And money. Five million. Cash. Payable on handover."

Artyom whistled low. "Moving you from Egypt to the UK in three weeks with a travel ban affecting much of Europe is no small feat. The rest, weapons and money is easy." He clicked his fingers a few times while looking down to his feet. "You selling the woman to my government means a great deal to them. They were prepared to offer you a great deal more, money things. The travel will be difficult but you have my word, in three weeks you'll be stepping onto British soil." Artyom spat into his hand. "Shake and we can have a drink."

Brutus shook the offered hand, then overtly wiped his hand along his shirt.

"Ah, Brutus my friend. You never minded your hands getting dirty."

"Blood doesn't smell as bad as your breath, Arty." Brutus considered asking Artyom to join him on the endeavour he planned, but his Russian friend no longer placed himself in danger's way. He ran business, traded and got fat.

"We'll drink now, yes? I shall meet you in a few days when things have been arranged." He thumped the dashboard of the Land Rover. "I shall also see to new plates for this. You've been sloppy since being here, Brutus. I need to protect my investment. People are looking for you."

"What makes you think someone is looking for me?"

"You wouldn't be asking for help otherwise, my friend."

"Perhaps you're right. When does the transfer take place?"

"Soon, Brutus. I'll contact you with where and when. Be ready to leave with an hour's notice."

***

Brutus gathered his team in the largest of the rooms they rented, a space covered with bags and sleeping rolls. It was a far cry from luxury but it was quiet, out of the way and crap enough to keep them uninteresting. It suited their needs.

Conversation amongst the team was not upbeat. No surprise after recent events. Payday and home were the only things spoken of, and even they were discussed with a commonplace tone. The bombshell Brutus was about to drop would test their trust in him. They watched him in silence, some stood and others sat. Brutus stroked his beard, more unkempt than he usually maintained. Opportunities to tend appearances were infrequent of late.

"Things have gone from bad to worse in recent times. That isn't what I had planned for us. I thought it would be an easy payday. Instead, we've lost friends and we've been hunted."

"Not to mention those infected, Brutus." Ash Gibbons leaned against the rear wall, arms crossed, munching into an apple.

"Apologies won't change things here. A solution may. And I think I've found one. The incident in the Sinai didn't occur the way they told you. The outbreak was not something identified by the Egyptian Government. In fact, I suspect that they have no real idea what occurred there. Our employer and his group, The Owls of Athena, engineered the outbreak specifically."

Roy cleared his throat. "Craig and I talked about this while we were observing the village. We both agreed that an outbreak could not have taken place there naturally. Too isolated with only a handful of people going in and out."

"The Owls of Athena are some shadow group, with aims I don't fully understand. They want to see outbreaks of the Carrion Virus and I got us tangled in their web. I know all of you want to go home. Since you were assembled here in Egypt that has become almost impossible. Travel restrictions are in place around the UK. The infected girl we captured from the village, I've done a deal, and we're selling her to an interested party. We'll receive enough money to see us covered for the money we were expecting, and assistance to return home."

Freddo flicked the blade of his combat knife with a finger. "Who are these people in this party? I'm all for going home, Brutus, but I want to know who you're getting us mixed up with. We're already tangled with The Owls. Who next?"

"The Russians. Some of you will remember my friend Artyom. He's still connected, and the Russian Government is anxious to acquire a sample of the Carrion Virus in a live host."

"Goddamned Russians," spat Magnus Munson. "He's pushed us into the claws of some shadow organisation and now we're jumping into bed with the Russians?"

"Calm down, Magnus," urged Niall. "We're already in trouble. Brutus has a way to get us back home with a ton of money. Then we go our separate ways. We don't need to see each other again."

"Not quite," said Brutus.

"What do you mean, not quite?" demanded Magnus.

Ordinarily, Brutus would bully or intimidate people into compliance, but he needed his team onside. "I've spoken with Andor Toth."

Niall and Freddo passed knowing looks to each other.

"He has suggested The Owls of Athena are planning to intensify the outbreak to the point of a pandemic. We're looking at this happening within a few years. Imagine an outbreak in every major city in the UK. We'd be overwhelmed."

"This is crap!" Magnus stood from his chair. "You need us more than we need you. You've got yourself into some trouble you can't handle on your own, and you're looking for someone to watch your back."

"Stay here all you like, linger in Egypt. I'm trying to pay you all back and get you prepared for what's coming next. We can't stop this. The Owls are burrowed into multinational corporations and ingrained in the military. When this storm comes, we can either be prepared or watch everything die. That's a fact."

"So what are you suggesting we do?" asked Stuart Taylor.

"The Owls have prepared bases in the UK, some place where the select few can wait out the infected, self-contained sanctuaries, stocked with enough supplies for several years. When the outbreak comes, and society is breaking down, we strike, and take one of these places for ourselves. I'm giving you a chance to keep your family and friends alive and safe." Brutus was not a man to care for another human being. Anyone he called *friend* could be terminated at any time if necessary. That was his law of the land. But to secure a bastion on his own was a big ask. He needed these men, needed them if he was to survive the future's pandemic. He knew to mention the safety of their families, was another way to ensure their support.

"How do we know he's telling the truth?" Magnus asked of Brutus. "How do you even know Toth is telling you the truth?"

Niall stepped forward. "Before the outbreak in Aberdeen, what, three months ago, you wouldn't have believed the infected were real. I think Brutus is telling the truth."

"The Russians will provide us with weapons, enough to take and secure one of these bastions. Bloodlessly if we can, if not, well, if not we do what we're trained for. I know you don't want to believe this is true, but I wouldn't be wasting my time if it wasn't. Who's with me?"

Magnus was the only man not to raise his hand.

"This is crazy, Brutus."

"Can't argue with that."

"I don't understand what's going on. I don't want to die for half-promises and other people's gain." He looked at the rest of the team, one by one. "Ah, shit. These guys trust you. I might as well, too. Let's go home."

***

The Russians were good to their word. They met with Brutus on the second day, all dialogue conducted through Artyom. He was flanked by a group of ten soldiers, heavily armed and silent. Spetznatz. Special forces, probably.

Brutus and his men were flown on a Russian military plane to Cyprus, where they boarded the freighter vessel Askold. In fourteen days they would be close enough to Britain, and would board an inflatable from the freighter and make landfall at night. The ship's crew was charged with security of the weapons locker. Should the ship be boarded by unwelcome forces, the weapons were to be thrown overboard. Brutus was in possession of the money and supplies. Everything was going according to plan. Brutus kept Andor Toth with him. The two captured mercenaries were no longer a logistic to consider. They were taken care of in Egypt. A bloody but brief end. Toth was valuable and resigned himself to incarceration. He mourned the fact he was taken, and proposed repeatedly that death would come for them both. No doubt The Owls were looking for him, but would they be looking on a Russian ship travelling through the Mediterranean?

The cabins were small and cramped, bunks stacked with a communal bathroom. It did not matter. They were going home. Enthusiasm was present. They chatted, laughed, and lamented the loss of their comrades. Brutus was not sure they fully believed the outbreak would be a pandemic in a matter of years. That did not matter either. Soon, there would be all the evidence they needed when the infected were tearing apart their neighbourhoods.

Brutus slipped from his bunk, landing light. He stepped out onto their balcony, a private area away from the crew where one could take in some fresh air. The commercial passengers section of the ship was locked away from the rest of the ship. The Russian crew had minimal contact with Brutus and his men.

He closed the door behind, the cold steel of the balcony cold on his feet. He pulled a cigar from his pocket not intending to light it, more just having it to hold. He leaned on the rail. The ship cut a steady path through the water, the constant drum of the engines and the breaking of the sea the only real sound. It was peaceful in a way. Quiet, but not enough for Brutus to relax. Brutus would never be able to relax again. Not when he knew what was coming.

The door behind opened.

"You kept your word." Niall joined Brutus at the rail. He leaned over and spat.

"Everything I've said is the truth, Niall. As farfetched as it sounds, I wouldn't have gone to all this trouble to get back home if I didn't think we needed to."

"Home. What is home to you, Brutus?"

"It's wherever I don't need to carry a rifle twenty-four-seven. Where I can sleep with my eyes shut."

"A few of the others think your intentions are good, but that things aren't as bad as you paint them."

"And you?"

"I don't think you care what I think."

"You're right. But humour me."

"I believe you."

"If they'd been in Aberdeen, they wouldn't doubt it."

"But they haven't. They've seen some infected and it shocked them. To think that anyone would release the virus to the world, it just doesn't make sense to them. But I'm trusting you, with everything. If the virus spreads from Aberdeen then we've got a problem. I want to keep my family safe. I'll follow you, Brutus."

Brutus lit his cigar, and blew out a long stream of blue smoke. "This is something new, but we're soldiers, we make a living from death and war. I'm a survivor, and I always will be."

"All what we've seen reminds me of a quote I heard somewhere. The strong do what they can, and the weak suffer what they must. We just need to make sure we're not the weak. I'm with you, Brutus." Niall clapped him on the shoulder. "Come inside. We're going to crack open some beers."

"I'll be in soon."

Niall left him alone with his thoughts. Brutus had learnt to be a survivor and not depend on others at a young age. Brutus was eight when he realised the world didn't give a damn about him, or anyone. They were at a play park, his sister Marta and him. She was only five. A sweet, innocent girl who Brutus doted on. Their mum drank too much and left her in his charge for the day while she headed off to one of her hotels and the myriad of men that pretended to love her.

The dog, black and tan beast struck from nowhere. It grabbed Marta by the ankle, pulling her from the swing and threw her to the ground. Children screamed, parents scooping them up as the Rottweiler pinned Marta to the ground, its jaws clamping down on her arms. Brutus, himself crying shouted for someone to help. No matter where he turned, he saw horrified spectators. Not one person stepped forward to help. Brutus picked up a large rock at the edge of the swing area and charged the dog. It had Marta by the throat by the time he reached her. He struck out with his improvised weapon, and hit again and again and again until he caved in the dog's head. Beneath the swing the dog and Marta died.

The world didn't change that day. Brutus changed. Brutus saw the cold truth of the world. It offered no security, no promise of innocence maintained. He lost his sister and childhood, but gained something - a glorious burden. The knowledge of how to survive.

Screw the Carrion Virus. For the next fourteen days all he would care about was freedom from fear, fear of the infected. And beer.

***

With the toe of his boot Eric nudged a tray of dirty dishes left outside Holden's door, the remains of the doctor's evening meal. A half-eaten sandwich on brown bread, and a salad that looked as though a fork had churned the lettuce and taken nothing. The knocks on the door echoed. Eric had tried a number of times. Holden was not answering. Since back in Aberdeen the doctor saw nobody, only leaving his room to visit Jane. Food was provided three times a day, and three times a day the majority was left at the door for the cleaners.

"Eugene? I just want to make sure you're okay. Is there anything you need? Open up and we can talk."

Nothing. Not even muffled sounds of movement. Eric could not blame the doctor for his enforced isolation. He was an old man, used to lab work, and should not have been made to run through a forest or held hostage.

"You know where I am if you need to talk, Eugene."

A dark smudge marred the white door. A small handprint. For a moment, Eric wondered who it could belong to. He walked back to this room, the ruined carpet squelching under foot.

How many people were infected now, or dead as a result of the infection? Aberdeen's population of two-hundred-and-twenty-thousand could have suffered a dramatic decrease. The true figures would probably never be known.

Operations for Black Aquila were grinding to a halt, with all tasks and assignments taken over by the new surge of American military. Williamson lived in hope that Black Aquila would once again be called upon to take a lead role in the battle. Eric doubted this. Too many people died and too many mistakes were made.

He looked forward to home. The thought of seeing Jacqui and the kids filled him with hope of a different kind, a hope that things could still be normal in a life so very far away. Maybe soon he would be back there. In the interim, he would make himself available to Williamson.

Eric rounded a corner. Gemma stood at the door to his room, her arms crossed, back against the wall.

"You've seen what's happened?" said Gemma, pushing herself from the wall. "Have you been watching TV? The news?"

"No. I thought the TV signal was off."

"It's coming and going," she said, her face flushed. "I'll tell you what's going on. A reporter has made it through the quarantine zone and is reporting from inside the city. Inside the city, Eric. Williamson promised *me* that story. I was going to break it. I've got half a mind to march into his room and tell him just what I think."

"I don't think Williamson is in control of what happens outside this hotel. If he indicated to you that he'd let you break the story at some point then I'm sure it was genuine."

"But it's not fair. I've risked everything to get all this evidence."

"Gemma, Williamson has lost a lot of men. His company is in danger of folding, and may face criminal charges once this is all done. You're a tiny part, a minor part. I know that seems harsh but that's the reality."

Gemma wiped a hand over her face. "This was supposed to change everything for me."

"You're being paid for your time and effort, and not a small amount. If I was guessing I'd say that Williamson can manage to get you a pass out of the city soon. There's going to be no work for us here."

"Things were supposed to be different," she said in a whisper.

"Get some sleep, Gemma. It's late."

"What about you?"

"I need to go and speak to Williamson, then I'll turn in."

She wished Eric a good night, her eyes red and watery. He could understand her frustration, she had risked a lot.

Eric walked on past his door. He knocked on Williamson's door and let himself in. Williamson sat in his usual spot, in the chair, tapping slowly at his laptop.

"You look like something's bothering you, Eric."

"I bumped into Gemma Findlay, or rather she bumped into me. She's upset. Apparently, there's a reporter who's made it through the quarantine and is reporting from inside. She thinks that was her right."

"She's got a point. I did promise her the opportunity to break the story, a personal report from the heart of the outbreak. But I don't suppose the CAF will tolerate these broadcasts and will shut them down soon enough. Gemma doesn't know it yet, but with the footage and information she has, she's likely to make a small fortune."

"Might be worth having a word with her, you don't want her doing anything rash through frustration."

"Tomorrow, Eric. I'll speak with her first thing. Sit down."

Eric slumped into the chair, a familiar place. "What's been going on out there?"

"The same as always, Eric. I'm very much out of the loop now but I hear more than most. CAF forces are continuing to sweep and clear as they move inward through the city. Nests of infection spring up. They've shifted from containment to eradication."

"We always knew this would happen, didn't we?"

"It was always the most likely outcome. They've realised the only way to stem the tide of infection is to eliminate it. As morally wrong as it seems, it's the only practical solution."

Eric shook his head, then leaned further into the chair tilting his face to the ceiling.

"We're being stepped down, Eric. Soon the provision of this hotel will be taken from us, I'm sure. There's a huge surge in multinational military in the city. What use is there for a depleted private security firm in this ever evolving situation? Black Aquila in its present form will cease. We need to restructure and reorganise. I'll be lucky to come out of this with the company still in my control." He waved his hand. "Anyway, that isn't your concern. If we are to stand down, until such a time as we can honour our existing contracts, you'll be able to go home, get that time with your family that you've been craving."

"That wouldn't be a bad thing for all of us, Ben."

The doors to the room were thrown open. Carter, leg heavily strapped, carried two AR-15s. Eric was on his feet in a flash.

"What's this?" asked Williamson, standing.

"Trouble," replied Carter.

He threw a weapon to Eric.

"What do you mean?"

Short, sharp explosions rocked the building.

＊

Ryan Bannister burst through the veil of sleep, eyes fixed on the slow rotation of the fan above him. Ryan had not slept well since the last meeting with Hector Crispin. Each time he fell asleep, horrendous nightmares came. Falling from the summit of a mountain to the rocks below. Brushing his teeth, and one by one they yellowed and crumbled like chalk. In one, he saw his father outside the window, his hand weakly tapping the glass. His mouth moved but no words came. Ryan could not speak or wave a hand.

The next, he walked the streets of a world drowning under a tide of infection, and they all came for him.

There seemed no escape from Crispin. Ryan had come to regret every choice that lead him to becoming embroiled with The Owls of Athena.

He closed his eyes and wiped the sweat from his forehead, then pushed the thin sheets down. It was not so much the temperature in the building, rather the panic of the situation. Had this all been preordained by a father he hardly knew? Why? How? He would certainly hate his father, if he ever held a feeling for the man.

The bedroom door clicked open, the sound sudden and unwelcome. Ryan kept his eyes pressed shut, hoping beyond hope that a sudden breeze blew through the building, knocking the lock off its latch. Light footsteps scuffed along the wooden floor, growing louder as they approached. Whoever stood next to his bed set a glass bottle down heavily.

"Ryan, wake up."

Hector Crispin stood to the right of his bed, and far behind was Steven Rennie, his foot keeping the bedroom door open.

"You're awake. Good." Hector swayed slightly. The bottle of red wine he entered with was close to empty. Hector was drunk. He was without his suit jacket, his tie loosened and the first three buttons of his shirt undone.

"Is everything alright, Mr. Crispin?" said Ryan, pulling the sheet up to cover himself.

Hector sat down heavily onto the bed and Ryan shimmied over, giving the man some space.

"I've been drinking. Quite a lot if the truth be told. And I'll tell you why. One of our agents, one of the most important ones, Andor Toth has gone dark. He was the linchpin of this whole operation. We've tracked him with a sub-dermal implant, and he is on the move. This brings us to one of two things. He is either no longer taking orders from us, or he is being held against his will. Either forces us into a problematic situation. The Owls of Athena have voted to put into practice The Athena Protocol. Don't speak, Ryan, just listen. The Athena Protocol dictates that when one of our key agents in the field is compromised we move forward with the immediate release of the Carrion Virus. Despite all our assets not being in place, we can't afford to wait. It's times like these I wish your father was still here. He and I were lovers, you realise?"

Ryan sat up.

"And for a long time until he passed away, far too prematurely. Such a loss. If only he was here now so I didn't need to face this alone."

What the hell was this guy saying? His father was dead? His dead father was his lover? As far as Ryan knew, his father was working away, not sharing a bed with another man, not dead. Nothing made sense.

Rennie's eyes fell to Ryan. In warning? There was no need. Ryan had no intention of asking questions. He'd tried that before and regretted it.

Hector snatched up the bottle and took another mouthful.

"Things will happen rapidly over the next few weeks. You'll be put in the field, doing what you do best. Exactly what you did in Aberdeen. You'll be sent out into the world to orchestrate more outbreaks, and on a much grander scale. You see, I need people I can trust. Despite the relatively short time we've known each other, I need you, Ryan. On the reverse side, you need me and The Owls for survival." Hector laughed, a sound which faltered to the point that it could have been tears.

Hector pushed the bottle toward Ryan who tentatively accepted. "Now take a drink."

Ryan, sniffed the wine. He estimated half a mouthful remained.

"It's a celebration of the realisation of The Owls of Athena's purpose being fulfilled. It's also a toast to the end of all things to come."

Ryan sipped at the sour wine, just enough to satisfy Hector's insistence. He handed the bottle back. Hector raised it high, one eye studying the bottle. He shook it slightly.

"Get some sleep, Ryan. Soon, there will be precious little of that."

"Rennie," called Hector. "Send the team to intercept Toth."

Hector patted Ryan's leg. "If I had another bottle with me, we would make a toast, to the end of everything."

***

171

As he did every night, Dr. Holden walked through the corridor of the hotel, leaving the sanctuary of his room. Several key members had rapped at his door earlier but he refused to answer. He had kept the door locked, and a chair leaning against the handle. Everyone he could possibly come into contact with in the hotel wanted something from him, and there was nothing left for Holden to give. He was spent. Broken. Empty. Apathetic. The Carrion Virus robbed him of his fundamental trait to help others.

His nightly pilgrimage lead him to the canteen. It was quiet at that time. The only people venturing that way were catering staff and those who would rather not be alone at night.

In the canteen he pulled a blackened banana free from a bunch and placed it on a tray, moved along the counter, picked up yogurt, cereal and poured a steaming hot coffee.

Nobody seemed interested in his passing, most kept their own company or talked in hushed voices. All looked dreadful, stressed and tired. A perfect mirror for Holden.

Holden nodded to a woman in her robe. Her eyes were heavy, as if she was medicated. More than likely it was nightmares that kept her awake.

A ping from a microwave sounded near the kitchen. Holden shook a sachet of sugar and emptied it into his coffee. There were no spoons. He used a pen to stir. He pushed his glasses up onto his forehead, then wrapped his hands around the mug. The warmth was welcome and at the same time a little uncomfortable.

Holden had decide his course of action. He was still wanted by authorities over the breach in Aberdeen. Holden would surrender himself to the CAF forces and allow a thorough investigation to take place. He no longer cared about his reputation built on a lifetime of good work, now ruined by lies and consequence.

Eric would help him move from the hotel to the CAF barracks at the airport, he was sure. He would have to visit Jane in the field hospital and also thank Eric personally for rescuing him. Tomorrow would be a long day, but a welcome one, the day when Eugene Holden would be removed from the outbreak.

Holden sipped his coffee lost in thoughts of what would come.

An explosion erupted with the suddenness of overhead thunder. It rocked the building, and Holden spilled his drink, scalding his free hand. A second explosion forced Holden from his seat to his knees, and beneath the table. One of his companion diners screamed. The lights went out, plunging the room into darkness.

"Don't panic," shouted a male voice. "It's a power outage. The grid must have been damaged. That's what the explosions would have been."

"Has anyone got a light?" asked a female voice, seconds away from tears.

"We should all try to reach each other," the male said.

"No," shouted Holden. "Stay where you are. You can't see where you're walking. You could hurt yourself. Stay where you are until the lights come back on."

Beyond the canteen, someone screamed. Commotion, and raised voices. Strong, piercing beams of light moved toward them up the corridor from the reception area. The silhouettes of armed men in combat gear entered the canteen. They took up position at the door, standing either side. The torches moved along the canteen walls, and over the tables.

Why were they armed if they were there to help? The collective light from the new arrivals allowed Holden to see a small amount. One of the men who sat not far from Holden, stood and walked toward the new arrivals.

"You've got a lot of nervous people here, friends. We were starting to panic when the lights went out."

The soldier who seemed to be directing others stepped forward, and drove the stock of his weapon into the face of the approaching man. He crumbled to the floor with a low grown. The leader stepped over the fallen man.

"We are looking for Doctor Eugene Holden. If he is here, he should make himself known." He spoke with a heavily accented voice, possibly Afrikaans.

A stab of terror penetrated Holden's core. Why did they know him by name? And searching for him?

"Make yourself know, Doctor Holden, and everyone else may go unharmed."

More darkly clad men arrived. They brought with them Black Aquila staff gathered from the reception area. They were ushered over to the far side of the room, next to a long table.

"Doctor Holden? We are here for your protection."

A Black Aquila guard locked eyes with the doctor, and shook his head in warning, a slight movement not seen by others.

Holden stayed on his knees.

"You'll all be held here until we find the doctor. We cannot guarantee your safety."

"There!" The woman in the robe stood from her seat and pointed. Her outstretched hand shook. "That's Doctor Holden. There. On the floor."

The leader shined a light into his face.

"Stand up, Doctor."

Holden did as was bid, standing on legs that felt as though they could give way at any moment.

The leader gripped his face, turning it from side to side. "It is you."

"What do you want?"

The leader clicked off the light, leaving Holden blinded.

"From you? Nothing, Doctor. Nothing at all."

***

"What the hell was that?" Eric checked his weapon, making sure it was serviced.

Carter, grimacing with the effort of walking, leaned on the edge of the sofa.

"The hotel's surrounded. They've taken out our sentries."

"Who?" demanded Williamson, his face set to outrage.

"Doesn't matter. They're killing our people," said Carter.

"How many?"

"A lot."

Williamson opened a secured table safe, and pulled out a Glock and magazines.

"Eric, get us support from the CAF units at the airport," said Williamson.

Eric crossed to the table where several laptops were networked. He picked up a radio receiver, hearing nothing but the dead tone and slammed it back to the cradle.

"The line's cut. Satellite phone maybe?"

"We'd never get through. I don't think nine nine nine works anymore."

"We're on our own then," said Carter.

Heavy footfall came outside the room. Eric pushed himself to the wall, on the threshold of the door, holding his weapon ready. So much for quiet time, he thought. More people trying to kill him without apparent reason.

It was his team, armed and kitted out for a fight.

The lights in the room and corridor failed, plunging them into near darkness, the light from the laptop screens the only real source.

Williamson said, "We're being attacked by forces not yet identified. We've no choice but to engage lethal force. I'm not your employer asking you to fight, we're fighting for our lives, all of us. We fight. We win. You all go home."

There was a rumble of agreement.

"Move out, sweep the floors, top to bottom. You know the drill."

They filed out, Carter hobbling after them. Eric was about to follow, to take charge of his men when Williamson stopped him.

"Eric, when you asked about The Owls of Athena, I didn't tell you the whole truth."

"You've picked a difficult time to be honest, Ben."

He spoke quickly. "Brutus came to me, a few days into our deployment here. He talked about an agency with a lot of resources looking for an in to the city and virus. The money was almost too good to question. He offered it all, and for a seemingly small price to ourselves. We needed to share key information with them, and allow certain operatives to work under our Black Aquila banner. Obviously, I had my company to think about. I couldn't throw that away so I turned him down."

"Brutus was the facilitator?"

"Yes."

"The Owls of Athena and Brutus?"

"I don't know how deep it runs, Eric. I promise you that. You know Brutus and his quest for money. He'd do anything."

"He did everything, Ben. He killed your men. My men."

"I needed everyone. I needed his experience. It was my mistake."

"But Black Aquila has still been infiltrated by The Owls of Athena? That business with Doctor Holden in the forest and the research centre, they did it even though you turned them down?"

"If the money Brutus was offering was a fair assessment of resources they have access to, then I've no doubt they could pay off just about anyone."

"And when we rescued Doctor Holden that put Black Aquila in direct conflict with The Owls?"

"Yes."

"So the men outside are a kill team sent to remove us since we've now become a potential threat?"

"That's what I assume."

Eric shook his head. "If what you've told me is true, they'll never stop until we're eradicated."

"I've got some ideas on what we should do next, Eric."

"If we survive this, Ben, then we'll talk."

Ben loaded his Glock and followed Eric.

The two men reached the rest of the team. A few had tactical lights on the rails of their rifles. They shined their lights on a corpse, collapsed on the floor. A woman, her torso punctured by high-powered rounds. The window where she stood was cracked, two bullet holes sitting like beady eyes.

One of the team checked for a pulse. "She's dead."

"Move on," ordered Eric. "Check the windows, they've got spotters out there."

The team moved forward. More corpses littered the way. Eric squeezed through the narrow corridor, past his team standing two abreast. Williamson moved behind, heading toward the fore of the group. Eric turned and put a restraining hand on his shoulder.

"Forget it, Ben. You're sticking to the rear."

"You're forgetting who is in charge, Eric. You don't give the orders."

Carter appeared at Williamson's side. "Eric's right. If we lose you this whole thing falls apart. They're looking to cut off the head of Black Aquila, and that's you. Stay to the rear, take no chances."

"Carter, you stay with him."

"Damn," said Ben, letting the men traipse past him.

"They're restricted to the ground floor, we clear the second, secure the stairs and move down."

Eric moved forward, the team at his back moving silently behind. Events could accelerate into chaotic close combat in the dark. It would be messy, brutal and costly. Eric prayed Black Aquila moving on the offensive happened quicker than they predicted. If they could catch the assailants before they were organised, they might just get through this.

They passed down the corridor, ignoring the lifts rendered useless by the power cut. Holden's room lay open, the door slightly ajar. Eric signalled a halt, switched on his tactical light and opened the door fully. He swept in, scanning for a threat. The darkened room stunk of body odour and damp washing. Dirty towels littered the floor, the bed unmade and clothes strewn upon the sheets. He checked the bathroom.

"He's not here." Eric marched out of the room. "Doctor Holden isn't in his room."

"Find him," barked Williamson. "He's important to us. He can't have gone far, probably down to get some food from the canteen."

Eric cursed Holden for leaving his room. If it was to get food it fitted his mood of late, creeping about at night to avoid as many people as he could. Eric had rescued him once, now he had to do it a second time.

They proceeded down the stairs from the third floor to the second. A handful of Black Aquila support staff had been roused by the explosions. Eric directed them up to the third floor, and convinced Carter and Williamson to watch the stairs to make sure no assailants managed to sneak behind and make their way above.

Eric approached the stairwell and pushed open the door. It creaked, echoing around the void. He stepped in, moved to the rail at the summit and aimed his weapon over the edge, illuminating below with his tactical light. Nothing but retreating shadows. Eric switched to hand signals and waved his team to follow. Their footfall fell impossibly loud, though he knew they were moving as quietly as a heavily armed military team could. Halfway down the stairs, Eric rounded the corner bringing him to the last set of stairs before arriving at the ground floor. He focused on the door, watching for any movement of the handle. He gripped his weapon tight, his shoulders set ready to receive the recoil. He summoned his battle calm to focus every aspect of his mind and body on what lay ahead. Beyond that door, that simple wooden door, a well-equipped military team was slaughtering whoever they found.

Eric took the last step and moved toward the door. His team split into two, each half taking position against the wall on opposite sides of the door.

"Breach and clear," he whispered.

Brody and Cole approached the door, slipping their weapons down on their slings. Brody knelt by the handle, hand ready. Cole pulled a flash grenade from his pouch. The door opened up to the side of reception, to the right of the main entrance. If they were there in force then Eric and his men would be opening the door to instant battle.

Cole and Brody counted together. To three. Brody opened the door and stepped back. Cole threw the grenade, and stepped back covering his eyes. The grenade popped, a short dull explosion with an intense flash of light.

"Go!"

Cole stepped through the doorway, and into the dark. Eric followed close behind. The air ruptured with the hiss of weapon fire. Cole went down without a sound, riddled with bullets. Eric stepped over his comrade, and hunched his shoulders, bent his knees, making himself as small as possible.

Eric fired into reception, providing some much needed suppression fire. He rushed to one of the satellite reception desks, pushed his body against the reassuringly thick barrier. He pushed his weapon above the parapet and fired indiscriminately. Empty shells rattled across the tiled floor. More of his team joined him, all pushing themselves down to cover.

Wood and granite splintered and chipped above their heads where the enemy's fire ripped the counter apart.

Eric chanced a look behind. Only Cole lay dead, an arm extended out before him where he fell. Everyone else made it through. They were too close together. A few grenades could end them all.

"Brody!" Eric yelled over the gunfire. Brody slid over to Eric on hands and knees. "Take four and flank around. We'll provide covering fire. We can't get bottlenecked in here."

Eric and the remainder of his men popped up from cover and opened up. Shadows, the enemy in dark camouflage, stood resolute in the doorway, firing. Four of them firing MP5s. A handful of others were dotted about the reception area, clinging to whatever cover they could find.

One by the door fell, his weapon firing wildly before slipping from his grasp. Another screamed as a round cut through his neck. The dim light from outside and the erratic movements of the tactical lights caused a confusing strobe effect.

Brody and his four men leapt from cover and made a dash toward the lifts and the rooms beyond. They fired as they went and found more cover, an overturned table. The enemy at the door retreated. Good, thought Eric. If they wanted to wipe Black Aquila off the map then they would have to come back through the main entrance.

Brody and his men shot dead the last of the enemy in reception. Stupid bastards, they were attacked from two different angles. No chance of defending themselves. The reception went quiet for a moment, nothing moved. Eric reloaded and jumped the desk.

"We've pushed them back. Hold here, keep the main entrance secure. If they want us, they'll have to come and get us," Eric said to the men who remained with him. "Anything comes through the door, shoot it."

Eric walked over shattered glass and empty casings to Brody. The hotel lobby, once modern, warm and welcoming was reduced to a shell. All windows and glass fixings were shattered by stray shots. The searching beams of light turned the scene into a flickering hell. Eric kicked an MP5 free from the hands of one of the slain enemy. More nameless mercenaries, white ghosts like in the forest. There would be hell to pay when the full extent of this confrontation was discovered. The facility they located in the woods may never have been discovered, but this was in the CAF safe zone. An attack would quickly be discovered and investigated.

That was a problem for the future. The rear rooms still needed to be cleared.

"Come with me," said Eric, his voice ringing in his ears. "We've not found anyone from the ground floor. They're either in the rear rooms or they've been taken away. There could be more of them out here."

"Cole's dead, Eric. They got him."

"I know. We'll tend to him when we've secured this place."

Each member of the team formed up, Brody to Eric's left, AR-15s braced and ready. Eric scanned left and right, the tactical light illuminating the dark recesses as they went. They moved forward, slow, controlled. The winter wind blew in from the shattered entrance. Each room they came to had not been disturbed, the doors either locked or left open. No signs of disturbance.

Eric waved them on to the cafeteria. The doors were closed. Unusual. They were always open in Eric's experience. Always staffed, food was offered twenty-four hours a day. No matter the hour, someone was sitting sipping coffee or reading a book.

Eric broke into a run and reached the door with Brody only a step behind him.

"I don't hear anything," whispered Brody. He directed his tactical torch around the doorway and on the floor.

"Look, Eric." A footprint in blood marred the carpet. "Looks like they left. There's more than one set of prints."

"Be ready."

Eric levelled a kick against the doors, forcing those inward. They opened to reveal a charnel house beyond. The men stepped over the threshold, into a massacre. Bodies were piled up on the floor, some were shot where they sat. Everyone dead.

One of the team behind Eric and Brody muttered something to himself. They swung the torches around illuminating the full horror of the situation.

Eric stepped further into the slaughter. He held his breath as the stench of death hung heavy in the room, choking and oppressive. Spent casings littered the floor, blood and flesh mixed in with them. Eric pieced together what happened from the location of the bodies. A large group, fifteen or so must have been ushered to the corner where they were shot. Each corpse was riddled with bullets. The wall behind showed the scars of the execution. The others in the canteen were killed where they stood or sat. Eric walked around each body, shining a light on them in turn, checking for those he knew, checking for Holden.

Some he needed to roll over. Eric recognised almost everyone. The executioners were ruthless in their operation. Nobody had been spared. It did not matter if they were data analysts, or field operators. They did not discriminate.

Brody shouted Eric's name, and waved him over.

"It's Doctor Holden. I think I've found him."

Eric released the wrist of one of the fallen, a woman in a night robe. Was his hope to discover someone alive futile?

Eric crossed the distance, and knelt down next to a fallen body. He was facedown, slight of frame. Eric, with the help of Brody turned him over. Even in the dim light provided by the tactical torches Eric knew the dead man was Eugene Holden. The frail doctor's chest was punctured by three wounds, red gaping holes, the shirt he wore torn in several places. He looked oddly at peace, his face neutral, no hint of pain or fear, both of which would have dominated his final hours. His ever-present glasses sat on top of his head, the lenses cracked.

Eric reached to Holden's neck, and pressed two fingers, a forlorn search for a pulse.

Brody tapped him on the shoulder. "He's dead, Eric. I checked for a pulse."

Eric held on for a moment longer, his fingers pushing into the cold wetness of Holden's neck. Nothing. No glimmer. He was gone.

Eric swore as he stood.

"A lot of our people have died here, Eric. What makes Holden so special?"

Eric blew out a breath. "Holden could've been the key to unlocking this virus. I don't know anyone with his knowledge or expertise. Losing Eugene puts us back months."

Brody shrugged. "Someone else will take his place. That's one thing they're not short of, smart people telling us what to do or not to do."

In a simplistic way, Brody was right. Perhaps Eric was feeling some personal affinity for Holden. Williamson placed a lot of stock in what Holden could and could not do. The truth was Holden seemed unwilling to take any further part, a broken man who wished to be left alone, that's what the outbreak had done to him. He hoped wherever he was now, there was some measure of peace.

"We're moving out of here. Close it up."

They sealed the door behind them, and made their way back to reception and the rest of his men.

"Report?" Eric moved low until he was behind some cover.

"No contact since you left. We've seen nothing to suggest they're still outside. We think they've disengaged and pulled back. Any survivors back there?"

"All dead." Eric wiped his nose. "We need to be sure nobody is left out there. They could be trying to gain access from the rear."

"The rear doors were welded closed when we took up residence here. All ground floor windows had bars installed. If they're trying to gain access, they'd be making a lot of noise. It's quiet like the grave out there."

"Cover me." Eric readied his AR-15, jumped the reception desk and ran to the doorway. He ignored the cries of his team, urging him to return. Eric stepped out into the blizzard, expecting to feel the hammer fall of bullets. Nothing, only icy wind and incessant snowfall. His team had moved up to cover his mad dash. Of course they have, he thought.

He scanned with his weapon, alert for the slightest movement. Nothing.

"They're gone," he shouted back.

"Come back inside." Brody waved.

Eric peered into the snow a final time, then returned to the hotel. "Secure the perimeter. Fetch Williamson."

***

By the time Williamson came down from the third floor, Eric's men had set up battery-powered floodlights ready to be powered up. His team secured the outside and performed a sweep of the building. No enemy located. Large smoking generators rumbled to life and temporary lights illuminated the battle-scarred hotel. It worried Eric that a military force could strike in the CAF safe zone and then melt away.

Williamson took stock of the reception area.

Before Eric could speak, Williamson asked, "Is it true? Is Doctor Holden dead?"

Eric wiped his face free of perspiration and melted snow. It was not particularly hot inside, but the heat of battle clung to him.

"Holden is dead, along with a lot of our people. The canteen is a murder scene. These people weren't looking for anything other than blood."

"How did he die?"

"Three shots to the chest at close range. He would have died instantly."

Williamson remained still as a statue, his gaze down, fists curled tight. He seemed on the verge of tears. He whispered something. It was not meant for anyone's ears.

"What do we do now? Ben? The men are looking to us for guidance."

Williamson sucked in a lungful of air. "We need to identify everyone who was murdered, process the slain attackers and send a runner out to the CAF forces."

"Is that a good idea?"

Williamson shrugged. "We've no choice. We're done. Too much has been risked and lost. Black Aquila is ineffective." He looked up. "Have the men start packing up once the CAF arrives. You're all going home. Come and see me when all that is arranged. Bring Gemma with you."

***

Eric was the last to arrive. Williamson and Gemma sat talking. Small candles flickered, throwing meagre light into the room. Eric almost did not notice Carter sitting in the corner, his foot elevated on a low footstool.

Gemma had been crying. She dabbed at her eyes with a tissue. She must have been told of Dr. Holden's death.

"Eric, good. Close the door."

Eric perched himself on the edge of the table.

"I wanted to bring you here with Carter and Gemma for a reason. It's fair to say that I took a massive risk with our operations here, some of the decisions I made have put us into direct conflict with The Owls of Athena and that, in conjunction with the outbreak, caused us to suffer catastrophic losses. I'll have to answer for the course of action I ordered. CAF will likely investigate what happened here. We're standing down, effective immediately. I will protect all of my operators as much as I can from the fallout that's to follow."

"So that's the end of it? We're beaten and sent home?"

"We're beaten and you're being sent home, but it's not the end of things. The CAF is pursuing a merciless campaign in the city, surged by huge numbers of US and EU troops. There's little doubt in my mind that in six months the outbreak here will be brought under control. Civilian losses will more than likely be in the tens of thousands. The CAF isn't putting enough resources into following up leads, seeking to find the source. They're only treating the effects."

"You're not saying all. Spit it out," said Carter.

"What I'm proposing will either make a difference or it will get us all killed. We could be on borrowed time anyway. Covertly, we take the fight to The Owls of Athena. Seek them out at their source. When we have enough information then we pass on the information to the right military resources. We have a lead."

"Brutus," spat Eric, the name leaving a bitter taste in his mouth.

"If we find Brutus then we have a link, a fragile link to The Owls. We need to bring him back onside."

"You can't be serious? Brutus? You know as well as I do what he did to us and you want to try to bring him back? He deserves to die. He's as guilty as anyone for the deaths of our people."

"I know that," snapped Williamson. "If you don't have the stomach for this, Eric, then you're free to go home whenever you like. I just hope that The Owls won't pursue you or your family."

"Don't you put that on me, Ben." Eric pushed himself from the table. "I've gone above and beyond what you've asked of me. What you're planning won't work, you have no concrete leads. Not to mention the legalities of this. You're talking about bringing a private war to the streets of Britain."

"It's better than sitting at home watching the news and waiting to be picked off one at a time," said Carter, calmly.

"You too? This is crazy!"

"If these Owls are that powerful then none of us are safe. If we work together and take it to them, we're protecting ourselves and our families. It only takes one man with a gun to create a tragedy at home, Eric. Think on that before you answer."

"It's not crazy," added Williamson. "It is simply adding a contribution to combating the outbreak."

"Why not just go to CAF about The Owls, let them deal with it?"

Carter laughed, a bitter sound. "These Owls are hiding in plain sight, Eric. You think if one of us reported them that anyone would investigate it?"

"We've got proof."

"We have rumours and corpses, and there's already enough of them in Aberdeen. If we do this, we need to do it ourselves, at least in the beginning."

"What about me?" asked Gemma. "What do I do?"

"Go home, Gemma. Stay the hell away from Aberdeen, or any city. Keep your head down and wait for all this to blow over," said Eric shaking his head.

Williamson held up a hand. "Eric is perhaps painting more of a bleak picture for what comes next than is reality. It's true, if you want to go home I can arrange passage through quarantine. You'll be paid as agreed and free to construct your story as you see fit."

"They're reporting from within the city. Whatever I have will be of periphery interest at best. My opportunity has past. I'd like to know what you think comes next, Ben."

"Doctor Holden waited to see what was next, Gemma," said Eric. "He waited too damn long and got three bullets for his troubles. Be sensible, Gemma, please."

"And if I go home, will you protect me or my family? Will you stop the virus reaching my parents?"

"Gemma, all I'm trying to do is make you think."

"I'm thinking clearly, Eric. I need to be here. I need to help stop this."

"Gemma," said Williamson bringing her attention back to him. "I'll need you to shadow the team we're putting together. Investigate any and all leads, much like what you've been doing before but without being restricted to Aberdeen. You've a knack for this. You'll be paid very well and offered what protection I can offer."

"For my family, too?"

Williamson spread his hands wide. "I'll do everything in my power. You have my word on that."

"Okay, let's do it."

"I'm in, too," said Carter.

"You're all mad. Haven't enough people died? What can we do against an organisation that is so deeply embedded within the ranks of the powerful? In fact, I don't care. I'm going home."

Eric marched out of the room. He clicked on the torch to make his way down the corridor. Footsteps came from behind.

"Hey," said Gemma taking hold of Eric's arm. "What was all that?"

With only the light from the torch, he could hardly make out her features.

"I wasn't going to spend another minute listening to Ben's ingenious ways of getting us all killed."

"You don't want to keep your family safe? Or yourself?"

"I can protect myself and my family."

"From the virus and The Owls? I know it's not about that. It's about Brutus, isn't it?"

That name spoken aloud caused Eric to ball his fists, knuckles white.

"It's not Brutus."

"I know what he did, and what he almost did to me."

The events in Aberdeen, what Gemma had to do, what she experienced had hardened her to the world. Eric could see that. She probably would fail to recognise her previous self, for her naivety which was so apparent in the beginning was now replaced with a hard edge. She was like a soldier.

"The team needs you, Eric. Think on it at the very least. As I see it, we all stand a better chance together." Gemma walked back into Williamson's room.

"Damn," he whispered, knowing that she was right. As much as he wanted to go home and pretend the world was not falling apart he could not. "Damn," he said again and followed Gemma.

Chapter Eight
A Sort Of Homecoming

The Russian freighter slowed, the engines blow lessening. The original enthusiasm for returning home gave way to frayed tempers and irritation. It all stemmed from the cramped living conditions and limited space to find some privacy. Brutus acted as peacekeeper as best he could. It was a role he was not used to playing, nor was he necessarily equipped. Arguments erupted over trivial matters, flashpoints of manifest frustration soon forgotten once resolved. Brutus needed to keep the cohesion of the team together. He needed each and every one of them, and another hundred like them. Soon enough, they would be a precious commodity.

Andor Toth having resigned himself to his captivity opened up a little to Brutus. Little nuggets of information, probably quite mundane to Toth, Brutus made sure to record. Logistic issues. Names of people involved in the conspiracy. Places. Dates. All seemingly unconnected but Brutus knew better. The coming conflict would be an intelligence war as much as it would be a physical one.

One of the crew knocked heavily on the steel door to the cabin's common room where Brutus and his team sat.

"You will be ready to depart in ten minutes," he said with his heavy accent.

Brutus waved the man away. "We're going home, boys. The ship's slowing. We'll be put over the side into an inflatable and cruise to the shore."

"You say cruise like it's a pleasure trip," said Niall. "It's the height of winter, the sea won't be calm. We're in for some serious waves."

"We'll be fine," insisted Brutus. "We'll be less than thirty minutes in the sea then we'll hit land. Our journey is almost at an end."

The money the Russian's paid and the cash The Owls initially paid was sealed in watertight bags and placed into robust holdalls. It would be divided up when they reached safety.

Niall picked up his gear and led the procession from the common room. The door swung closed behind them, leaving Brutus alone in the portion of the ship that had been home for the past thirteen days. He picked up his own pack, and slung it over his shoulder. He started toward the door when a shrill ring sounded.

The satellite phone. Brutus threw down his bag, and tore open the flap, digging hands deep trying to locate the device. He laid his hands on it, right at the bottom, wrapped inside a dirty shirt. He pulled it free. The green screen flashed with the incoming call.

Throw it overboard, the cautious voice in him urged. Brutus never had paid much attention to it in the past, so why bother now? He popped the aerial up and pressed the button to answer.

"Who is this?"

"Richard? Is that you?"

The signal was terrible. The voice could have belonged to anyone with that much distortion. He was about to hang up when the voice broke through the distortion once again.

"It's Ben Williamson."

"What do you want?"

"We need to talk/ You're working for The Owls of Athena. They got to you, I know. You can't trust them, Brutus."

"You must be desperate, Ben."

"We both should be. You can't trust them."

"And you can't trust me. I'm ending this call. Don't call again. Nobody will pick up."

Brutus switched off the phone, and dropped it to the floor before stamping on it over and again until it lay in pieces. He scooped up the shards and took them to the balcony door. He opened it and facing down terrific wind and snow, hurled the pieces into the icy depths of the North Sea.

He closed the door, and returned his possessions to the backpack. Brutus hurried from the common room, down the length of the ship to where his team waited.

A heavy winch was extended over the side of the ship, a large inflatable swinging in its descent to the sea below. The captain of the ship, a heavily bearded man who never introduced himself stood silently, overseeing the deployment of the smaller craft.

Snow collected in his beard, his wiry hair matted to his forehead. Brutus leaned over the side in time to see the dinghy touch the water and drag in the waves. The sea threw the small vessel around like a toy, despite it still being tethered to the ship. Brutus could feel the worried gazes of his men, could feel his own beginning to form.

The captain barked gruff orders in Russian. His men moved a number of sturdy containers onto the winch. It would be the weapon cache.

"What the hell are they shouting about?" asked Brutus, above the wind.

Freddo, who was the only member of the team to have a splattering of Russian attempted to translate. "They're saying two of us need to be down there to take control of the weapon cache as it's lowered. Any volunteers?" shouted Freddo, with a grin.

Magnus Munson and Ash Gibbons moved toward the ropes hanging off the side of the ship. They would have to propel down the side of the ship, land in the dinghy and then control the lowering of the cache.

Magnus leaned into Brutus and said with a smile, "Sometimes I really hate you."

Magnus peered over the side, let out a string of obscenities. He spat on his hands, took hold of the ropes and eased himself over. Ash did the same, neither men looking confident. If either man slipped and fell into the sea, they were dead. The freighter would not stop for them. The cold would get them before drowning did.

They descended, slowly, the wind throwing them left and right. Waves kicked up to meet them, showering both in icy water. Ash dropped the final few feet to the vessel below and held the guide rope for Magnus. Both men landed safely.

Two of the freighter crew lowered the containers. Ash and Magnus worked tirelessly to secure the cargo before the winch was retracted. Toth, too weak of body, was lowered next by the winch, a heavy rope tied round his waist and under the arms. He yelped in pain and was dropped with no sign of care. The rest of Brutus's team went over the side and down via the ropes.

Brutus marched up to the captain and struck out a hand. The captain looked from Brutus's offered hand to his face. It annoyed

Brutus just how impassive the captain's weather-beaten face remained. He finally shook, his rough hand like hard, worn leather.

"Good luck," he uttered.

"Life jackets? Where are the life jackets for my men?"

The captain shrugged, a slow uncaring gesture. "Life preservers for my crew. We do not have enough for you or your men. You go now or don't go. Your choice."

No threats or bargains would change the situation now. The captain was a man of unrelenting openness. His word was law on the ship. Besides, if the small boat sank, they were dead anyway, life preserver or not.

Brutus went to the side of the ship, took one final look at the upper decks of the Askold, then threw himself over the edge and clambered down the side, his feet slipping against the wet hull. Mist from the waves chilled his every fibre. The muscles in his arms and shoulders burned. He kept going, muttering every swear word in his vocabulary, and there were many. Hands reached up and took hold of his boots and legs, guiding him down to safety. The dinghy and the team clung to the side of the Askold a moment longer. Roy Smart sat to the rear, and started the engine.

"Cut us loose," shouted Freddo.

The tethers of the Askold were released, and the small vessel was left to fend for itself.

Roy opened up the throttle, sending the dinghy thrusting through the mighty waves. The small boat rose and fell on the back of the sea's blustering. Nobody talked, everyone clung to safety ropes or each other. Ice waves blasted over them all. The sting of the water burned Brutus's eyes. He wiped at them but found little relief.

A sound came, faint over the roar of the sea and the hum of the engine. Roy clung to the helm laughing like a madman, half through terror, half through the exhilaration that a man experiences on the edge of death.

"Crazy bastard!" Brutus yelled.

The tiny vessel, alone on the belligerent sea, forged forward toward land.

***

The dinghy broke through the final waves and powered through the shallows. The hull tore through sand and stones, and the crew jolted with the last forward motions. Night had closed in, the snow fell unabated and only a hint of the moon revealed itself from behind high cloud cover.

Brutus leapt from the dinghy, his feet plunging into shallow water, the sand beneath sucking at his feet. The others jumped into the shallows and together they hauled the boat from the water onto the pebble-covered beach. Roy silenced the engine. For a moment, they were alone with the lapping waves in the dark.

Each man switched on their torches. The beach was a desolate, long stretch of coast, tall dunes protecting the coast.

"Ash, Roy. Get up on one of those dunes and get our location. Send the signal to the contact. We need a pick up ASAP."

Brutus had a contact who was to collect them, and transport them to a secure location. Due to the unpredictable nature of their arrival it would be impossible to offer anything but the roughest of locations. Once the signal and their location was sent they potentially had a few days to await pick up. It meant uncomfortable nights on the beach. The Russians provided survival equipment and gear, enough to make sure they wouldn't freeze to death, but not enough to provide comfort.

Both men looked exhausted, soaked through, but set off without protest. They raced toward the dunes, disappearing into the dark. Only the light of their torches remained visible for a time until even they were swallowed up by the night.

"Get the equipment unloaded. We need to move up the beach."

Brutus helped move the crates from the dinghy to the beach, each one heavily laden, requiring two men to each. Brutus dragged the final holdalls and packs free, then reached into the compartment next to the wheel of the vessel and pulled a small canister of fuel free.

Toth stood a little behind him shivering. "What are you doing?"

"Getting rid of the evidence of our passing."

"What if we need that again, to go back or something?"

Brutus flicked the cap off the canister and dashed the liquid over the small ship. "Our sea journeys are over, Andor. We don't go back from here."

Brutus pulled his lighter free. He flicked the lid and ignited the flame. He turned to Toth. "To moving forward," he said with a smile, and tossed the lighter into the vessel.

Despite the snow, the flames caught quickly. He turned his back to the pyre, picked up the two holdalls at his feet and shoved Toth toward the dunes and the rest of his men.

"I bet you never expected to make it back to Britain, Andor. You never thought it was possible."

"You've taken a dangerous path, Brutus, yet for all the obstacles, here we are."

Brutus was about to reply, but something was amiss. Torch light was nowhere to be seen. He could not hear chatter, nor detect the location of his men.

A shot broke the winter's night. Toth's back exploded in a cloud of red and he slumped to the sharp stones of the beach. Brutus threw himself down, a matter of instinct. He crawled to where Toth lay, less than ten feet.

Toth gasped for breath, somehow still alive despite the gaping wound in his chest. "It's them. The Owls," he rasped. "They're here." A strangled gargle followed then his body fell limp.

The sound of crunching stones under foot came. Too late. Dark figures emerged from the gloom, weapons aimed at him, night vision lenses attached to helmets.

"I'm a British citizen," said Brutus still lying on the ground.

The lead soldier kicked him to the side of the head, a blow that sent fireworks exploding in his mind. Not CAF or British forces, he thought. Strong arms picked him up and dragged him over the stones. They cut through his clothes, slashing at the skin beneath. He wasn't in pain, everything dulled by the cold and the savage kick.

Stones were replaced by wet sand. It poured into every opening in his clothes, and into his mouth, his nose, his eyes. The soldiers released their hold. His breath came in short gasps. He pushed himself over to his back. The moon provided enough light to make out his surroundings. Freddo lay near to him, his face bloody, clothes torn. His chest moved in slow rises and dips. His team knelt in the sand, their legs and arms lashed together. All were blindfolded. Ash Gibbons and Roy Smart? Nowhere. Brutus tried to speak but nothing came out.

If Ash and Roy eluded the clutches of The Owls of Athena then there was still hope. Otherwise, Brutus and his men would be unlikely to see sunrise.

***

Eric watched Jane sleep. The temporary infirmary housed patients with the more minor injuries. Her lips sat apart, and she grunted softly. An IV line snaked from her arm to a bag of fluid suspended above her head. It was late and only a few staff buzzed about. He did not have much time. Williamson had arranged for the surviving members of Black Aquila to be flown out of the conflict zone and back to a staging area before being allowed home ... until they were called upon again. It still did not sit well with Eric, though little did in these times.

Eric felt the need to break the news of Dr. Holden's death to Jane personally. He owed her that at the very least, a familiar face in a world of confusion.

Jane's arm was cool to the touch. The large medical tent the patients sheltered in kept the worst of the weather out but was by no means comfortable.

"Jane," Eric whispered. "Jane, wake up."

She opened her eyes. "Eric? What are you doing here? What time is it?"

"It's late." Eric sat back in the chair. "I wanted to come and see you before I go."

"Go where?"

"I've got some bad news, Jane. It's Doctor Holden. He's dead."

Jane's focus remained on Eric, her eyes unblinking, a glistening beginning to appear. "How did he die?"

Eric thought up ways to tell her how he died. Peacefully in his sleep was what he thought to say. Something in Jane's steely gaze forced the truth from his lips.

"He was murdered, Jane. Killed by a rogue element of Black Aquila. We couldn't get to him in time."

She looked away. "He gave everything to fight the outbreak, Eric. Everything he could. At the end, there was nothing left for him to give. I could see it in his eyes. He was broken." Jane wiped the tears from her eyes. "So what happens from here? I don't know what to do."

"You need to get your health back and when the time comes we'll get you home."

Eric knew she would likely end up in a displacement centre. Nobody knew when the mandatory quarantine would end.

"But you won't be here, will you?"

Eric shook his head.

"So I'll be left with the CAF people?"

"I'd say so, yes."

'What's going on? Why are you all leaving?"

"We've lost too many people, Jane. We don't have enough left to work effectively."

Jane simply nodded. "Has any of what we've done made a difference, Eric? All the death and pain? Was it worth it?"

"Is it ever?" he said, standing. "I'd better get going, Jane. I'm sorry that I was the bearer of bad news. And now I'm running out on you."

Jane picked at one of the blankets at her lap. "I regret ever volunteering after you saved me from the hospital. Do you regret your work?"

"Regrets and hindsight can only bring you down." He patted her arm, and gave a brief smile. "Sometimes events take you along for a ride, and you either hold on or fall off."

"Poetic words. Not like you, Eric."

"Said by someone dear to me, not too long ago. Take care of yourself, Jane. Be sensible. You know the signs to look for."

"Signs? I feel like you're trying to tell me something."

"I am," said Eric. "I'm telling you to be sensible and to take care. See, nothing poetic."

A roaring din rocked the small tent, several high-powered engines roaring overhead. Jane pulled her covers up. The few medical staff exchanged questions. A phone began to ring, and one of the staff rushed to answer.

"I'll be back." Eric ran through the maze of beds, to the exit, pulled the flap aside and stepped out into the storm.

He shielded his eyes from the snowfall in time to see two explosions rip apart a section of the security fence that ringed the airport. A fighter jet, little more than a blurred movement of light banked and turned heading back out toward the coast. A pair of attack helicopters swooped in low. They unleashed a salvo of missiles into the explosion area, followed by a torrent of cannon fire.

The wave of heat from the conflagration hit Eric, dull in the snow but he could imagine the intensity if he had been caught closer.

An alarm. An air raid siren sounded. Lights sprung up over the airport. Armoured vehicles, American Humvees raced toward the inferno, search lights shooting out terrific beams. Eric could now see figures milling about the fire. Infected. It had to be. It was the only thing in the world that could elicit such a response from the military.

Parts of the security fence, reinforced since the outbreak, swayed rigidly. Figures heaved against the fence. The CAF forces raced to intercept them, but there were too many besiegers and not enough defenders. Time to get the hell out.

Eric returned to the makeshift infirmary. Two females dressed in blue scrubs stood near the phone.

"Are there any weapons here? Anything at all?"

"This is a hospital, of course not."

"Get on that phone, tell them that you need a security detail here immediately. The infected have broken through the perimeter."

Eric made a snap decision. He did not trust the CAF to secure all their assets in the airport. Jane would come with him. Three more explosions impacted, not so far off.

"We're getting out of here. This will nip." Eric yanked off the tape securing the IV line to her skin and pulled free the needle. She let out a hiss. Blood spurted from the tiny hole. Jane watched the blood leak from her, dripping down the length of her fingers onto the floor. Eric pulled a wad of gauze from the treatment table next to the bed, pushed it against the area and taped it in place.

"Can you walk?"

Jane nodded, and threw the covers back. Eric pushed the safety rail down from her bed and she swung her legs over the side. She reached out and Eric supported her as she stood. She wore only a hospital gown.

"Clothes?"

"They took them away. I have nothing."

Eric wrapped Jane in one of the bed blankets. She grasped it tight beneath her chin. It fell to just below her knees. She slipped her feet into thin hospital slippers. Walking outside in them, in the temperature and snow would mean losing toes. They did not have time to search for more appropriate footwear. Eric took Jane by the hand and led her through the infirmary, past startled and panicked patients. He ignored all questions and pressed on. One of the nurses stepped in front of him.

"You can't leave! What do we do? I called and they said they're aware of the situation."

"Then sit here and wait for someone to help you."

"But you're not waiting."

"Look," said Eric. "I can't help you."

Jane let out a yelp as her unprotected feet disappeared into the carpet of white. The crackle of gunfire ripped through the night. High-powered, likely .50 calibre pounded in the near distance. Infected poured through the several gaps in the security fence. CAF forces engaged them where they could, but there simply was not enough of them. A group charged through the snow toward the infirmary.

"Time to leave," said Eric, scooping Jane up in his arms.

Eric ran, and Jane clung to him, her arms tight around his neck. She was not heavy, but pushing through the snow and wind made the five-hundred-metre dash to the car painfully slow. He knew what the infected were capable of, what they could endure. They would not be likewise hampered.

"It's cold," she stammered. "So cold."

"Think about the summer. Imagine you're on a beach somewhere."

"You're joking, right?" Her teeth chattered.

"Then try a cruise ship."

They raced through the airport grounds to where the car was parked. Eric's breath burned in his chest. He was unable to speak. He laid Jane on the ground and patted down his pockets, searching for the keys. For one, horror-filled moment he believed he had left them in the infirmary. He found them in his pocket, a single key attached to a ticket with a number. One of the pool cars available to Black Aquila. He unlocked it and opened the door, and threw Jane into the back. Eric got in and started the engine. Another attack helicopter flew overhead, low. He put the car into reverse and turned.

"This cruise ship is mighty uncomfortable," Jane said.

"It's the best I could come up with."

"I can't feel my toes."

It would not be a long drive back to either the hotel or the Black Aquila Chinook which would be flying them out of the city. *Wheels up* was scheduled for very soon. Eric decided to head for the Chinook first. With Williamson being so well-connected he would no doubt be aware that the perimeter had been breached.

Eric checked behind. Jane was propped up on one elbow, sprawled over the back seats.

From Eric's periphery, he saw the approaching shadow too late. The impact jolted the entire vehicle. The driver's airbag inflated with a bang. The car flipped throwing the two occupants about like ragdolls. Eric landed heavily, smashing his shoulder against the door. Behind, Jane screamed before falling silent. The car rolled a few more times then came to a rest.

Eric groaned, letting his vision return. A dull calm settled on him, the world beyond forgotten. Blood dripped from a scalp wound. He wiped at his forehead. Jane! He turned where he lay. Jane lay still, breathing but unconscious. Eric moved, wriggling himself to the door of the car. He kicked out at the buckled hinge, knocking the door free. He pulled at Jane's arm, not softly, and dragged her between the two front seats and out of the passenger door. He scooped her up and slung her over his shoulder.

The Humvee they struck had been knocked off course, the front wheel slightly buckled. Two soldiers inside, attempted to restart the engine.

He moved on, Jane's weight feeling as though it had doubled. Eric scaled a small embankment and went down the other side. Two-hundred feet in front of him, the landing area where Black Aquila embarked for operations. The black Chinook waited, rear door open. Men moved about outside, loading boxes onto the aircraft. Shouting would be pointless. Eric moved forward with all the speed he could muster, knowing full well that hell snapped at his heels. His feet left snow-covered grass and landed on tarmac. Carter stood at the edge of the ramp, waving for Eric to hurry.

"Who's that?" he asked.

"She's coming with us."

"You're both hurt. We can't take her out with us, you know that. Everyone on this aircraft has been screened. She hasn't."

"I'm not leaving her, Carter. Get out of the way."

Williamson stomped down the ramp. "Stop pissing about and get on board." He pointed to the skies. "It's starting to get a little busy up there."

Aircraft were taking off in rapid succession, large cargo planes for the most part.

"He's trying to take this woman out with her."

Williamson looked between Eric and Jane. "We can't just leave her here. Take her on. Hurry."

Eric moved up the ramp. Williamson assisted with Jane. They lowered her into one of the chairs and strapped her in. Her arms and legs were heavily lacerated. Thick shards of glass protruded from several of the wounds.

"Can you feel your toes now?"

Jane shook her head.

Eric took the seat next to her. Williamson next to him. Carter closed the rear hatch and gave the signal for take-off.

The Chinook shuddered, then the ground fell away.

"We don't know how this happened, Eric. The CAF was caught unaware. We didn't know such a large migration of the infected could move without being detected. The weather probably masked some of the movement but this is a disaster. We got the order to bug out ASAP."

"What about the hotel?"

Williamson smiled. "Nobody came. I guess they've got bigger issues right now."

The events at the hotel not being investigated was a stroke of luck in the grand scheme of things. It meant less scrutiny for Black Aquila. Eric pulled a thermal blanket free from beneath his seat and covered Jane, tucking it tightly against her.

"We're flying to the coast and following it south. If there's ordinance being dropped into the airport we will try to miss the worst of it," said Williamson.

Eric turned to the window. His shoulder burned. Below, the airport burned. New explosions popped every few seconds. Whatever was happening down there, it was murder. He thought about the nurses and patients in the infirmary, he did not even try to save them. Were they dead now? If they were not dead now, they soon would be.

The Chinook banked and turned to the coast. The sea stretched out below, opal and twinkling. A fleet of ships from many nations lay at anchor. Brief flashes lit the decks as missiles sped from the military vessels into the city. Fighter aircraft launched from an American aircraft carrier. All flying toward the city, all seeking to stem the tide of the advance of the infected. Eric leaned back, welcoming the altitude the Chinook provided. Eric was leaving Carrion City behind.

Only a select few knew that The Athena Protocol was initiated. The terrible carrion outbreak that ravaged Aberdeen would soon become the pandemic academics feared. It was coming for them all.

CHECK OUT OTHER GREAT APOCALYPSE BOOKS

WHITE OUT
by Eric Dimbleby

An apocalyptic snowstorm sweeps the globe. Experts predict this freak storm will be "The New Ice Age." Electricity is gone, as are all forms of communication and road travel. As each member of a divided family tries to survive in their own way, they must deal with a snow-driven madness that has gripped the underlying evil in the hearts of men. In an epic struggle to get home and reunite, they will find that terror lies around every snow drift... and even in their very own backyard.

NIGHT PLAGUE
by Rowan Rook

Humankind will soon be extinct. A mysterious pandemic cut through two-thirds of the population in just four short years, and within another four, it will decimate everything – and everyone – left.

The last days are ticking by, relentless and ruthless, and the reclusive Mason Mild finds himself torn between a peaceful end and a brutal immortality. Between his hopeless, but comfortable days with his family, and something new...something violent and wild.

Have the fang marks above his heel dealt him an early demise or a second birth?

 SEVERED**PRESS**

CHECK OUT OTHER GREAT APOCALYPSE BOOKS

XY
by D.S. Lillico

An iron fortress protected by automated gun turrets is the only world Elsie has ever known.

When tragedy strikes, Elsie is forced to leave the sanctuary of her home and out into a brutal new world. A post-apocalyptic wasteland filled with savage mutants.

Hunted and alone Elsie stumbles into the care of a giant named Punch, but the world is now full of worse things than giants. Cannibals are starving, bandits are roaming and war is coming.

Elsie's arrival plunges the new-world further into darkness... and is there really something hidden inside of her?

SANCTUARY
by Ian Page

Deeta Nakshband, a Connecticut physician is attacked by a local surgeon while on duty in the hospital. Her friend, Janelle Jefferson, has similar experiences in Miami. Both of them become aware of an increasingly violent world as acts of isolated brutality escalate into civil unrest. They grapple with their paranoia as family members and coworkers become dangerously unpredictable. Worldwide, military units go rogue, war begins in Korea and cities implode as people slaughter each other in the streets. Martial law is declared in an attempt to maintain order. People are arrested, detainment camps are set up and interrogations end with tragic consequences as modern civilization crumbles. Deeta and Janelle band together with family friends and coworkers to save each other and find sanctuary.

SEVEREDPRESS

f facebook.com/severedpress
twitter.com/severedpress

CHECK OUT OTHER GREAT APOCALYPSE BOOKS

THE DEAD FAMILIAR
by J.D. McKenna

In the twilight hours of a failing world, one man seeks to bring his loved ones to safety. Jack Hightower: Marine, bar-keep, and doomsday prepper. He knows of the coming calamity, and on the final night of an old world he seeks a new beginning.

This is the story of that night, the tale of how Jack and his survivor's colony in the north came to be.

DOMINION
by Doug Goodman

Dominion has been taken from man. Now, six friends must cross an apocalyptic wasteland dominated by a hell's me-nagerie of mega-fauna. Their middle-class suburban skills are no longer applicable to the world they live in. To find a safe haven in this world they will need to develop a new set of survival skills and fight the mutated denizens of the animal kingdom for every step of their terrifying journey.